THE WEB IS NOT ONLY FOR SPIDERS

Leon Bari

Grosvenor House
Publishing Limited

This book is published by
Grosvenor House Publishing Ltd
Link House
140 The Broadway, Tolworth, Surrey, KT6 7HT.
www.grosvenorhousepublishing.co.uk

This book is a work of fiction. Any resemblance to people or events, past or present, is purely coincidental.

A CIP record for this book
is available from the British Library

ISBN 978-1-80381-502-2
eBook ISBN 978-1-80381-503-9

Dedicated to
The girl from Yorkshire.
'Jack's Story'
Inspired by
Jennifer.

PROLOGUE

Jack was a man of mature years, he was in the best of health, fit and still sports minded. When his wife passed away – it was the big C – it came as no surprise to Jack or his children. There had been other health issues and when the end eventually came it ended his wife's suffering, she was now at peace.

No, Jack was not surprised by his wife's death but what did come as an unwelcome shock was the void that followed.

After a long marriage the emptiness and silence of the house was unbearable, it was spooky, it was unendurable... Of course there was the Camera Club, the weekly meetings helped, but what was a fit mature chap to do to fill his time?

It was when a neighbour suggested, "Why don't you go on one of the dating sites on the web?" Jack's mind went into overdrive... Dating sites? What were they? Jack had used the web, it was for shopping and for research, but dating? What would they think of next?

CHAPTER ONE

Jack Tomlinson gazed down at the elongated mound of earth; at one end of the mound was a small wooden cross, it was just a marker, a temporary sign until the headstone was erected, on the cross were the words;

Sylvia Tomlinson... died 8th December 2016

Placed carefully on the mound, spelled out in white flowers, was the word MUM and at each side of the mound were bunches of flowers of different hues.

A few days before, a crowd of family and friends had gathered around to watch the coffin being lowered into its final resting place, but on this cold winter's morning Jack was alone.

The cemetery was empty save for a small black and white dog sniffing at one of the gravestones, Jack's eyes sought the owner of the animal but there was no-one, 'he's alone,' thought Jack, 'I know exactly how he feels'.

A single tear rolled down Jack's cheek, his eyes were moist and red, he had shed many tears during the previous few days and he wondered if there were many more, but each time he thought of the future, the emptiness of the days ahead, he would feel the emotion of grief and he was unable to stop the flow. He removed a handkerchief from his trouser pocket and gently wiped the tear away.

Not one hundred yards away was the grave of his son, David, laid to rest five years earlier.

David was 'autistic', somewhere towards the upper end of the scale. He had been a prolific writer of short stories, derived for the most part from personal experience; but the voices in his head, the voices that refused to leave him during his waking hours, had been the principle reason for his writing. The concentration of applying the written word enabled him to push the voices to the back of his mind, but, they were always there, lurking, waiting to invade his thoughts once again.

Apart from the short stories David had penned many poems, both rhyming and in prose. There were two pieces that had always been to the forefront of Sylvia's memory, two pieces that brought tears to her eyes, two pieces that made her recall the plight of her eldest son, the son she had never been able to help.

The first was a short story that he had written later in his life; a short story that he had entitled, "In the blink of an eye". The story recounted the day of his tenth birthday, the day when the realisation dawned on him that he was different, different not only from the others in his school class but different from everyone. That realisation had happened in an instant, or as David had aptly titled his short story, In the blink of an eye.

The other piece of writing that had made such an impression was a piece of prose that David had written describing how he felt, how he related to the rest of humanity, how he lived his tortuous life, a life ended by his own hand. He now rested in oblivion, the perfect state that he needed to attain for the peace that he craved.

Jack had revisited Sylvia's grave on this day to tell her that she was now reunited with her loving son, they were together once again.

He pulled the folded page from his pocket, his eyes were damp as he read the words aloud, there was no-one else in the cemetery but he knew that she could hear him. The words he read were David's, his story set down in the way only a writer can adequately describe to the reader, A poem that he had entitled:

'A Way Through the Brambles';

There is a perfectly paved path,
It began as all things must,
Once upon a time,
And marches forth towards the horizon
To a place where many feet traverse the path.
There are;
Black shoes, white shoes, shiny shoes,

Shabby shoes, large shoes, baby shoes,
Backless slippers, high heeled shoes,
Bare feet with bells on their toes,
They all pass across my eyeline.
I was discarded.
Kicked from it by the differing,
Yet identical sets of feet.
This path lays flat atop an embankment
With a ditch either side,
The side which I inhabit
Is filled with brambles;
Thorny devils woven together in a virtually
Impregnable matrix taller than I can stretch.
Presumably, the other side is just as inhospitable.
Every day I inch through the barbarous forest
At one hundredth the pace of the feet above me,
Marching to their soft rhythm.
And as darkness descends my clothes are torn,
My skin is scarred and my determination
Is less than the previous night, nevertheless
At sun-up I orchestrate another assault
On the blockade, desperate to reach the
destination,
The feet, which eagerly head forwards in
streamlined
fashion,
Is there a castle on the other side, filled with
riches?
Or a beautiful maiden betrothed to me?
Will there be luxuries, entertainment or
tranquillity?

Or will I be too late?
Above me the feet pass with veritable ease
And eventually go out of sight,
Night will shortly fall. Already exhaustion and futility
have taken their toll.
Perspiration drips from my brow, stinging my eyes,
Magically blurring my surroundings.
Tomorrow will be my eleven-thousandth
Five hundred and sixteenth day
Battling these fiendish weeds,
I know not how near I am to my prize.
I need to rest; I lay down upon the thorns.
Winding my limbs through the loops and
Strangleholds around me,
They have provided me with bedding
For as long now that any discomfort
I may once have felt
Has been replaced by a sense of belonging.
There probably isn't any end to the brambles,
Best I just lie here and dream.

It was the way that David felt, he was different, so different that he was alone, he didn't fit in, he never would. He was never close to his mother; some autistic boys aren't but his mother somehow felt that she was to blame for David's condition; it was a self-blame that she took with her to the grave.

Jack folded the piece of paper and replaced it in his pocket, he gazed at the mound of earth and flowers and under his breath mumbled, "David has found his way through the brambles; he is with you now and someday we will all meet again."

But the weather and air temperature were the winners, Jack's fingers and toes were tingling, as regretful as it was it was almost time to go home, just a few more minutes.

Jack, now in the Autumn of his years, had been married to Sylvia for many years, many short years, looking back they seemed to have passed, as David would have said, in the blink of an eye. But the future stretched in front of him seemed bleak and empty; he was now as alone as David had been, he now understood David's sense of isolation.

They had two children, Laura who was forty-two and Peter who was five years younger, two mature and busy children who had their own lives to lead; lives that by their very nature had meant that visits to their parents had become somewhat infrequent.

Laura, married to Brian, a successful architect, had children of her own. Paul and Simon, they were twins, eighteen years old and just beginning their university education.

Laura was tall, one hundred and seventy centimetres, she had long, shoulder length wavy auburn hair, her eyes were brown and her features, although slightly drawn, were attractive and gave her a regal, haughty look. She did not have either of her parent's features, favouring her grandfather in appearance.

On the other hand, Peter was very much like his mother, blonde hair, blue eyes and a couple of centimetres shorter than his sister.

Laura had never been close to her mother; she had visited infrequently and had always been too busy with her family. She was one of those individuals whose emotions were quite shallow, she did not appear to have any strong feelings about anything; perhaps they were hidden or deliberately buried, it was safer that way.

Peter in many ways was the opposite, tears were always not far from the surface when he watched a sad film or saw an animal mistreated, he was easily angered and very tactile when it came to family, he had many of his mother's attributes.

Jack took a step back from the grave, he ran his fingers through his grey hair, he was lucky that it was still comparatively thick, except perhaps for a little thinning at the crown.

As he stood by the graveside he recalled the words of his father at his mother's funeral;

"With every couple, married or not, one must pass before the other, when the death of the one happens earlier in life, the other has time to recover and start again; when the tragedy occurs late in life the one remaining has a much greater challenge. That is why belief in a God is so important, it does not matter whether God exists or is just a figment of man's desire to explain the universe, it is the faith that there is something beyond. That faith is the force that enables the remaining one to continue life".

As he stood there contemplating, Jack became acutely aware of the cold December breeze, His ears tingled, as well as his extremities and his nose indicated the fall in temperature, the weather was just as the forecasters had suggested, but Jack had been too desolate to take any notice of weather forecasts, in fact Jack had been in no mood to take notice of anything at all.

At just under one hundred and eighty centimetres tall he was an imposing figure. He was still sport active, he was athletic with few signs of the wear and tear of his mature years. His gentle blue eyes and square jaw indicated that the ageing process had been kind, as Sylvia had often laughingly told him as she stroked his cheek.

He remembered the gentle touch of her hand and the knowing smile; it did not seem feasible that they were gone forever. Perhaps she would be waiting for him when he got home; Jack shook his head at the stupidity of the thought.

Jack had retired a few years earlier, a lifetime behind a desk was more than enough, he had wanted to pursue his hobby of photography on a more professional level and he had often dreamt of exhibiting his work, perhaps with Sylvia's help he could have attained his dream, she had always been encouraging... but now?

During those last months when he had become virtually housebound because of Sylvia's advancing debilitating condition, he had turned to his other love, the written word.

He had read most of David's work and he accepted that he would never reach his son's wordsmith ability, but he had written several articles for the photographic club magazine and there were a number of unpublished short stories that he hoped one day someone else would read and appreciate.

Jack's eyes began to fill with tears once more, he looked around, there was no-one else in the cemetery, he was alone. He considered those words for a moment, yes, he was definitely alone in every sense of the word.

He felt desolate, abandoned, deserted, a figure in an endless wilderness, a wilderness from which he could see no escape. He knew of course that he was not unique in being the one left behind, following the passing of one in a long marriage, but being left is just not the thing that anyone considers; it is not taboo, it is an inevitable consequence that is always pushed to the back of the mind.

He pulled his short winter jacket around him more tightly, he should now go home, but what was home, there was no one there, it was empty, there were only memories and each memory tore at his heart because there could be no more.

Jack had never considered what 'being alone' really meant. The world was full of people who lived alone, some lived a lonely life through choice, with others it was pure circumstance, but either way Jack would never have thought that it was a hardship.

Now he knew better, he was the wiser, loneliness was a physical state that was worse than anything that he could ever have imagined. It hurt in both mind and body; it was a pain without cure.

One of his friends had told him a couple of years before, following the death of his wife, that he could not imagine the days ahead when she would not be there, he could not get it into his head, his mind, that he would never see her again. But two years later he still lived, she was not forgotten but he had friends who had helped him with his grief and the pain, the ache had become bearable.

Jack turned and made for the cemetery gates, home it had to be, what he would do when he arrived he had no idea, just sit and remember he supposed, perhaps a cup of tea, food was out of the question, he had no stomach for anything solid.

He dreaded turning the key in the front door, but what else was there to do, what alternative did he have? None.

As Jack entered the hallway his landline began to ring in the living room, Jack quickened his pace, reached for the cordless phone and pressed it against his ear,

"Hello."

"Hi Dad, it's Peter, I've tried to call you a couple of times, are you okay?"

"Yes, I'm fine, I've just got back from the cemetery."

That was not quite true, Jack was far from fine, but what else could he say, he did not want his son unduly worried. Peter worked in IT and was always incredibly busy, he had his own life to lead, a life that rarely included his father; why should it?

Peter had taken his mother's death with tears and grief, but with his own heavy responsibilities and his family life to deal with, the initial shock and loss had to take second place. He now accepted that one of his parents was gone, but he had his own challenges ahead.

Peter had been married to Susan for five years, they had no children, both seemed to be too career minded to want or need a family, Jack was sad that there were no small grandchildren to babysit, to enjoy with Sylvia, to spoil and watch them grow but now that she was no longer with him it did not seem to matter quite so much, in fact nothing mattered.

"I'm on lunch break and I was wondering if there was anything I could do."

Jack thought for a moment, there was of course something that Peter could do, he could be in the house to alleviate the terrible loneliness that Jack had felt over the past week or so, but that was out of the question. Peter lived fifty miles away, he worked long hours and when he wasn't working, he was entertaining or he was sleeping.

"No Peter, I don't need anything at the moment, will you be coming over?"

"I'm really busy at the moment Dad, but I'll try and drive over for a couple of hours during the weekend. Oh, by the way, I've been in touch with the stone masons and they tell me that mum's headstone won't be ready for a few weeks."

Jack nodded then remembered that he was on the phone, "Thanks Peter, I'm just going to put the kettle on, perhaps you could give me a call tonight, I'm not going out, I'll just watch some television before I go to bed."

"Okay Dad, I'll give you a call later."

The phone went dead, and Jack replaced it in its holder. Going to bed had become another problem, Sylvia had passed away ten days earlier and each night since then had seemed like an eternity. In fact, he dreaded going to bed, the sheets were cold and empty, and it took forever to go to sleep.

Jack filled the kettle, it would be Christmas in seven days, his first Christmas without Sylvia, the thought brought tears to his eyes once again. He was dreading the coming holiday, it would bring back memories, happy memories it was true, but it would also enhance the "aloneness" that had struck and that had found prominence in his mind. He placed the kettle on its stand and switched it on.

The next three days passed more slowly than any Jack could remember, he occasionally switched the television on but failed to concentrate on the picture on the screen or the sound emitting from it.

At odd times, a Waitrose cottage pie was cooked in the microwave, it sufficed, he didn't really feel hungry, his stomach clenched at the thought of food, he only ate because he felt he had to, and to appease the nagging of his children.

Jack had picked up his camera a few times and ventured out into the garden, then he changed his mind and returned indoors. He had no heart to call any of his friends, why impose his misery on them.

Never mind, it was Saturday tomorrow, perhaps Peter would drive over.

At ten o'clock Saturday morning Jack received a call from Peter, he was on his way, ten minutes later he received a call from Laura; "Hi Dad, how are you, Peter has been in touch, he says he's coming over".

"I'm fine Laura, Peter's on his way."

"The twins have asked about you, they're missing Grandma Sylvia already."

"Tell them I'm missing grandma too and I hope I'll be seeing them soon, perhaps during a break from Uni."

"I'm sure they'll see you soon Dad, keep busy if you can and I'll try and get over to you shortly, Oh the front doorbell is ringing, I'll call you back later."

"Okay Laura, talk to you later."

Jack replaced the phone and waited for Peter to arrive.

In the two weeks since Sylvia's passing Peter had seemed to come to terms with the loss of his mother. It was not possible for him to understand how his father felt, how lonely he was or how bleak the future felt.

Jack had always been self-sufficient, independent and secure, now that everything had changed, his rock had crumbled, he was walking on quicksand.

When Peter did finally arrive, his presence brought relief to Jack, having someone else in the house made an enormous difference; in an instant the house lost its cold and gloomy atmosphere, it was transformed. It hadn't occurred to him before but a three-bedroom, three living room house was going to be far too big for a man on his own.

"I know it's early days Dad, but you must try and keep yourself busy, have you been to the photographic club since mum died?"

Peter's question was intended to help, but Jack did not need reminding of what to do, or should do, all would come in time, in Jack's time.

"No son, I just don't have any enthusiasm for anything at the moment, maybe next week I'll give a couple of my friends a call. They have already told me that they would be there for me if I needed them."

"That's good Dad, you should take them up on their offer, it'll be good for you."

"I'll think about it son."

Peter stayed for an hour then made his excuses and left, he had never stayed long, even when his mother was alive. It almost seemed that the visits were duty bound, visits necessary from a family point of view but visits that interrupted his normal routine and prevented him from doing something more important. Therefore, by necessity, the visits had to remain short.

On Christmas Eve Jack was on his own, he had arranged Christmas dinner with his son the next day and he was going to spend Boxing Day with his daughter, but if truth were told he wasn't relishing either; without Sylvia both days would be empty, and he was praying that the festive holiday season would pass quickly.

Both of his children would be acutely aware that their mother was absent, absent for the first time. There would be awkward moments, awkward silences and feelings held back for fear of upsetting their father. Without doubt Christmas would be a testing time. Best that it was over soon.

Jack's lack of appetite and indifference to alcohol meant that there was no possibility that he would be able to gorge himself or down the wine and spirits that were the usual part of the Christmas celebrations, the mere thought made him wonder how he would get through it; but for the family's sake he had to put on a brave face.

His mood was strange, he wanted or needed to be alone, but on the other hand he was desperate for company, it was an indecipherable conundrum.

New Year came and went, but nothing changed, the loneliness was as acute as ever, the grieving was a little easier, but his heart was empty, so very empty. He was living in a vacuum, one from which he could not escape, it appeared to him that it was one from which he would never escape.

By the end of January two thousand and seventeen, things were getting a little better, the natural grieving process was continuing, the sense of loss had not diminished but Jack had developed a sort of routine. It was a routine created by necessity, it consisted in the main of finding something, anything, to do during the daylight hours, pushing something into the microwave in the early evening, then turning on the TV until his eyes closed of their own accord. He was existing but he wasn't living.

He was back at the photographic club meetings and he was occasionally lunching with his friends. Perhaps 'friends' was too strong a word, they were acquaintances, people he saw on occasion when he indulged in one of his hobbies.

His son and daughter rang him each day to check on his well-being, he always told them he was okay, but the acute loneliness remained, the void in his life was always there, no matter how much he filled his time, the hours passed slowly, and the vacuum was never filled.

Jack's neighbours were a help, they knocked on his door from time to time to see if he needed anything, he always declined any offers they made but he was grateful for their care.

One day Bill, the neighbour on his right, a man in his sixties who although living alone did have a partner with whom he spent a great deal of time, knocked on the door, "Hi Jack, I know you've been very down since Sylvia passed, look I'm cooking for myself tonight, why not join me, it's just as easy to cook for two as it is for one."

Jack was surprised at the call, he had spoken to Bill on many occasions as they passed each other coming and going from their houses, but he had never seen the inside of Bill's.

"Thanks Bill, nice of you to ask, I could do with the company, what time do you want me to come over."

"Shall we say about seven?"

Jack nodded, "That would be great, I'll be there".

Jack closed the door as Bill disappeared down the driveway, he did not have much of an appetite these days, in truth his stomach had probably shrunk, the less you eat the less you want or need to eat, but just not being alone was going to be a pleasant change.

It was only just after lunch, there was still the rest of the day to consider. There was however a need to restock some provisions, the food cupboard was looking sorry for itself, it had definitely been neglected; he was low on milk, breakfast cereals, cheese and dishwasher tablets and so a trip to the local supermarket was necessary.

Shopping was a chore he tended to put off until the last minute, but it was something to do.

Jack's children were continually asking him to pick up on his hobby, photography.

During her last visit Laura had chastised him in a gentle way,

"Dad, your last photos were really exceptionally good, I thought that you were going to put together a sort of social history with your visual images."

Laura was correct, that was Jack's intention, but it had to be in his own time.

"Don't worry Laura, I'll get there, I just don't have the motivation at present."

"I know Dad, but we worry about you, are you eating properly, your face looks thinner?"

"Please don't worry, I'll be fine soon."

That had been the course of several conversations, but to be honest, through the grief and loneliness, he was aware that he was losing weight. Much of the problem was eating, he just never felt hungry, he was satisfied with the occasional snack, but he just could not be bothered with the process of preparing a meal.

That evening Jack knocked on Bill's front door, Bill was waiting and ushered him into the dining room. The table was laid, and Bill went into the kitchen to bring in the various dishes of meat and vegetables.

Jack had not realised that Bill was a very good cook and the meal looked quite appetizing. Unfortunately, as soon as Jack began to eat, he realised that he had no stomach for food, each small mouthful became a problem. After a time, Jack had to admit defeat, he was unable to force any more food down.

"I'm sorry Bill, the meal is delicious and I'm really grateful that you invited me to share it with you, but I just can't eat."

Bill shrugged his shoulders, "I know what you are going through, my dad was the same when mum died. He couldn't get over it, he seemed to lose the will to live, he passed away himself three months later... Oh sorry Jack, I didn't mean that you..."

"That's alright Bill, I know what you mean."

Jack gave a nervous laugh, "No chance of that happening to me, I only need some time to adjust and then I'll be fine. You know Bill, Sylvia and I were together for such a long time and we hardly ever spent a day apart".

Jack paused, sighed, "It's very tough trying to get used to being on your own. I understand that, as my own father told me, in every long marriage one or other of you has to die first leaving the other one alone, but you don't think of it, do you?"

Bill nodded in apparent understanding. "No, I suppose you don't, in my case Janet and I divorced five years ago, we had only been married six years. We'd persevered during most of that time knowing that it wasn't working, then Janet met someone at work and that was that."

Bill refilled his wine glass and took a sip, "Want some more wine Jack?"

Jack shook his head, "No thanks, I haven't eaten much, it'll go to my head".

Bill gave a wry smile, not in connection with Jacks reply but in something that had crossed his mind.

"The Hindus say that everything happens for a reason, they're right. The divorce was always on the horizon and if it hadn't happened, I would never have met Barbara."

Barbara was Bill's long-standing partner, they didn't live together all of the time, each preferring to maintain their own premises and their own independence, but they slept together each time they visited each other, which was regularly each week.

"How long have you known Barbara?"

Jack was now making conversation; he wasn't really interested but it was polite to ask.

"You know Jack, it seems like forever, it's about two years. We were introduced by a mutual friend and from the first moment there was something, I can't explain what and I wouldn't expect you to understand, but I somehow knew that she was the one."

Bill took a sip from his wine glass.

"I do understand Bill, but it wasn't that way between Sylvia and myself. Thinking back and it was a long time ago, I remember we started dating after we met at work and sort of drifted into a relationship, then it seemed only natural that we should get married. It was only in a Registry Office, so I don't even have any photos to look at."

Jack paused as if reflecting on his past, "Maybe we should have made a big thing of it, you know, the church, reception, bridesmaids and the rest, if we had I'd have something to look back at now".

Bill was silent for a moment or two then he said, "Jack, you have a lifetime of memories to look back on, think of all those happy times you had".

Bill was right, it was a natural response, one that everyone offers when given the circumstances, but it didn't apply, there was a mental block.

"That's the problem Bill, Sylvia was so ill during the last few months, she needed care and what with the constant 999 calls for an ambulance and the bedside vigil for the last nine or ten days, that's all I can really remember."

Bill took another sip of wine while he considered Jack's predicament, "Don't worry Jack, give it time, it'll all come back to you, just give it time".

Jack merely nodded; he didn't say anything because others had said the same.

A little after ten that evening Jack said his goodbyes after apologising for not eating more and returned home. HOME was the operative word because there was no one there, it was silent. It had been a home, but now it was just a place to stay, comfortable yes, but a place that only echoed the memories of the past.

As Jack sat alone and disconsolate in the living room he thought, "This must be how it feels to be in solitary confinement, but those in their cells are only there for a short time, my solitary confinement is for ever, for the rest of my life".

As the thought passed through his mind the black cloud of depression descended.

On Thursday morning the second of February Jack received a phone call from Stan, a fellow member of the photographic club. Stan was a couple of years older than Jack and was as enthusiastic in his photographic hobby as Jack.

"Jack, it's Stan, I'm just giving you an early morning call to see if you have any plans for later. The wife's gone to visit relatives and won't be back until tomorrow morning, I've been let off the leash."

Jack was pleasantly surprised by the call, the club had been far from his mind, but Stan's voice came as a welcome reminder; "No, I haven't any plans, what did you have in mind?"

Stan responded, "Well, the weather forecast is good, and I know how keen you are on photography that has social significance, so I thought we could go into town tonight and take some shots of the West End at night. You could get some interesting shots of the lights, the general bustle of the centre of town, the guys who sleep on the streets and if we're lucky maybe shots of guys passing out the stuff, you know hash. You couldn't get more social than that".

Jack thought for a moment, in all honesty he didn't have any motivation for anything at all, but it would mean getting out of the house that night and that would be a welcome relief.

"Okay Stan that sounds good, what time would you like to meet?"

"What about after the rush hour, say seven thirty at Paddington Station by the underground entrance, we can get the Bakerloo to Oxford Circus?"

"That's fine Stan, I'll see you at seven thirty, I'll look forward to that."

Jack was still depressed, it had become a permanent state of mind, a mood that he was unable to shake off, but he was glad he had friends.

He made himself a cup of tea and two slices of toast, merely for the sake of eating something, it was a bit of an effort getting them down.

It was only seven weeks since Sylvia had died but it seemed like seven months, in reality it WAS seven months. Since the cancer had taken hold Sylvia had become a different person, she was not the Sylvia he married.

There had been a couple of occasions when she had been delusional, almost certainly caused by the drugs, the chemotherapy, but it had been quite scary, the awful but inescapable truth was that he had lost Sylvia months ago, maybe that was the reason that those months were all that he could remember.

The day drifted by slowly, he looked out of the kitchen window, the grass needed cutting, it could wait, he just couldn't be bothered. The children phoned to check how he was, as usual he told them he was fine. Jack turned on the TV, it was the usual daytime stuff, he looked at the screen without taking anything in, it passed the time.

At long last six-forty rolled around, he needed forty-five minutes to get to Paddington, he picked out the appropriate camera but before he left the house he reached for his smart phone, it was better for taking photos in dark corners or doorways.

By the time Jack and Stan reached Oxford Circus the rush hour was more or less over. It was an early February evening, so it wasn't as busy as it could have been, but the weather was fairly mild and so there was still plenty of activity.

The theatre goers are always about, and the West End lights were a good photographic shot, but Jack was more interested in the figures huddled in doorways, the homeless. This was his forte, this is what he liked to do, show the world just how bad things were, how civilisation still had a long way to go.

For a couple of hours Jack managed to forget how lonely he was, that was until they had exhausted their places to explore, then he remembered that he would have to go home.

Stan did manage to drag him into a fast-food place for a bite to eat, but still the thought of going back to an empty house played on his mind.

Two hours later Jack turned the key in the front door. it was dark inside, he also noted that there were no lights in the neighbour's houses either side, this accentuated his feeling of isolation. What could he do to alleviate this feeling, this lurch in the pit of his stomach? He had no idea, perhaps he would eventually get used to living alone, many people did, but it didn't feel like it at the moment, hopefully one day...

Most of his friends and family could or would not realise that the grieving process was now virtually over, the last few months had seen to that, they did not understand that it was the loneliness, just the terrifying loneliness.

Jack had never been on his own before, that is, he had never lived on his own before, he could never have realised just how depressing it was. His children merely believed that he was going through the grieving process and all would be well when it was eventually over, but it was not that at all.

"Why not join something Dad, you know, local senior clubs, walking clubs, maybe you could take up art or something."

Their voices, helpful voices, concerned voices, echoed in his head.

They were trying to help, Jack did know that, but he did not have the motivation or the interest to do anything. His mind and his body were lethargic, his life was empty, his future uncertain, he was in a vacuum.

Nevertheless, in an effort to drag himself out of the bog that engulfed him, he did decide to join the local over sixties club, just to see if it would help. The phone number was on the web and when he rang the number listed, he got through to the secretary; "We are always pleased to sign up new members, we meet on Wednesday afternoons at two-thirty at St. Mary's Church Hall, that is the last Wednesday of each month. We do have an excursion down the Thames tomorrow it goes from Windsor and there is a small lunch provided on the boat.

"We've organised a coach to take us to the boat, it leaves at nine-thirty from the bus stop outside Waitrose. If you are interested our treasurer lives in your road at number twenty-four, why not go across pay the club's annual subscription and the charge for the boat trip".

Jack thanked her for her help, it sounded interesting, at last perhaps this could be a start, something that would help to pass the time, it was certainly worth a try. He wasn't a natural socialiser; he made the effort, but in normal circumstances he allowed the other party to make the running. This time he would have to be the conversation instigator.

Jack was lucky, the treasurer was at home when he called, so he paid the subscription and the excursion fee for the next morning, he was actually looking forward to it, perhaps he would meet people in a similar situation to his own.

He slept pretty well that night, not totally through the night as he did wake up a couple of times, but better than usual. Next morning, he was at the Waitrose bus stop on time. When he arrived, he noticed two elderly couples sitting on the bus stop seat, Jack nodded in their direction, but they ignored him and carried on talking between themselves.

Over the next ten or fifteen minutes a few other elderly people arrived, many using walking aids and all with someone, there did not seem to be anyone on their own. More worrying was their ages, Jack was old enough, but these over sixties were very much older and none of them seemed to be as fit as Jack.

The boat trip was about two hours long and although Jack tried, he could not engage in any meaningful conversation, the other club members seemed to only be interested in their medical ailments or the delivery of their mechanised walking aids.

All in all the excursion was an unmitigated disaster, there was no-one in the club with whom Jack had any kind of connection.

It was evident that the over sixties club was not for him, however the experience encouraged Jack to check the web for other local groups, art, walking, in fact anything at all.

There were many such senior groups, all met just once a month, the drawback was that Jack lived a little off the beaten track and all of the groups seemed to be very poorly attended. In addition, he noted that most of the attendees were women, there did not appear to be many men at all in members listed for current meetings.

Jack wondered if it was because men are bad joiners or perhaps there were many more widows than widowers. Either way he decided to put the idea on hold, at least for the time being, he could come back to it later, meanwhile he still had his photography.

The next day Jack wandered into his study, most of his material was in his computer but there was still a mountain of paper and photographs scattered around the room. He would need to sort it out when he had time.

"How ridiculous," he thought, "I've got all the time in the world".

There were a number of half-finished projects he really should look at, if only he could find the motivation. There was his local school project, it wasn't a new idea, but he had in his mind to mentally draw a circle around the nearby school, covering about a mile in diameter and on A4 size paper photograph most of the local trees and include on the same page a photo of the leaf and a photo of the fruit or seed of the tree. Then to put the photos in a scrap book so that the children on their field trips could seek out and identify the trees from the photographs, it would increase their natural history knowledge.

There would be a lot of legwork and research involved to complete the project and one day soon he would get to it, but not today.

Jack's mental lethargy was worrying, even to him, but he just couldn't shake it off. He was unable to stop the depression of loneliness, it was constantly there, and it was magnified each time he returned to an empty house. In any case the house was now too big, he would have to do something about that, at some time.

During the past months, whilst Sylvia was ill and incapacitated, Jack had learnt the mysteries of the washing machine and also how to cook, (with the exception of using the frying pan, he didn't want to set the house on fire), Sylvia had been unable to do any of that, but they were both chores that he did not enjoy.

Laura and Peter phoned every day, it was only a few minutes each time, but it was contact with the outside world. It wasn't enough of course but it was something, it was nice to know that they were concerned.

Two days after Jack's photographic excursion to the West End, Laura called, "Hi Dad, I thought I'd call you to see what you intend to do with mum's clothes, I know she had wardrobes full of all sorts of stuff".

Jack hadn't even given the matter any thought, everything was still in the same place, nothing had been moved. The thought of disposing or giving away Sylvia's clothing or other personal effects seemed like an act of betrayal.

"To be honest Laura I hadn't given it any consideration, what would you do with the clothes?"

"Well Dad, they serve no purpose left in the wardrobes, I was the same size as Mum, I could probably wear some and the rest should be given to the charity shop. There are lots of people who would make good use of them."

Jack considered Laura's words, she was right of course, but it seemed like early days to be thinking about changing anything.

"Dad, Mum had lots of handbags, do you know where they are?"

"Yes Laura, they're in the cupboards above the bed, I haven't looked but I know they are in there."

"I liked some of them, so I would like to take my favourites before you decide to get rid of them; is that okay?"

"Of course it is Laura, why wouldn't it be? I'm sure that Mum would have been delighted if you took some".

"Thanks Dad, I could use three or four, there were some nice dressy ones and if I remember they matched a couple of day outfits. There were also two new leather jackets that were perfect for any occasion."

Jack had now heard enough, it was almost like robbing a corpse, he'd seen a lot of that on TV, it didn't seem quite right, he didn't know why, after all they were only 'things', but they were Sylvia's things and she'd only been gone a couple of months, it just seemed too soon.

However, Laura was not only his daughter she was also Sylvia's daughter and he was sure that Sylvia wouldn't have minded.

"Alright Laura, come over whenever you can, take whatever you like."

"Thanks Dad, Mum wouldn't have minded she always said we should share. I was just a bit worried that you might throw things out without realising that I may want them."

"I had no intention of throwing anything out Laura, it hadn't even crossed my mind."

"If you don't mind Dad, I'll come over tomorrow morning, I'm not working, and I'd like to see you."

Jack said that he would be expecting her and replaced the phone. He did wonder if she really did want to see him or was she merely visiting to see what she could get.

"God I'm being so cynical," he thought.

Laura came the following morning and after a cup of coffee she suggested that they check through Mum's wardrobes. They both went into the main bedroom and opened the wardrobe doors but seeing all the clothes that Sylvia used to wear, including her favourite ones, proved to be too difficult for Jack and he decided to leave his daughter to it;

"I've got a few things to do Laura, have a look through, take those that you like, and I'll chat with you when you're done. There are some carrier bags in the utility room, there should be more than enough for you to pack the garments in".

Laura nodded, said thanks, and began rummaging through the wardrobe as Jack left the bedroom.

Jack went back to the kitchen and with a sigh sat down on one of the kitchen chairs; Laura would be some time, but Jack was in no hurry to do anything in particular, merely sitting and thinking was enough. However, his thoughts were interrupted by the ringing of the house phone.

"Hi Jack, it's me, Bill. I've been thinking, I know that you are not happy about staying in the house on your own, and after you mentioned that you were lacking the motivation to join local activity groups I came up with an idea. It goes without saying that you need company, someone to go to a restaurant with or the theatre, whatever, well I haven't told you how I met Barbara, perhaps you could meet a companion the same way."

Jack looked a little nonplussed. "Okay Bill, what are you suggesting."

"Look Jack why don't I come over a bit later and I can explain."

"That would be fine Bill, I'm not going out, just give me a ring when you're coming."

Jack did not have any idea what Bill was talking about, he had not given any thought of how Bill met Barbara, he didn't much care, but now, thinking about it he imagined that they were introduced at some gathering, a party perhaps. In any case it was difficult to see how that would help him, he had no party invitations on the horizon.

Jack had never been a party animal, he normally stood to one side and waited for someone to come to talk to him, initiating a conversation was always difficult, it seemed inane approaching someone with the line, "What wonderful weather we're having," or "isn't it a lovely party".

In any case Jack was not one for idle chit chat or gossip, both bored him.

Nevertheless, it was true, it was possible to meet someone at a party, how else did people meet these days? That was one topic that Jack had not yet contemplated, meeting someone... Meeting whom? Another woman? A companion? Jack mused at the idea, it was still early days but being alone was hurting, really hurting and he needed something to take away the pain. Laura interrupted her father's thoughts,

"I've put a couple of Mum's things in a bag, but I can't reach the cupboards over the bed, can you help?"

During the next hour Jack pulled out all of the handbags from the cupboards, there were more than he had imagined, Laura picked out three, she called them 'classic', the rest Laura thought were old fashioned.

After his daughter had said goodbye and the remainder of the handbags had been put away, Jack sat at the kitchen table, head in hands and with furrowed brow, wondering what Bill had in mind.

CHAPTER TWO

The ringing of the hall telephone interrupted Jack's train of thought… It was Bill; "Jack, if you're ready I'll come over now".

Jack concurred, and his brow furrowed as he tried to imagine what plan Bill had in mind; "It's probably a friend or acquaintance of Barbara, maybe someone from work, or perhaps a widow from her wide social circle".

It could of course be anyone from anyplace, Jack did not have any idea, however his curiosity was sufficiently aroused to be interested in hearing Bill out.

Whatever Bill had in mind, it was connected with an introduction to a member of the opposite sex. Jack wasn't sure that he was ready for that. Would it be unfaithful to Sylvia, would she understand? They were of course rhetorical questions, there was no direct answer, but Jack mused that if any introduction merely led to company, to companionship, someone to share a meal with, then there could be no harm in that.

One thing was painfully obvious and that was his loneliness and his desire to end it as soon as he could.

Life at present had no significance, no meaning, perhaps Bill had an idea how to help.

But there was one small complication, Jack didn't know about women. Yes he had been married for many years, but that was the problem, he knew about ONE woman, not women in general. Naturally, Jack, along with most husbands, would not admit to that, every husband who has been married for many years would profess to be an expert. In fact it is the "lothario" who has the greater knowledge. Jack was greener than a twig in spring, he knew little, it would have to be Bill's job to warn him of the pitfalls.

It was just a couple of minutes later that the front door chimes peeled out their melodious tune.

Bill stood on the doorstep, he held his iPad in one hand and his iPhone in the other, 'curiouser and curiouser' thought Jack. He held the door open and waived Bill inside. Jack presumed that the communication devices were to be used, maybe they were going to make a call now.

Jack ushered Bill into the living room and the two devices were laid on the coffee table, but Bill thought that it would be more comfortable at the table in the kitchen. He explained that they would not have to bend over to observe the sites they were going to visit on the web, it was easier to view the iPad at eye level.

Jack made no comment, he did not know what Bill had in mind; he had no notion why Bill had brought his iPad but he was quite content to allow matters to take their natural course.

Looking and sounding quite upbeat it was Bill who opened the conversation; "Before we start Jack, it would be a good idea if we tanked up with a couple of beers, what have you got?"

Jack smiled, Bill was hitting the right note and they hadn't yet started; "Not a lot Bill, just a few cans of Fosters".

"That'll do Jack, get out a couple of glasses."

In the next couple of minutes two glasses were full of the amber nectar, the fact that the glasses were marked Coca Cola did not detract from the cool taste of the lager.

Bill downed a third of the glass with his first gulp, he was obviously winding himself up for something.

He placed his glass back on the coaster and turned to Jack; "I've never mentioned it before, that's probably because the subject has never come up, but I actually met Barbara through a dating site".

Jack nodded, waiting for the follow up, so far nothing had been said that aroused his interest, in addition the mention of a dating sight meant nothing to him.

He was obviously aware that such organisations existed, but he had assumed that they targeted young people and had no connection to those of pensionable age. Jack had seen the advertisements on television and they all appeared to target the generations that were younger than himself, but to be frank most TV adverts were a break, time to put the kettle on, and he never really gave thought to their content.

Bill continued; "I realise that you would have had no reason to check out such sites, but many of them, the genuine ones, exist for the purpose of putting together lonely people for companionship. You know, widows, widowers, divorcees and such like. The ones I'm talking about are for older people, people like us who find ourselves suddenly living alone".

Jack listened in silence, he now had a good idea where this was going but his interest had now been aroused and he decided not to interrupt Bill's flow.

When Jack was young there were many ways to meet members of the other sex, there were dances or discos at most church and community halls on a regular basis; for the younger generation there were plenty of youth clubs.

Jack had long since recognised that society had changed; the advent of TV and the computer had all but destroyed sociability, entertainment for the large part was now in the home rather than outside.

Bill went on; "I'm talking here about the sites run by quality newspapers and the more serious radio programmes Jack. The people who join these sites are interested in real companionship and perhaps even more".

Bill looked at Jack to see the reaction to his last remark, but Jack did not display any emotion...

Bill continued; "When I joined the site some years ago, I was very lonely, I was going around the bend, I needed close companionship, someone I could be with, someone who I could share my life with, really a reason to be alive. I have never understood those people who are happy with their own company, who are happy with solitude, who are happy being alone. That was never for me, I needed another human being with whom I could relate and of course being a man, it was important that the other person was female".

There was still no response from Jack, but Bill could tell that he was listening.

Jack was indeed listening and he was also thinking, Bill had suddenly awakened his thinking processes, he was imagining himself with someone other than Sylvia, it was unimaginable, he began wondering if there was anyone out there with whom he could spend quality time, a strange woman, a different face but he just could not contemplate being with anyone other than his beloved Sylvia, it wouldn't be right.

In any case who would put up with HIM, was there anyone out there who would find him interesting enough?

Being married to one woman for almost a lifetime made him doubt his own ability to be able to physically or mentally attract anyone else. When you are married for so long everything comes naturally, both the silences and the chatter, there is no need to think and no need to force conversation.

So, as Bill was about to describe his own meeting, Jack's mind turned somersaults as he tried to imagine a new friendship, a new relationship, a new female in his own life.

"So Jack, I decided to sign up for a dating site in an attempt to fill the loneliness that I felt. If you like, it was the last chance saloon, as I thought. I'd talked to a few people beforehand and they really couldn't understand my reticence, 'go for it' was their advice and that is exactly what I did."

Bill paused; he was waiting for some sign from Jack but there was none.

"Have you got another beer Jack?"

"Sure, I'll get one from the fridge."

Once settled, Bill continued, if he were to convince Jack that a dating site was the best option to overcome his loneliness he would need to relate his own experiences, he would need to show that the entire process would not only be painless but could also be very interesting.

"Once I'd entered all of my details and indicated the sort of person I would like to meet, I received details of ladies with whom I matched. Some were a ninety-five per cent match some a little lower. They all had photographs on their sites together with their profiles, well not all but most, so at least I could see if there was any sort of physical attraction, not that it was vitally important but a pleasing appearance is always a big help for the initial meeting."

Bill raised his glass, took a swallow and replaced the glass on the coaster.

"Anyway, I looked at a few, read their likes, dislikes and their preferred male types and left them messages. They were able to see my own profile and photo so if they thought that I appeared acceptable they would respond.

"The first answer I received was, thank you for contacting me, but I am now seeing someone. Sometimes this is a polite way of saying, 'I saw your photo but I didn't fancy you'. The next one was polite but told me that she did not believe we were a match, I received no response at all from the third, she obviously did not like the way I looked, but the fourth one said that she would like to know more."

Bill glanced at Jack, he was checking to see if there was any response, he had been through this entire scenario himself over a considerable period of time, but he was acutely aware that this idea would be totally foreign to Jack, it would be strange, something he had never considered and he did not know how Jack would react. He did not even know if Jack was ready for the concept or if he was able to take on board the idea of a new relationship. All that he really knew was that, even if Jack did not go for it, he needed something to help with his loneliness.

Bill was in full flow so 'carry on regardless' came to his mind; "That did seem to be a positive reply and I was encouraged. When she said she wanted to know more, she obviously meant more about my hobbies, past life, current situation etc. So, I sent back some details".

Bill paused once again still waiting for some response, he wasn't disappointed, Jack was becoming intrigued, he wanted to know more. He knew where Bill's information was leading and if truth were told, he was becoming interested. Jack leaned forward.

"What happened next Bill, was the fourth one Barbara?" Bill gave a chuckle; he was getting through.

"No Jack, Barbara was some way down the line. When you enter info into your profile one of the questions is about the distance you are willing to travel, you know ten miles twenty miles, fifty miles, anyway I believe I just put in worldwide and the lady who responded lived in Wales. To be honest I didn't mind, a night in a B&B was not going to deter me if it turned out that she was "The One". As it turned out, although she was nice and although I had a pleasant weekend it was obvious to both of us that it wouldn't work out. She is still on my Christmas card list."

Bill paused, he realised that he had Jack's full attention.

"Putting in worldwide is not ideal for most people, but I travel a lot and I really didn't mind meeting someone a good distance away. To be honest the people on the sites usually restrict the distances they would like to go for a meeting, you know, ten miles, fifteen miles, that sort of thing, but I wanted to cast my net as wide as possible, I suppose I was desperate. Though I don't think it would be appropriate for you Jack."

Jack nodded as though he fully understood, travelling for hours to see someone for the first time was not on the agenda, it wasn't going to happen. However, at the moment Bill's experiences were personal to Bill and were not relevant to him. Nevertheless, it did seem that Bill was inferring that he, Jack, should indulge in similar excursions through the same medium, the dating site, and this Jack found to be interesting enough for him to hear more.

“What happened next Bill, presumably there were more dates before you met Barbara?”

Bill was only too pleased to continue, he liked to recount his meetings, his experiences, his ‘girlfriends’, it was good conversation and in this case, he was attempting to impress upon Jack that if he really wanted to deal with his loneliness then this was a good route to take, and even if it took time to meet a suitable companion, the journey itself was interesting so he went on;

“Yes of course there were Jack, it would be a miracle if you met the right person straight away. There are thousands of people on these meeting sites, people of all ages and persuasions, I suppose in a way it’s like looking for a needle in a haystack, but I can promise you that somewhere on the web there is someone with whom you can empathise and who would be a great companion.”

Jack crossed his legs and muttered, “That would be nice”.

Bill could see that Jack was not fully convinced, but he also noticed that he had generated enough interest to enable him to introduce Jack to enrolling on the site he had in mind.

"Look Jack don't expect to find a replacement for Sylvia, you're not ready yet, but you do need someone who is easy to talk to, has similar interests or will share in yours and someone who is looking for an amenable companion. You can't, and you shouldn't expect more than that at present".

Jack was silent, but he nodded in agreement, he couldn't argue with the obvious. Then with a sign of the anguish that he felt, he turned to Bill; "I feel so guilty about wanting female company so soon after Sylvia's passing, I do hope she will understand and forgive me, we were married for so long, I feel like a traitor even considering going out with another woman".

Bill could see that Jack was troubled but he wanted to reassure him.

"Jack, you are not being disloyal, you have lived with Sylvia for very many years, you have never been alone, it is perfectly natural that you would want to spend time with someone else now that she is no longer with you. That is what companionship is all about, a friendship that will help with loneliness.

"I know that you have the photographic club, but how often does that meet? Not often enough to be of any real help."

Bill hoped that Jack's concerns would be overcome by his need of sharing his life with someone.

Bill had himself wondered if being alone was better than being so desperate that the first thought of companionship made one choose the first interested party who came along, that choice would be likely to lead to an undesirable liaison. That was his reason for the wide boundaries he had entered on his profile. He was aware of his weaknesses, his enthusiasm for accepting the first person who came along who intimated an interest, he had needed choices to prevent him from making a mistake. Desperation forces errors.

Jack replied; "Thanks for that Bill, so what happened next?"

"Well, I told you that I did not put any restriction on distance and the next message I received on the site was a lady who lived in Switzerland. I gathered that she travelled to London quite a bit and thought that it would be nice if she had someone in town with whom she could team up during her visits. To be honest that was not what I was looking for, but I believed that the match made in heaven would come from the most unlikely source, so I decided to respond in a positive manner".

Bill paused for a moment, gazed at his empty glass and in a somewhat pained tone asked, "You wouldn't have another lager, would you?"

Jack revisited the fridge, pulled out another can of Fosters and handed it to Bill who continued.

"Anyway, the lady from Switzerland, who turned out to be called Candice, arranged to meet me in the Dorchester coffee shop. Actually she was quite attractive and friendly in a nice way. We had a long chat and I discovered that she was a woman of considerable wealth, properties all over the place, a portfolio of investments and, from what I could gather she had a considerable income, all courtesy of her deceased husband.

"She had never been on the London Eye so that was our first port of call, after that, as it was a nice day we strolled around the West End before finally finding a restaurant for our evening meal, all in all it was a very pleasant day."

Jack could see that Bill had enjoyed the day but as he was no longer with Candice he was interested to hear the downside, there must have been one otherwise Barbara would not be Bill's partner. "Did you see Candice again?"

"Yes! I saw her the next time she came to London; it was a couple of weeks later. She was very pleasant company and that was the problem. She was just looking for an escort during her UK trips and nothing more; that, in the longer term was not what I wanted so I explained that I was looking for a serious relationship and not just a casual friendship."

"So, what happened Bill?"

“Candice understood perfectly, I have an idea that she had been through this before. Anyway, we agreed to remain friends and I did see her once more a month or so later, in fact we still exchange Christmas cards.”

Jack pondered the info that he had received and concluded that Bill must be spending a fortune on stamps come the festive season, he also wondered why Bill bothered to keep in touch with someone once a meeting had ended with no prospect of future meetings on the agenda, it didn’t make sense to him, still each to his own.

Jack was already getting the feeling that this potential new adventure was not quite as straight forward as first thought, but he needed to hear more.

“Did you have any more dates before you met Barbara?”

Bill was revelling in his reminiscences, he really enjoyed talking about them, and in Jack he had a willing ear.

“Oh yes Jack, several, I can’t remember the exact number, but I do recall that I arranged a meeting with a lady from Cardiff. She seemed a good match according to her profile and as I didn’t mind travelling I went to Cardiff to meet her. This time I wasn’t disappointed, her name was Alwyn and she was as pretty as a picture and an extremely nice person. In reality she was the type of person that I had been looking for. We got on well and I met her brother, in all I saw her four times and to be honest I would have been happy to make our friendship a closer one."

Bill sighed; it was apparent that this was the one who got away; "Why didn't it work Bill, it seems from your description that you had found your needle in the haystack?"

"I thought so too Jack but obviously she didn't see it that way. She explained to me that we lived too far apart, and her feelings were unlikely to be strong enough to satisfy a long-term relationship. I guess she was just being kind as she said that it would be better to end our friendship at that point before it progressed further."

"shame."

Bill stood up and pointed towards the toilet, "Before I go on I just need to go to the bathroom".

As Bill left the room Jack gazed out of the living room window onto the back garden. The garden had always been Sylvia's pride and joy, she loved to keep it looking pristine, manicured lawn, not a weed in sight and each and every plant given as much love and attention as a new-born child. Alas Jack was no gardener and already weeds were sprouting here and there, the lawn needed mowing and all in all the garden was looking a little tired. Tired or not Jack had not been able to motivate himself to spend time in Sylvia's province, in fact since his loss Jack had not been able to motivate himself to do anything at all.

Jack took his eyes from the slightly depressing scene outside and became lost in thought. He recalled the constant advice provided by his children and by others, "Jack, the best thing that you can do is keep busy, get out there with your camera, contact your friends, join local clubs," and so on; but none of them understood that keeping busy was NOT the answer, the answer was in his mind. Joining clubs was not going to help if his mind was not interested, the same argument was appropriate for everything else, he needed to WANT to do those other things, otherwise they were not the answer to his loneliness dilemma. Jack was not sure what the answer was, all he knew at the moment was that there was an enormous void in his life and he had no idea how to fill it. Perhaps Bill had the right idea, perhaps not, he really didn't know, but he was determined to listen and if Bill had found himself as low as Jack was now feeling and had found a solution then it had to be worth a try.

Bill sauntered back into the room and sat down.

"Where were we Jack? Oh yeah, my dates. Well after my excursion to Wales and the end of my potential romance with my Welsh beauty, I wasn't about to give up hope. You do realise Jack that there are more lonely ladies on these meeting sites than there are men, at least that's what I understand, so there is bound to be someone who fits the bill, I wasn't going to let one failed meeting deter me from trying to find that someone special."

Bill checked to see if he still had Jack's full attention; he had.

"I continued to receive messages in response to my initial intros and I continued to converse with several possibilities. I suppose that they were doing exactly the same with other guys. Anyhow, because I was happy to travel I went to Scotland to meet someone and I went to Ireland. On both occasions I had a great time, but they were not meant to be, either I was not interested, or they were not interested in a second meeting."

Jack nodded in understanding, "I take it that after your travels to Scotland and Ireland you then made contact with Barbara?"

"Not quite, there were a couple of other meetings, but they did not amount to anything. I must have been on the site for over six months before I sent my usual message, following my examination of the photos and profile, to Barbara. I had no expectations at that time, I merely wanted to chat to see where it led. You really can't tell from a photo what a person is like, and sometimes the camera does lie."

Jack reached for a tissue as he stifled a sneeze, "I suppose you then arranged to meet?"

"Not straight away, we messaged each other a few times asking each other about our interests, background, history and the like, then we arranged to meet for a coffee."

"Talking about coffee that's just what I need right now, do you want a cup Bill?"

"Yeah, that would be great, white no sugar, thanks."

Jack sauntered off to the kitchen, while he was making coffee he mulled over in his mind everything that Bill had said thus far. He was definitely coming around to giving this idea a shot, it had to be better than remaining as he was, perhaps it was unfaithful to Sylvia, but he was sure that she would want him to be in a better place than he had been during these past months.

A few minutes later with two cups of coffee on the table in front of them, Jack continued where they had left off; "Was it sort of love at first sight?"

"Nothing like that Jack, but I must admit there was something, some connection, at least sufficient for us to arrange to meet again. We met several times after that until we were meeting several times a week, and of course the rest is history."

Jack knew of course where this was leading, what Bill was going to propose, and he was grateful that there may be an answer for the gap that Sylvia had left behind, but was he ready? That was an unanswerable question, he really didn't know, perhaps he would never know, but the thought of those lonely nights with the knowledge that the following day would be desperately empty, was enough to keep him listening to Bill's advice.

Jack's thoughts were interrupted by Bill, "Jack, I am not suggesting that you will find another Sylvia, nor a replacement for Sylvia, all that I am suggesting is that you may find some pleasant acceptable company who will help you get through the days, months ahead, can that be bad?

I've watched you moping about, not knowing what to do, where to go and going without a decent meal. You must have lost a stone in weight over the past couple of months, it really is time to call a halt and look ahead, don't you think?"

Jack thought to himself, "look ahead to what, I'm alone what future is there, I just can't believe that Sylvia is no longer here, not in the next room".

Jack shook his head, not in refusal but to remove the morbid thoughts. He was an intelligent man and he knew that life must go on, as unpalatable as it may appear to be at present.

"Okay Bill, if you think that the meeting web site would be helpful I'm prepared to give it a go. I've never dated anyone before, except Sylvia of course, I wouldn't know where to start, I'll need your help."

"Of course I'll help, that's the reason I brought in my iPad, just in case it is needed, but we will have to join the site from your laptop."

Jack left the room and within a minute or two re-emerged with his Dell laptop. He entered his password, pushed aside Bill's device, pulled up his chair and placed the open laptop on the table in front of them.

Bill smiled and typed in the name of the website he had used.

"This site specialises in matures, not exclusively but mostly."

"You mean pensioners do you Bill?"

"Well yes, but pensioners who are seeking a new start, a new beginning, a new relationship. Pensioners who haven't given up on life and who are looking to enrich their everyday existence, in the same way that you are Jack."

Jack smiled, he had been sarcastic, but Bill was right, there was one thing that he really did need and that was something to fill his every day.

Bill was now ready to launch Jack, it was the reason for his visit and he knew that it was what Jack required.

"You can sign up for the first month free of charge but after that there is a fee. If someone does appeal to you in that first month you will need to become a fully paid-up member before you will be able to pass on any communication details."

Jack nodded; "I can see that it makes sense, after all the dating business must make money, that's what the world is about".

"Don't be cynical Jack, you are not going to regret this and whatever the fee it will be well worth it, believe me."

Jack accepted the mild rebuke it was well intentioned.

Bill completed his typing and turned to Jack; "Ok, I'm in the site now, we have to enter all of your personal details including your likes, dislikes, personal preferences etc. The object of the exercise is to match you with someone who shares the same interests and who matches your physical preferences".

"I understand Bill, it makes perfect sense, mind you it sounds like a lot of hassle."

"There's no other way Jack, if you want to meet someone who meets even half of your expectations you have to go through the detail required. You know what they say, No pain, No gain."

He smiled at his own wit.

"It isn't that difficult Jack, each question gives a list of alternatives, for instance they ask for hair colour then there is a list of the choices, brown, black, grey, bald and the rest, all you have to do is tick the one that is appropriate, how hard is that?"

"Okay Bill, point taken, you're right it doesn't sound too difficult, let's go for it."

Over the next forty-five minutes the pair went meticulously through all the questions asked until they reached the final piece of information requested and that was a description of Jack, as he saw himself.

"What in God's name do I write here Bill?"

Bill thought for a moment, reflecting on what he had written when completing his own profile.

"Hmm, let me see if I can remember what I wrote, it was quite a while ago but for you I would say, 'As a photographer I enjoy both countryside and the city, I enjoy walking and socialising. I also like to visit the theatre and local restaurants.

'I am looking forward to spending time travelling to new places with a likeminded person.

'I am romantic and like to hold hands when walking. I am very fit and in good health. I would be extremely interested in sharing any hobbies with someone else.

'Although my initial aspirations are for companionship and good company I would not be disappointed if the friendship led to something more serious'."

Jack listened with interest, it didn't sound too bad, it was what he may have written himself, except of course for the last sentence, he probably wouldn't have added that. Still if that's what it took to create interest.

Jack was now sensing a feeling of nervousness, he hadn't even joined the site as yet but already the thought of meeting, taking out, socialising with strange females, was daunting. It had been so many years, he just couldn't envisage himself with anyone else, what would he say? What could he say? The mere thought of what he was embarking on was making him shiver, he was beginning to wonder if he could go through with it.

Bill was blithely unaware of the worry going through Jack's mind.

"You could write more if you wish, but probably that would be enough."

Jack was positive that it was enough, it was most likely too much, it sounded so personal.

Bill continued, "Now Jack comes the important bit, your photograph for your site profile. I'll take several on my iPhone and send them to you, you can then add the ones that you like to the site".

Bill glanced at Jack and wrinkled his nose, "Jack you look a little old fashioned for the photos, you need to present yourself in the best possible light".

Jack looked down at his attire, white shirt, grey worsted trousers, grey socks and brown brogue shoes. He had no idea what Bill was talking about, everything looked fine to him.

CHAPTER THREE

Jack had always considered himself a reasonable dresser, he didn't wear designer suits or very modern garb, but he always tried to be smart. This was probably due to a life in office administration, it would not have been appropriate to dress any other way.

As a senior executive it was beholden to dress in a manner that set an example to less senior staff, he was in effect a member of the old school. In recent times, even in City institutions 'dress down days' were a popular concept and in Jack's view the old standards had been dropped. However, he accepted the march of time and his wardrobe did contain modern garb for weekends and 'off duty' days.

In the twenty-first century, senior citizens were having some difficulty in coming to terms with the dress code and the attitude and the behaviour of 'modern youth'. Jack knew that this had always been the case, each generation rebelling against its predecessor, but Jack's intention, his desire, was to meet someone from HIS generation.

Now Bill was suggesting that his current outfit was not suitable for a dating website photo. He was tempted to say, "if they don't like what they see they can go to hell," but he decided to go along with Bill's judgement and take his advice; although at this juncture in the 'dating' process, he was wondering just who he was trying to impress.

Bill was attempting to be patient, he had considerable experience in the necessity of presenting the right appeal to a waiting female audience. He explained in a friendly and non-condescending tone; "Jack, even more mature ladies like their men to be up to date. Most will be knowledgeable with current fashion trends; women tend to move with the times and they expect, or would prefer, to meet a man who is modern. In general they are not seeking a 'pipe and slippers' man.

"Perhaps you could put on a pair of jeans and a check shirt or maybe a turtleneck sweater, that would create the right impression".

Jack pulled a wry face, he did have a couple of pairs of jeans, but they were usually worn for gardening, the turtleneck sweater was not a problem. He was not stupid and he saw the wisdom of Bill's words, he had to give this venture a decent crack of the whip, otherwise there was no point in carrying on.

"Ok Bill I'll go and change."

Dressed as Bill had suggested the photo session was about to begin, Bill was hesitating, he turned to Jack and said;

"We need the right background; we also need you to change into a different outfit for at least a couple of the photos. I'll take a number and you can choose which ones to put on the site. We will need something to show you relaxed, something to show that you are active and perhaps one outside in the front garden".

Over the next thirty minutes photos were taken of Jack reclining on a chair, Jack in the garden spade in hand, and Jack standing by his car with one hand on the bonnet, all very casual, all meant to be endearing to the viewer.

However, Jack had no illusions regarding his appeal to the opposite sex and he doubted that there would be many ladies who would find him interesting enough to make contact, he had never been photogenic and he didn't like to see himself on paper, but he had to have the photos for the site, there was no option.

"*C'est la vie,*" passed through his mind.

So, the job was done, Bill forwarded the pictures he had taken on his iPhone to Jack's laptop and after choosing what he thought were the best of a bad bunch, the photos were put on the dating website alongside the profile, now it was a case of waiting for any responses.

"Thanks Bill, I really appreciate your help, but I wonder just what I'm getting myself into. I don't think I've actually dated anyone before, apart from Sylvia of course, I just hope I'll know what to say."

Bill understood exactly where Jack was coming from, he had been there himself. He was now relaxed about the dating site and the contacts and the responses that it brought, but in the beginning… "Jack just be yourself, there's no need for any airs or graces, be natural and it'll work out fine, don't forget your dates will be in the same position as yourself".

"Easy for you to say Bill, you're settled now but it's new for me, it's like starting all over again like I was a teenager, in fact it feels extremely weird."

Jack wasn't exaggerating, in the beginning Bill had indicated that they were embarking on an adventure, but Jack was sure that he was embarking on an ordeal, a trial by fire. He had wondered if it was worthwhile, his life had been boring, mundane, but it was safe. Those had been his thoughts as he posted the photos on the website and as he activated it, his doubts multiplied.

However, on reflection, after he had made the decision to go ahead Jack knew that it was the correct decision, he had to deal with and overcome his loneliness, his life was no life, it was unbearable, it had to change. Bill had helped him to choose a new path, he just didn't know yet whether it was the right path.

Bill noticed the frown on Jack's brow and he guessed that he was worried; "It was the same for me Jack, it took time for me to get used to the dating game but after the first couple of times you will take it in your stride. I would advise one thing though, don't restrict yourself to talking to one person at a time, if you receive several responses then talk to each one. Unfortunately, there are those who are quite satisfied with just online chat and who do not really wish to meet, whilst there are others who are looking for meal tickets. You'll just have to make your own assessments when you come across them".

"Thanks for that Bill, it didn't really help my confidence."

So, the waiting game had started, Bill had indicated that it would only be a day or two before his entry onto the site was up and running. It would be interesting to see just who matched his criteria, his profile, and who would make contact. On second thoughts perhaps it was up to him to make the first move after viewing the photographs and descriptions. It was odd that although he was only seeking companionship, someone to keep him company, their appearance was important. Just why this should be the case he couldn't fathom; it shouldn't make any difference. As long as she shared some of his views and interests her physical appearance was, or should be, of no consequence; but it was.

Jack had deliberately omitted one thing from his profile and that was his interest in, 'the circle of life, the circle of existence', he had not wanted to appear weird.

The fact was that both he and the person that he hoped to meet were both in the final chapters of their lives. Chapters that he sincerely hoped would not be wasted, it needed to be fulfilling. Nevertheless the end of his chapters were not that far distant and he had wondered what comes next if anything.

Ancient civilisations had believed that nature was circuitous, everything was born and then reborn, there was no such thing as death. Modern man, in his wisdom, his intellect and his education had still not concluded if death meant the end of existence for an individual, they wanted or perhaps needed to believe that the soul or the psyche lived on. Jack's interest was in the philosophy of the conjecture.

It was by its nature a deep subject so Jack was hoping that he would be able to meet someone who was his equal in considering the more sombre side of life's existence, whilst also was capable of fun, light-heartedness and caring.

He did not know if such a person existed, he hoped so. But Jack still felt that he was being unfaithful, not so much to Sylvia but to their long marriage. She had been gone for such a short time, but he was so lonely, perhaps the fact that they had been together twenty-four seven was the reason.

Since he had been on his own, sleeping in a bed without the comfort of someone alongside had been an issue. Consequently, from the very beginning he had placed a pillow beside him in the bed, to give him the comfort, the feel that Sylvia was there. It helped him sleep, at least a little, but it was never a sleep that was satisfying, it was always a sleep of exhaustion arising both from grief and his inability to drift without effort into oblivion.

It was the next morning, after his session with Bill, that Jack awoke with the feeling that it was the day that his online experience was about to begin.

He peered through the bedroom curtains on to the back garden, it wasn't raining, that was a good start, but he quickly looked away, there was work to do to bring the garden up to scratch and he wasn't in the mood. The garden had been Sylvia's province, her pet love. She spent hours pruning and weeding, getting everything neat, tidy and in order, Jack didn't have the interest to follow suit. His only consolation was that it was the end of winter and spring had not yet had the opportunity to take over.

He turned over and gazed at the wall, he would get up in a minute and get himself ready before switching on the computer, there was no hurry.

As he lay there his thoughts drifted back to the day of the funeral. He had reminded the mourners of Sylvia's favourite Psalm, she hadn't been religious, in fact in all of their years together they had entered a church on only a handful of occasions, just deaths and marriages. But as he stood in front of the tearful gathering he had spoken the words that had meaning for Sylvia, Psalm twenty-three;

> The Lord is my shepherd; I shall not want,
> He maketh me to lie down in green pastures
> He leadeth me beside the still waters
> He restoreth my soul, he leadeth me in the paths of righteousness for his name's sake.
> Yea, though I walk through the valley of the shadow of death
> I will fear no evil, for thou art with me, thy rod and thy staff will comfort.me.
> Thou preparest a table before me in the presence of mine enemies;
> Thou anointest my head with oil,
> my cup runeth over,
> Surely Goodness and mercy shall follow me
> All the days of my life
> I shall dwell in the house of the Lord, for ever.

Sylvia had learnt the words from the Bible during her early school days and her father had spoken the words of the psalm at her mother's funeral, it was fitting that he did the same at her funeral.

Jack lay in bed mouthing the words, the tears returned to his eyes, he thought of the future, a bleak and empty future. He could not turn off his mind, he could not move on.

The reading of the Psalm had been even more poignant because on reaching the age of senior maturity, life and death had leapt to the fore of his thinking. He believed that he was fast approaching the end of his life; he had lived it in the biblical sense and now he had begun to think of the end of his existence; it was morbid but often after the age of fifty many people did consider that their particular end was fast approaching.

With the passing of Sylvia he had now been touched by death, it stood in front of him… waiting.

However Jack did have the slightest of consolations. When confronted with the question, "Does death mean the end of all TIME for the person who has passed away?"

He had given it some thought and had come up with his own philosophy, a philosophy that helped him with the passing of Sylvia. He had written his notion, as improbable as it was, in prose form, it had helped him come to terms with the future; he had called his piece TIME;

What is TIME? Is it just a measurement?
A description of a life span, a made-up word?
But what is a life span? Everything has a life span,
a human, a tree, an animal, a planet, a sun,
a galaxy, a universe. They all live and die.
Or do they? Planets, suns, universes and everything
on them is constantly reborn, reformed,
to live again, as it was before,
in a constant process, in perpetuity.
When our own sun dies, somewhere in the universe
a new sun will be formed, in fact there will be
countless suns born, and when they die there
will be countless others, many with planets and
many with life as we describe it.
Nothing, and if we accept the new concept that
matter can be created from energy,
then it follows that throughout
the universe the same energy must be used over
and over again, in the process of recreation.
It further follows that the death of something
of anything, is merely just part of the process of
recreation. In consequence nothing truly dies,
everything is recreated in some form.
Nature is circuitous, a perpetual and everlasting
death and rebirth, a movement or transition of energy
without end. If energy cannot be destroyed then
there can be no end.

Like a circle it is everlasting, always there, always existing.
Even the 'big bang' theory relies on the existence of a singularity, an enormous amount of energy.
Therefore if nothing ever 'dies' and time is a measurement of a life span, then time itself does not, cannot exist,
it is merely a word used to describe relativity, a word
used to describe what we see in our insular world, but not a word that describes reality.

It is NOT real.

Jack was a thinker, and apart from his uneducated and probably nonsensical views on 'time', he had often wondered about the word GOD, what exactly did it mean. One famous theologian had paraphrased it as; "God is unknowing and infinite".

That meant nothing to Jack, if he/she/it could not be known and was infinite, then as far as the human mind was concerned God could not exist, at least not in the way taught by any of the religions.

Jack smiled to himself, his mind was overactive, anyone who met him from the site would probably think that he was bonkers, she would have to put up with a great deal.

Jack turned over in the bed, everything was what it was, nothing was in Jack's control. Bill was trying to help and for that Jack was grateful, he should just go with the flow and try and eliminate the depressing thoughts from his mind.

The last days and weeks had been a real struggle for Jack, he had to accept tomorrow and not dread it, perhaps the dating site would help in that respect.

CHAPTER FOUR

Today was not like any other day, not in the normal sense at least. It was a day when Jack was about to embark on a search for someone, that someone being female, a woman with whom to share his future life, or at the very least a part of that life.

Those thoughts were a little optimistic but he needed to approach this 'dating site' venture in a positive mood. It could be a cure all for his unwanted solitude, that was the idea and he needed to hang on to that notion.

Jack had put aside his early morning morbid thoughts, dressed, eaten and approached the table that supported his laptop, the door to his future. In this case it was the table in the kitchen, many would say the most used room in any house.

In the recent past Jack tended to spend most of his day in the kitchen, it was the room that led to the conservatory and ultimately the garden. It was also the room where he was unable to slump on to the settee, an unhealthy tendency if he happened to wander into the living room, the room that had been the centre of his grief.

He had spent so much of his time following Sylvia's death, lazing, snacking and watching TV, because it was easy, he didn't have to think, he just had to lay there and stare at the cavorting images on the screen and allow time to pass, he had become almost comatose, a way of dealing with the situation that had been thrust upon him.

It was not as though there was nothing better to do, it was merely that he had lost the motivation to do anything, what was the point?

Depression had been his state of mind for too long, it had never been a problem before, but he had never been alone before.

With Bill's help, he was now about to discover if someone had responded to the profile he had entered into the dating site.

He felt a little apprehensive as he mused whether a lady may have answered his call, a lady who may fill the void that permeated through his entire being, perhaps a lady with whom he could laugh, a lady in whose company he could feel relaxed and with whom he could share a glass of wine whilst engaging in light conversation.

Jack smiled as he realised that his attitude, his mental approach had become juvenile, he was acting like he had acted on his very first date all those years ago, he was being presumptive, there was most likely no message waiting at all.

His life had become a life of 'perhaps', but that was significantly better than a life full of nothing.

Of course, it had also occurred to Jack that the 'someone' he was thinking about may not actually exist and even if she did exist there was no reason that he could think of that would attract that someone to him.

After being married for so many years the idea that the special relationship that grows after a long time period, a relationship built on shared experiences and common interests, could in any way be replicated in the time he had left, it was difficult to conceive that it was possible.

The dating site was the first step towards his search for companionship, of a future, or a path that when travelled would enable him to reach a destination of contentment. Of course pessimistic Jack had also considered that he may be unable to find anyone that was interested in him. He knew that his looks were passable, but they were just that, 'passable' and in truth he believed that most female subscribers would be seeking something more.

Jack was under no illusion that he would be a good catch, just the reverse, since her passing he had wondered how Sylvia had put up with him for so long. The more he thought about his own inadequacies, his idiosyncratic nature, his daily requirements, the more he convinced himself that no-one would be interested in an old photographer with little to offer.

But in truth he really did not know what his responders, if any, were looking for.

Jack settled himself at his desk, opened his laptop, waited forever for the ageing device to respond then tapped into the dating website.

He noted with some surprise that he had received one response and it was with a great deal of trepidation that he read the words on the screen.

To date he had not fully registered on the site, this meant that he could only receive or send one-line messages, he could not at this stage make arrangements to exchange telephone numbers or email addresses, any mention of either was redacted by the site, however he could relay and receive sufficient information to begin meaningful correspondence.

The message read;

> *Saw your profile we seem to have a lot in common perhaps we could talk.*

This was Jack's first taste of a conversation with a member of the opposite sex, a conversation that was intended to be more than just a casual reference to the weather or the political state of the nation. It was the first step towards a potential meeting for the purpose of getting to know someone of the opposite sex in a more intimate way than he had ever envisaged during the past fifty years.

It was quite scary, he would need to see who had sent the message, he would then need to consider a reply, a reply that would not make him sound like an idiot or make him sound like a newcomer to the dating experience.

He brought up the profile of the sender of the message and was disappointed to discover that there was no photograph, Bill had advised him that this was sometimes the case, either the subscribers had not discovered how to load the photograph or they were newcomers themselves and had not had the time to do it, nevertheless he decided to respond;

I'd love to chat; do you have a photo?

While he waited, he decided to check the profiles of other females who were on the site. He did not know if the sender of the message was currently online, but it didn't matter, there were pages of potential possibilities, pages of ladies that according to the site builders had profiles that matched his to varying degrees, based on one hundred percent for a 'perfect' match.

Jack had not mentioned anything to either of his children. He wondered what they would think if they knew that he was trawling a dating site. They would most likely be slightly disgusted, a man of his age; what would he want with another woman?

Since the children had reached adulthood the family had drifted apart, both geographically and mentally. In itself that was not unusual, but children, even though distant from parents still held the old-fashioned view that their elders had to be paragons of virtue, which meant everlasting mourning and no new partners.

Daughters had in general a less approving attitude to their remaining father or mother spending time with a member of the opposite sex. It was absolutely fine in a friendship sort of way, but they could never imagine anything more.

Sons on the other hand were not more tolerant they were merely less sensitive.

His mind went back to his own parents, they had divorced when he was eighteen. His father, Edward, which was Jack's middle name, had been an aggressive drinker; many a Saturday night he had arrived home after the pubs had closed, in a foul mood and had immediately picked an argument which invariably ended up with something being smashed. He never hit Jack's mother, his anger was always directed against objects, anything that was within reach, but it was still a frightening anger, it was always a possibility that he would lose control and strike out.

Some heavy drinkers fall asleep, others are happy and sometimes silly, while others, fuelled by the alcohol, need anger management. That was Jack's father, a few glasses of beer and he wanted to fight the world.

Jack recalled that he had never seen his parents in a loving embrace, he was sure that they did embrace but in the old-fashioned way, 'not in front of the children'.

Nor could he remember ever having had a real conversation with his father. They had not been close and had little in common. Although he did recall that when he was about thirteen his father had handed him an adult novel, a slightly risqué novel, not overly sexual but a little more adult than any book he had read thus far.

It was his parents attempt to provide 'sex education', but Jack already knew far more than the book portrayed. 'Sex', in an educational context was never again mentioned; it seems that in those days it was almost a taboo subject between children and parents, it was left to the schools or the playground.

Because of his father's drinking Jack had withdrawn into himself; by necessity he became very self-sufficient, relying on no-one and needing no-one. He also found it difficult to show his true feelings, they had been suppressed and they had remained buried, until he met Sylvia.

It was an odd thing that after the divorce it was his father who suffered the most with the loss of a supporting wife. He appeared devastated and looking back Jack realised that he never really recovered. Maybe he realised that he was the instigator of the divorce, that it was his actions that resulted in the breakdown of the marriage.

His mother had begun a new relationship within twelve months to a man whose personality was the opposite to his father. A man with a gentle nature, a man who only drank on social occasions, a man she felt comfortable with and in whose company she felt no fear.

That had been the final straw for Jack's father, there was no going back, no reconciliation, no future for him.

Jack recalled that his parents' divorce did not create within him any form of despair or sadness. He merely accepted it as a matter of course, he was more interested in arranging to leave home, in striking out for himself and whatever arrangements his parents made were their choice and responsibility, they were of no concern to him.

On reflection it now seemed to Jack that as a young man it was a rather callous reaction, but we are what our circumstances and experiences make us.

Following the divorce Jack visited both of his parents from time to time, but their break-up was never discussed, his father never really recovered from the divorce and only ever lived alone afterwards.

His eventual death was painful insomuch that a lung disease, brought about by heavy smoking, left him with limited ability to be active, and gradually his mobility had been reduced to shuffling around the house.

Jack later learned that the lung disease and inactivity was brought on by emphysema and was caused, so the medical profession deduced, by a lifetime of smoking, apparently the lining of his lungs hardened until he could not breath in sufficient oxygen to sustain movement.

At the end Jack felt more warmth, sorrow, pain and compassion for his father than he ever had whilst growing up.

Now Jack, at this late stage in his life, was looking for someone to replace his children's mother; Of course that was really not the case, she could not be replaced, but he knew that it would be the view his children would take.

They would be wrong, he was looking for companionship, he was seeking a relationship that would fill the void in his life and the only connection that it had with Sylvia was the fact that she was no longer there.

Nevertheless, he could not allow his children's views to deter him, the alleviation of his loneliness had to be Jack's priority.

*

The website had organised for its subscriber's, their MATCHABILITY, which meant the similarity they had to other members, that is to say how individual profiles were similar in their desires, needs and aspirations, to each other.

Jack had entered his own details and details of the person he was hoping to meet regarding height, age, location, etc, etc. He was therefore pleasantly surprised to discover that there was someone with whom he had a 100% match, a match made in heaven, one would suppose.

"I can't believe that I've been so lucky at my first look," thought Jack, "Perhaps Sylvia is giving me her approval".

The notion was immediately discarded as stupid and Jack brought up the profile of his perfect match. He read her detail carefully, she had entered; Location... anywhere in the world.

Height...... 5 feet to 7 feet
Age...........50–100
Hair.......... any

And so it continued. It was obvious that every male registered with the dating agency would be a 100% match with this particular lady.

Jack was unsure what to think, either the lady was desperate, wanted to meet as many men as she could, or had registered tongue in cheek. In any event it did not matter because she had not posted a photo.

Jack realised that not only did he have a lot to learn but also that his search may prove more difficult than first thought.

"Bill was right," thought Jack, "patience is a virtue, I'll just have to bide my time, make no assumptions and see what happens".

A ping from the laptop interrupted his thoughts. A new message had been sent; it was in response to his first one-liner.

> *Why do you need to see my photo, I don't show myself to everyone I talk to?*

Jack thought for a moment, the response came as a surprise, he had logically thought that everyone would attach a photo to their profile. However, he did not want to appear rude, so he responded,

> *Please do not take offence, it is that I find it easier to talk to someone who I can see, do you wish to know anything else about me?*

Jack sat at his laptop staring at the monitor, he expected an immediate reply, but nothing happened for a full five minutes. The lady must have been considering her response.

With a sigh he went back to the site, checked a few more profiles and left a number of one-line messages announcing his interest in starting a conversation.

Following the first dip of his toe in the water he had little confidence in any positive responses to his messages. He was fully aware that people were not online all the time and that it may be hours or even days before his contact one liners were read so he waited a few more minutes but his computer continued to remain silent.

Jack decided that it was time for coffee, he didn't intend to give up yet, there were many more profiles that he could read and hopefully there was someone out there who was in similar circumstance to himself, someone who desired a listening ear, someone who needed companionship, someone who was lonely and had their own void that they wished to fill.

Jack returned to the table, placed his coffee on the left side of his laptop (leaving his right hand ready to respond) and began reading through the online profiles.

He was amazed at the number of ladies that were seeking 'friendship or more', however many seemed to be looking for men both taller and younger than himself.

He typed out several more messages, making sure that the profiles matched his own and that the ladies in question were not seeking a Hollywood movie star.

Jack gazed out of the window onto his back garden, it was early in the year but the winter sun was shining in a cloudless sky, the lawn was still glistening with the morning dew and the evergreen shrubs were looking in good order, it was the type of day when at other times he would be out, either walking with Sylvia or pottering around the garden, there was always something to do. But today he had no desire to do either, sipping a cup of coffee and checking his laptop was enough.

He remembered that it was only the previous autumn that he had written a poem for the photographic magazine, a poem that was printed beneath an autumn landscape view, a photograph taken by his club friend Stan, he had titled it 'The Leaf;'

The tree stands tall in golden splendour
The autumn leaves will soon be gone,
On one small branch a rustic dancer
Clings to life, its duty done.
A gust of wind will test its valour,
Should it's strength fail, there will be none.
But leaf holds fast although it's shaken

And turns it's face to autumn sun.
The gust of wind blows hard in anger
It knows the branch has only one.
A single leaf that must be taken
From its hold, it's had it's fun.
The autumn wind will not be beaten,
It puffs it's cheeks and makes it's run.
The branches shake, but leaf holds firm,
It still remains, the battles won.

In the back of Jack's mind the poem was not only about autumn it was also a reflection of life, at the time Sylvia had been very ill, she was battling the cancer that had invaded her lungs.

They both thought that with determination and faith the cancer could be beaten, but cancer is a formidable enemy, it takes more than willpower and a strong constitution to beat it. In the end, with all resistance and willpower taken by the irrepressible disease, Sylvia succumbed, she had become too tired to battle further.

*

Jack sat gazing at the screen, saddened by his thoughts, saddened by his neglect of the garden; was it only last autumn that he had written those words?

It was but a few months yet it seemed another lifetime. It is amazing the effect that one death can have on an individual; death destroys dreams, it breaks the heart, it takes away all those small pleasures that used to bring joy and comfort. It always comes as a surprise and it always seems to come at a time of vulnerability. They say that love, pleasure, wealth and prosperity are wasted on the young, but death is the ultimate waste.

As Jack sat daydreaming a message appeared at the corner of the screen, there was someone interested in making contact. Jack clicked on to the message.

Thank you, please tell me more.

It was another online communicant, someone new, someone who had seen his photos and read his profile, someone who was replying to his one-line question. Jack immediately replied,

What would you like to know?

There was a short delay, although the profiles were quite informative, they were not fully comprehensive, they gave little or no indication of feelings, intent, long term desires or integrity.

There were cases of married men joining sites to find girlfriends, or young men seeking the company of older mature women for personal gratification. Consequently, it was more than reasonable for ladies to want to make sure that they were contacting a genuine companion seeker.

This lady had used the name of 'Southern Rose' as her site *nom-de-plume.*

What is your real name?

A direct question, a question raised by a seasoned campaigner, Jack replied.

Jack, I used my real name.

Southern Rose came back with;

Are you fully prescribed?

Jack replied;

Yes.

This was a response from someone with limited conversation ability, however Jack could sense that Southern Rose was not shy, she had been here before;

Good, then we can correspond properly, how long were you married.

Jack slightly resented the directness of the questions, it felt like the third degree and it also felt like an intrusion on his privacy from someone he had never met. Nonetheless, nothing ventured nothing gained so he decided to reply with honesty, albeit with a touch of indignation;

40 years, my wife passed away last year from cancer and I'm living alone now, a lifestyle I'm struggling to contend with. I have hobbies and belong to a photographic club, my next-door neighbour has been a great comfort but I must admit I miss female company, I hope my late wife will forgive me for that. I write a little and I do take time to keep fit. I belong to a bowls club; I find that a little competition gives the adrenalin a nudge. Do you have any hobbies?

Jack took a sip of coffee; the conversation was faintly exhilarating even though it was only by email. He wondered how many others Southern Rose had spoken to and how many she had dated. Her tone and her approach indicated that she was experienced but obviously unattached, Jack was curious why.

The messager replied within a few minutes, she was obviously online and that made the exchange of responses a little more personal and that much easier.

It was enlivening for Jack; it was the first time that he had been engaged in a conversation with a member of the opposite sex, a conversation where its sole purpose was to forge a relationship that was not just a casual friendship.

Jack was in a place that he would never have imagined that he would ever be, his interest was aroused as he read her words;

My husband died many years ago, my daughter lives with me and my two dogs keep me company.

Jack thought for a minute, he needed to keep the conversation going with meaningful dialogue, and then replied.

You didn't mention if you have any hobbies?

That was the extent of his 'meaningful' dialogue, but the situation was so foreign to Jack that even online he was somewhat tongue tied. But Southern Rose did not seem to notice as she replied;

Oh yes, I belong to a number of groups, water colour painting, flower arranging, walking and others.

The responses came back quickly, it was apparent to Jack that his intuition was correct and that she was a seasoned member and used to these exchanges.

Jack thought for a moment, he had not been put off by the profile photo that he had seen, just the reverse, Southern Rose looked younger than her 65 years, her blond hair was shoulder length and her features were attractive, it was a photo that would have, should have, attracted a lot of response from the males on the site.

But somehow, for some reason which he could not fathom, Jack was losing interest, the conversation was becoming boring. He decided to move it along a little.

Would it be out of order to ask for your real name?

There was again no hesitation, perhaps he had her confidence.

My name is Moira.

There did not seem to be any reason why he should not cut to the chase so Jack responded with a direct approach, a bold move for him;

Moira, I would like to talk to you properly my mobile number is ...., if interested, would you give me a call?

It was no surprise when she replied;

Yes I will do that.

The link was ended, and Jack wondered if Moira would indeed call.

Bill had already warned him that there were a number of ladies who seemed only interested in online chatter, a sort of pen pal and that was the last thing that Jack needed.

As he pondered he noted that he had another message, this time it was from 'Sunshine Smile'.

Jack needed something a little stronger than coffee, a lager would break the chit chat for a few minutes and he needed that time to reboot before he became involved in another conversation.

As he poured, Jack remembered that he had not received any further messages from the lady with no photograph, thinking back he could not recall that he had been anything other than polite, perhaps she had rechecked his photo and decided that he was not worth the effort of a follow up. Never mind, he would see what Sunshine Smile had to say.

CHAPTER FIVE

Jack woke with a start; he glanced at his bedside alarm clock; 7:30.

His sleep had been fitful, he had dreamed, disturbing dreams, he knew that they were disturbing although he could not remember the content.

Jack glanced out of the bedroom window on to the back garden, it was a bright day but it looked cold, the deciduous shrubs were still naked and uninviting, they were bare and colourless, a little like the way he felt. He turned over and pulled the covers up to his chin. He had been in the habit of laying a pillow in the bed alongside him, it gave him comfort. He reached out and touched it, he still could not get used to sleeping alone.

He was now fully awake but made no move to get up, he thought for a minute, what day was it? The days merged one into the other, there was little difference, it was a few moments before he realised that it was Monday.

Then he remembered that he had forwarded his mobile number to a lady called Moira, there had been as yet no response.

Following the online chat with Moira and her positive approach he had expected a call the previous evening, she had seemed genuinely interested.

In some respects Jack was surprised that he had received any interest at all, he wasn't being particularly negative he genuinely felt that a man of his age and circumstance had little to offer.

Bill had taken the photos for the site, but Bill was no professional photographer and Jack was of the opinion that the photos did not really do him justice, not that he was particularly photogenic, but aside from the inability to produce a photo that improved his appearance, (the camera frequently lies), he was no great catch and he felt that any ladies online would have higher expectations.

He checked again on the message received from 'Sunshine Smile' It merely thanked Jack for his interest but advised him that she was seeing someone else on the site and was therefore not available at this time. Bill had already warned him that those words, more often than not, were a polite way of saying, I've seen your photo and I don't think that you're my type.

So much for leaving a few messages and spreading his net wide.

It was with a pleasant surprise that he discovered that he did have another message, a response to one of his introductory one-liners, it would appear that Bill was right, swamp the site with messages and someone, somewhere, would eventually respond.

Although he had received a refusal from Sunshine Smile, he decided that he should still adopt a positive approach, it was early days and it had taken Bill forever to find someone who was the mirror image of the desires he had listed on site, she was 'compatible'.

Compatible was an odd word to describe someone with whom you 'connected', it was more in line with internet products, and it did not indicate what dating site subscribers were seeking; in general they needed a great deal more than compatibility, they were looking for close companionship and of course love.

This message was from a lady called Caroline. Jack went back to her photograph and profile, staring back at him was a short haired blonde with passably attractive features, she certainly did not look her age of sixty-five. Although the face did not pluck the strings of his heart, (most people have a propensity to be drawn to a particular look, a particular shape of face, particular features; beauty is indeed in the eye of the beholder).

Notwithstanding, he decided that a conversation would certainly be worthwhile, there was nothing to lose.

Jack went back to his messages and typed in,

Thank you for your interest...

He went on to describe his situation as a widower and briefly explained his main hobby as a photographer and his interest in creating 'social interest' photos that may have an impact on the people looking at them. He also told of his interest in nature and the photography that he hoped would instil in others the encouragement to see the wonders around them.

Jack had barely finished writing his response when his mobile gave its familiar ring.

"Hi, this is Moira, you gave me your number."

Jack was silent for a moment, he was nonplussed, he had not really expected a call, he then gathered his thoughts, reflected back mentally on his email messages with Moira and in an attempted casual voice replied;

"Oh, hi Moira, thank you for calling, I read your profile and it seemed compatible with my own and following our online chat and exchange of histories I thought that we may have similar requirements for companionship."

Jack hesitated for just a second, his choice of words seemed to him to be a little lame, they were not the way he would naturally express himself but as he was about to embark on something that he had not done for almost half a century he ploughed on, regardless;

"I was wondering if perhaps we could get together for a coffee or something, it would be nice to meet you face to face, it's difficult to reach any conclusions about the person you are talking to if it is only carried out over the phone or online."

Jack's words still seemed laborious and forced to him, the situation was odd, it was strange even weird, he was asking for a date with a complete stranger, not only something that he never envisaged but something that had already proved to be quite disastrous.

He had always been a good communicator, as a senior administrator it had been necessary to host conferences, to encourage staff, to assess and draw out the best in those he worked with; he was never short of ideas and never tongue tied. In the work environment he had been confident and sure footed... but this was different, very different.

Moira responded with the confidence of someone who had a great deal more experience with online dating than Jack. He was not her first meeting, that was quite apparent, she sounded very relaxed and without concerns as she replied;

"That would be fine, I know a very nice pub in a small village near Henley, is that close to you?"

Of course, Moira would not know where he lived, there were no addresses or communication details on site, members had to be protected, and until they were fully paid up no address or phone details could be exchanged.

When Jack was building his profile, Bill had sardonically advised him that for some ladies 'dating' was almost a way of life. They enjoyed being with men, being wined and dined, being placed in romantic settings, it was for them a perfect pastime.

There were no close ties, no promises, no long-term commitments, just fun and good times. They used the dating site, not for companionship or a long-term relationship, but for a brief flirtatious interlude with someone new every so often.

Unfortunately, there was no way of determining the intentions of a date until it was too late. Jack would just have to go with the flow and use his instincts.

*

Henley was in fact, only a thirty-minute drive for Jack and it was a very convenient location, but Bill's words echoed through his mind as the arrangements were made to meet at lunchtime on the following Wednesday, just two days hence.

Moira explained that she would be driving a silver Audi and there was a parking area directly opposite the pub. She asked if he had been there before, but the pub, and the village were new to Jack; Moira acknowledged Jack's unawareness of the area and responded;

"That won't be a problem, it's the only pub in the village you can't miss it."

So, the die was cast, his first attempt to enter a new and nervous phase in his life. It was like starting again at age nineteen, gone were the comfortable feelings that a long marriage creates, trepidation was the only feeling that Jack now felt.

He was still unsure if he were doing the right thing, his children would definitely not approve, he hardly approved himself; he wondered if Sylvia approved and if she was annoyed with him. He felt strangely uncomfortable with what he was about to do, no it was more than discomfort, it was guilt. But he could not stop himself, he was angry at his own weakness, other people lived alone quite happily; they got on with their lives, followed their hobbies, met their friends and did not seem to need that close relationship with another person; so why did he?

It was a question without answer, everyone was different, everyone's needs were different, it was nature. But no matter what guilt he felt he knew that he had to go ahead with the meeting.

Wednesday dawned, fortunately the weather forecast was dry and sunny with average seasonal temperatures, that meant semi-casual wear and a sweater. Something reasonably smart but not over the top for that venue and that time of day. The truth was that Jack had no idea what to wear it was an occasion that was totally foreign to him.

As he sat behind the wheel of his car his stomach felt knotted, he was nervous, almost afraid. It was his first 'date' for half a century, he had no experience and worse still his stomach was in such turmoil that he knew that he would not be able to eat. He was going to lunch and he would not be able to down the food, how ridiculous was that? He would probably make a fool of himself, he had visions of shovelling some of the lunch into a nearby flowerpot when her back was turned to make it look that all was well; Jack gave a nervous grimace at his own stupidity, but this meeting was rapidly becoming an unwanted ordeal.

However, suitably adorned, suitably as far as he knew, Jack gripped the wheel and drove through the country lanes to the appointed meeting place.

He found the village without difficulty, it was a typical English hamlet, a short main street, a church and a pub. And as Moira had described, directly opposite the pub there were parking places. It was quiet, the meeting had been arranged for twelve thirty and it seemed that the village had not yet woken up.

There was one other car in the available spaces but Jack could not detect the driver, he was probably downing a pint.

He was early, only by fifteen minutes, but he guessed that Moira would be on time or a little late. His limited experience with the opposite sex told him that.

Jack parked the car and strolled across the road where he sat on a wooden bench, one of two each side of the main door. There were a couple of empty hanging baskets on the outside of the building, but the pub did seem to be typically oldy worldly and typically British. It had been newly painted white with pseudo-Tudor black beams which in all honesty gave an attractive appearance. It was the type of pub that he frequented with Sylvia.

Sunday had always been their traditional outing for lunch, but Wednesday was okay. Nevertheless a pub lunch, something that he had always enjoyed with Sylvia was now being undertaken with someone else, was he being a traitor?

Bill, the experienced Bill, the unromantic Bill had already warned Jack that the very first date would be his most difficult, after that it would be all downhill as far as nerves were concerned. Every subscriber to the site had to have a 'first' date, some would sail through with aplomb, others would be nervous and edgy. It was a fact that many 'senior' men were unsure of themselves in the circumstances that Jack found himself. They lacked confidence in their ability to converse and verbally entertain the woman that they were with. Bill explained that it was natural, but after a couple of meetings Jack would become blasé, he would become confident and even amusing as he charmed his 'new' friend.

At the time Jack smiled, he realised that Bill's intent was to cheer him up, make him feel at ease, but deep down he had his doubts.

*

Five minutes after the agreed time a silver Audi appeared at the far end of the high street and pulled up on the opposite side of the road, Jack remained seated, he waited.

The car door opened, and a mature lady emerged wearing a calf length plain blue flared skirt and a dark blue jumper, it was Moira. She wore her dark brown hair as a frame for her face, it was short enough to do that.

She pushed the car door closed and pressed the remote car locking key, turned and began crossing the road to where the now standing Jack waited.

As he had always been acutely aware, first impressions were important if only because they left an imprint that was difficult to erase. Jack's first impressions were, 'Her head looks a little too large for her body'.

Jack as a photographer had studied anatomy through the camera lens. He noted large men, in large he meant tall, who had heads that seemed to be too small for their frames; men and women whose bodies seemed to be extraordinarily long compared to their legs and of course vice versa, in effect he had noted all types of body and head sizes; most fell into the 'average' range but some had unusual proportions. Jack realised that not only was everyone different they were also more, or sometimes less, appealing to the onlooker. Jack's personal preference may not be, in fact would not be, the preference of someone else.

It IS strange how first impressions can actually be lasting impressions; it is also strange how first impressions can also form the basis for our positive or negative thoughts.

In Jack's case the thoughts were extremely negative. He knew at once that no matter how nice Moira was going to be, she was not the person with whom he intended to become friendly. It was an unfair reaction but an undeniable one.

Jack immediately felt elated, he knew that this 'date' was not a date at all, not in the true sense of the word, it would be a casual meeting of two strangers that would not be repeated.

He was off the hook, his first 'true' date would be the one where there was a modicum of mutual attraction and where a further meeting would be proposed. That was not going to happen today, he was still true to Sylvia.

Moira crossed the road, she recognised Jack immediately and held out her hand in greeting.

As it turned out Moira was a very pleasant person, easy to talk to and the pub meal was consumed in a relaxed atmosphere. Jack was relieved that although his first date would also be his last date with this particular lady, it had not been an unpleasant experience. He sure that it would not be long before his first 'date' found an acceptable companion, but it would not be him.

After the meal Jack escorted Moira to her car, thanked her for a pleasant time and mumbled that he would be in touch. This of course was untrue but, in the circumstances, he did not know what else to say and he did not want to appear ungentlemanly.

The car radio kept Jack company on the way home, he felt slightly elated, he had sailed through his first ordeal unscathed; now all he had to do was be relaxed and confident next time.

Back home, sitting at the table in front of the closed laptop Jack reflected on the day's events. He decided that it would be unfair to call the day a disaster, no, it was an experience, one which Bill had warned could be one of many.

The day was still young, it was not yet evening, perhaps there was a further message for him on the site, one that may bring a little cheer.

Jack gazed around the empty living room, the last thing he felt was cheerful, relieved yes, but 'cheerful' not exactly.

There were jobs that required his attention, laundry, cleaning, calling his son and daughter, but he just could not rouse himself to tackle any of these at that moment; they would have to wait. So with a sigh he raised the lid of his laptop and pressed the indented 'on' button.

The computer took its usual few minutes to activate, Jack mused whilst he waited for the password indicator to light up, "it's getting old, like me".

He was suddenly feeling a little sorry for himself. When he was able, Jack tapped into the dating site.

After his first excursion he was no longer confident that anyone of interest would be in contact. It hadn't mattered on this occasion, it was he who had dismissed any potential future meetings, but on another occasion, if he did show an interest, the shoe may well be on the other foot. This dating business was not only tricky, frustrating and nerve-racking, it was also totally hit or miss.

The site providers had attempted to eliminate the randomness as much as they could, but with very limited success.

Bill had told him that there were several times more mature females seeking males than the other way round, Jack wondered where they were because that did not seem to gel with his experience, nevertheless the predominance of females could be his salvation.

Jack was pleased to note that he did in fact have a message. He had originally forwarded several 'feelers', one of which was to a lady who had called herself Caroline but he saw that the response came from 'Pat' and in brackets was the name Caroline.

The site had advised all participants to use a 'site name' to protect themselves. It was apparent that Pat had read his profile and had reached the conclusion that he was genuine and it was safe to use her real name. Jack recalled her photo immediately; the lady with the short blonde hair and young looks.

His interest was aroused and without hesitation he messaged that he had received her email and would be pleased to meet over a coffee at any time that was convenient.

In most instances the email would be picked up when the recipient was next online, in this case it was obvious that Pat was online at that very moment because the response was immediate,

I am free the day after tomorrow, can we meet.

There followed a few exchanges and it was eventually agreed that they would meet in the cafeteria of a garden centre that was convenient to both. Pat had explained that if they met mid-afternoon the cafeteria would almost certainly be quiet, and he should have no difficulty in finding her. Arrangements were finalised and Jack's second date was lined up, 'second time lucky,' he mumbled to himself.

The next evening was a normal bowls night, he should have no problem organising a game. On his last appearance his performance was disappointing, that was due to lack of practice, he decided to use the following night to address this problem, he knew that he really did have to motivate himself.

The rest of the evening was spent channel hopping on TV, munching salt and vinegar crisps and wondering why time passed so slowly when there was nothing to do... and so to bed. Jack woke early the following morning, he looked out of the bedroom window on to the back garden, it looked cold and bleak, although he could not see any threatening rain clouds in the sky it was grey, it did appear likely that rain may follow.

The lawn grass had not yet begun to grow, it was still quite short, but Jack noted that those irresistible weeds had forced their way through here and there, they seemed to survive no matter what the winter had produced, they were as tough as nails stronger than any of the perennials he had planted.

The rockery and fishpond lacked colour but the small rockery plants, although not in bloom still retained their green hues. Jack could not detect any goldfish or koi near the surface, not that the heron would care, he always came down in the morning desperately trying to get his long beak through the netting, and no matter how many times he was frightened away he always came back.

'Time to get up,' thought Jack. He felt warm where he was, but at the same time he was not one to sleep in late, for some reason lazing in bed made him feel guilty even if there was no pressure to rise.

An hour and a half later, following his usual cup of tea and slice of toast, he sat in front of his laptop and lifted the lid.

Although he had arranged his second date for the following afternoon, he decided that he would check a few profiles and leave his usual one liner message hoping for some responses. He slowly one finger typed,

> *I read your profile and saw that we seemed to have many things in common. I am an amateur*

photographer and an active fit walker. If you are interested in having a chat please respond.

Jack always added the part of being fit because Bill had advised him that ladies did not want to be a carer for men of a certain age, in fact many of the ladies on the site were seeking companions who were younger than them.

The one-line message was sent out to several possible candidates before Jack noted that he did have one reply from 'Francesca', (most likely not her real name), she must have responded late the previous evening from one of his earlier mailings.

This lady wrote that she would like to learn a little more before making any direct contact such as telephone calls or meetings.

The request was not unusual, probably because many on the site did not want to waste time meeting or talking to candidates who were totally incompatible. Profiles often were either inaccurate or they omitted factors that may be considered unpalatable to the other subscribers.

Therefore, in response to Francesca's request Jack sent as many personal details as possible that he considered to be appropriate and of course details that he believed may be appealing.

It was quite early in the morning and he knew that he was unlikely to receive any reply until later in the day or on the morrow; not everybody checked their computers every day, unlike Jack they had lives to lead,

The rest of the morning passed slowly, it was a workday for most so Jack resisted the urge to ring his son, he didn't want to disturb him at work. Instead he mulled over the morning paper that had been delivered, reading slowly to make the time pass, but the news appeared to be mundane, there was nothing of particular interest.

Although he did not wish to disturb his son there was no reason why he could not contact his daughter, particularly if he waited until lunchtime when she should be available.

Fortunately, Laura was home when he called, she seemed pleased to hear from him and asked how he was. They exchanged pleasantries and caught up with each other's news. Jack did not of course mention his lunch outing the previous day. They chatted for almost an hour, quite long for his daughter, however the call used up a little of Jack's 'idle' time and he was grateful for that.

That evening he did find a game at the bowls club, a match with a friend called Alan; friend was probably too strong a word, they were acquaintances, they met each other at the club but they had never socialised outside those hallowed walls.

At the end of the evening they decided to stay on and chat over a couple of pints. It was only during that conversation that Jack learned that Alan had been diagnosed with cancer, Alan was not specific but after that meeting Jack never saw Alan again.

The next morning Jack carried out some of his domestic duties. When you are performing tasks that you do not enjoy time moves very slowly, the hands on the clock appeared to be frozen, he was killing time and time was killing him.

It was an age before Jack decided that it was opportune to get ready for his journey to the garden centre to meet Patricia. It was only a fifteen-minute drive and as the parking lot would most likely be half empty with no difficulty finding a bay, he decided that he would calculate the journey to arrive only a little early.

As before he felt a little trepidation, this was his second meeting from the dating site and he hoped that it would be more fruitful than the first. However, seeing a woman in order to create a relationship was still alien for Jack, it was something that he never thought that he would have to contemplate, he wondered if he would ever be able to accept it as a new way of life.

Jack parked his car in the garden centre car park but sat contemplating for a few minutes before he gathered himself and entered the open doors.

He looked around and found the sign indicating the way to the cafeteria. Once inside his gaze sought the short blonde hair that would indicate Patricia's presence; but although there were only a few people dotted around the room there was no-one matching Patricia's description. It was obvious that she had not yet arrived.

Jack made his way to a vacant table and then noticed that he was being closely observed by an elderly lady with dark hair. He looked more closely and found the woman's face vaguely familiar. A second glance convinced him that this was Patricia but with dark hair not blonde and at least twenty years older than the photograph posted on site.

Jack was both perplexed and disappointed, nevertheless he approached the table with a forced smile, held out his hand and said,

"I'm Jack it's nice to meet you Patricia?"

There followed an uncomfortable sixty minutes when coffee was consumed and pleasantries exchanged. It was obvious to Jack that this was to be a one-off meeting.

A little later when Jack arrived home, still disturbed by the 'date', he gave Bill a call and relayed to him the circumstances of his latest excursion. Bill was amused, he advised Jack that it was not unusual for people on site, both men and women, to post photographs of themselves at a younger age; perhaps they really believed that they had not changed very much, who's to say, but Jack had to get used to the idea that not all of his meetings would mirror either the profile or the photo of the person that he had arranged to date.

Jack's first two meetings had left him with no confidence that dating was going to be his salvation. But, on the other hand 'dating' was the only way that he was going to meet anybody, there were no unattached females at either of the two clubs he had joined.

CHAPTER SIX

Jack woke early the next morning, Francesca, he thought to himself, that doesn't sound German. He had double checked the profile that 'Francesca' had written on her site details and she had stated that Germany was the country of her birth. The name sounded more Italian to Jack, she sounds interesting, he thought, but as he had already discovered from the disappointments of the site introductions, he realised that he would have to approach the meeting with no pre-conceived ideas, he would just have to 'go with the flow'.

He was still daunted by the thought of dating but he had already cast the dye and he knew in his heart a long period of loneliness was not an option, he needed company, not necessarily romance, but someone with whom he could share his time.

Francesca had suggested a meeting in a pub car park near Marlowe. Jack knew the pub although he had never eaten there. The meeting had been set for noon, presumably a time that would enable them to meet before the lunchtime rush when it may be difficult to find a table. Jack was comfortable with that, it seemed sensible and it was always difficult to talk in a crowded and noisy atmosphere.

It was eleven fifty-five when Jack pulled into the car park, it was only one third full so he chose a space that enabled him a full view of the area.

Within ten minutes the small dark blue Ford pulled into a space close to the entrance. Francesca had previously described the vehicle in order to avoid confusion, so Jack was in no doubt that his arranged meeting had arrived.

He watched with both curiosity and expectation as an elderly woman emerged from the driver's side.

His first thoughts, as before, were disappointment, Francesca was somewhat pear shaped, not that her shape was any reason to suppose that she was less than attractive, it was just that this first impression was not conducive to a feeling of possibility. No matter what anyone says, first impressions can determine the success of an encounter, and this encounter did not auger well for Jack from the outset.

Francesca, or as it turned out Mia, her real name, was a most agreeable lady, well-educated and well informed. Her conversation was interesting and Jack felt immediately at ease. Mia was a person that would make a pleasant friend, but Jack could not get over the feeling that she reminded him of an elderly aunt.

This train of thought left him a little bemused, Mia was the same age as Jack but somehow her demeaner made her appear older, a little mumsy, not Jack's cup of tea. It was conceivable that they could be friends but Jack was fully aware that the ladies who joined the dating site were generally not seeking a casual friendship.

As he sat talking Jack felt himself hoping that time would pass quickly so that he could bring the meeting to a pleasant and amicable end, with no feelings hurt with the potential of amicable conversation in the future.

It was a shame but this third meeting left him wondering just what he was seeking. He had persuaded himself that it was pure companionship, now he wondered if he was deluding himself.

As they parted company Jack promised Mia that he would be in touch. He was honest in his intent; however he was also determined that he would be honest in that he would tell Mia that friendship was the only agenda for him and that the sort of companionship that she may be seeking was not a possibility.

It was an hour later as he sipped a cup of tea at his laptop that the phone rang, it was Bill.

"Hi Jack, I was just wondering how things are going, on site I mean; any luck so far?"

Jack relayed the details of his three meetings forgetting that Bill was already aware of the first two. He advised Bill of the pessimism he felt at the possibility of meeting anyone who matched up to Sylvia. Not that he was trying to make comparisons, but the meetings so far were so disastrous, he rephrased, disastrous was too strong a description, but that it was difficult to imagine who out there would prove to be compatible.

Perhaps there was no one, perhaps it was just too late, perhaps he was just too old to expect that life could be resumed after the loss of his wife. Bill listened with some impatience;

"For God's sake Jack, you haven't given it a chance. I did tell you from the outset that you may have to meet dozens of women before you found anyone with whom you could relate. As far as being too old, no-one is ever too old to look for close companionship, everyone needs someone".

Bill paused for a moment; he was frustrated with Jack's lack of patience. Perhaps Jack wasn't ready to start looking for someone to share his life, Sylvia hadn't been gone that long. But then he recalled Jack's despair at being alone, his depression and fear of solitude, it was quite apparent that he did need companionship, not romance, but someone with whom he could share his life on a daily basis. It had occurred to Bill that the companion need not necessarily be female but from his own experience female companionship was very much more fulfilling.

"Jack, It took me some years to find my match, I'm not saying that it will take you as long, but believe me there is someone out there who will be just right for you, just as you will be right for her. Don't give up now, the journey is just beginning, be patient, carry on with the dating and do not expect too much at the first meeting You will probably need to see someone several times before you realise that you would like to be with her or at least see her on a frequent basis. It took a couple of months before I knew that Barbara was more than just a friend."

Bill ended his well-intended speech but he needed to be persuasive.

Jack knew that Bill was right, he hadn't given the site a fair crack of the whip, he needed to keep going; then Bill continued,

"I've never believed that there is only one woman for each man, Jack, I'm sure that's a fallacy, no-one is unique, not even Sylvia".

Then he thought for a moment,

"Well maybe Einstein, mind you there is bound to be some budding Einstein's in the future, so not even him. Jack she is out there somewhere, keep looking, you will know when you find her, but for goodness' sake give it more than just one meeting".

Jack nodded then he thought for a moment, even his beloved Sylvia had not happened at the very first meeting. There had been, of course, a physical attraction, but it took a little time, until they had got to know each other that Jack had thought, 'she's the ONE, and even then they had tended to drift into their marriage'.

Jack thanked Bill for his time and muttered,

"Don't forget, as soon as you can find some time we'll go out for a beer, I certainly need to get out of the house, I'm fed up spending my evenings staring at the box".

The phone call did have the desired effect, it cheered up Jack and gave him the encouragement to go back to his laptop for another check on his messages. Bill had made him feel a little more optimistic, what the hell if some of his dates ended up being a waste of time, surely, eventually, it would be well worthwhile?

As luck would have it there was a response from one of his short messages,. This time a lady called Samantha had left a short note saying that she would be pleased to talk. Jack brought up her profile on screen.

He was pleasantly surprised to see an attractive blonde; she had the shape of face and features that he found appealing. At age sixty something it would appear that ageing had been extremely kind, assuming of course that the photo was current.

Jack looked carefully through the details of her profile; she was a dog lover, well that was okay, she loved to walk, that wasn't surprising because she had a dog. He went through the rest of the text and found nothing off-putting and, lo and behold, there it was, the photos had all been taken within the last twelve months.

Jack was encouraged, Bill was right he just had to be patient and more laid back, he should set his expectations lower and take things as they come. Without further ado he began typing his response;

> *Hi Samantha, thank you for your message, I've checked through our profiles and it does seem that we have much in common, in all honesty I've always owned a cat, cats were the favourite of my late wife, but I am also a dog lover and many years ago we owned a Dalmatian, it was a wonderful animal, child friendly, gentle but also a good guard dog, not in the sense that it would attack an intruder but in the sense that it would make a lot of noise, I always maintained that it barked to let us know but probably it was just excited. If you would kindly consider sending me your mobile number I will give you a call.*

Jack realised that he had gabbled on a bit but the message had been sent and he couldn't bring it back. He seemed decidedly cheerful, a great change from a short while ago when it was all doom and gloom.

Now, although he was destined to stay in that evening, a plate of shepherds' pie, a cup of tea and a couple of hours watching a film on Netflix appeared to be far more palatable than he had thought just a few hours ago.

The following morning Jack was up early, there was a little more bounce in his demeanour this time. Bill's 'lecture' had certainly made a difference.

He made a beeline for the computer, why he thought that there would be the message containing from Samantha with her mobile number, at eight o'clock in the morning, he had no idea. Of course it wasn't there, there were no messages. Jack cursed himself for being stupid and overanxious.

"Just cool it," he murmured to himself. "Be patient."

It was early, too early in the morning to trouble family or friends; he didn't want to go out, for one reason there was a chill in the air and secondly, although he chided himself for being a silly old fool, he wanted to keep checking his computer, just in case....

In his office desk drawer Jack had accumulated many photos, mainly black and white, some coloured, he had set aside the better ones for his dream of displaying them at a local gallery. His genre was social deprivation, poverty, hardship, or day to day matters of general interest, such as demonstrations, speeding police cars ambulances or fire engines, observational everyday things that nevertheless captured the imagination.

He decided to check what he had and put them in some sort of order, he had already concluded that some of the photos needed to be enlarged in order to get away from too much regimentation.

There was one particular photo of which he was proud, it was a colour photo of a hummingbird moth. Just outside his bedroom window in late spring with blossom abundant around the garden jack spotted the moth, not very much different from the bird in size or colour, hovering in front of a bloom. The moth was fully engaged in collecting the nectar, its proboscis fully buried in the flower on the shrub. As luck would have it the camera necessary to capture the instant had been used the night before and was still in the bedroom. The result was the rare image of a hummingbird moth hovering in flight. Jack was aware that these moths are not easy to discover and his resulting photo magnificently captured a rare sight.

He had never seen this moth before nor since, His son was taken by the photo which now hung framed in a prominent position in his son's living room.

Most of his other photos were in the drawer waiting for someone to appreciate them. He had captured images of rough sleepers, elderly female beggars, poorly clothed and shoeless children in Naples, taken whilst on holiday, and even an image of a booted farmer climbing into a tractor, an image that, in Jack's mind, reminded him of the second world war 'dig for victory' campaign.

As he poured through his collection the memories came flooding back, particularly on those occasions when Sylvia had accompanied him, the others had been taken whilst with one of the members of the camera club.

As he looked Jack became determined to get back into his hobby, a hobby that had been sorely neglected these past few months. In the past his enthusiasm with the camera was all encompassing; he viewed his photographs in the same way that an artist may view the image on his canvas. He saw modern life art, through his camera lens; he hoped that sometime in the future his pictures would enable those who saw them to learn the truth from the past.

Now it was time for a late morning cup of tea and a computer check. His expectations of any site responses were low, but he was wrong, there it was, a reply from Samantha giving her mobile number and advising Jack that she would be out during the day but expected to be back at about seven o'clock,

Jack did not wish to appear too eager, so he waited until eight thirty before making the call. He was always interested in the voice; it was an underestimated asset in the popularity stakes. The voice can be a sensuous weapon in anybody's armoury. When Samantha answered the call she sounded very pleasant and spoke quite freely without any sense of nerves or hesitation.

'She's been here before,' thought Jack, but he ploughed on, attempting to match her 'matter of fact' approach, and they finally agreed to meet on the following Saturday at the entrance to a large store in a shopping centre that was not too far for either of them to travel.

Jack was confident that this time the 'date' would not end as the others had.

Rosina (Samantha's real name} appeared to be entirely different from the others that Jack had encountered so far. Her natural style had immediately put Jack at ease and he felt quite relaxed at the thought of the forthcoming meeting. However, it was apparent that she had been on site much longer than Jack and without doubt had been on many more dates. He could not fathom why her meetings had not been successful, no doubt he would find out in due course.

On the Friday evening Bill called and the two of them spent a relaxed evening at the Dog and Duck, a pub that they had frequented over the years, Jack was in a particularly relaxed mood, he was relaxed because he was looking forward to the morrow with high hopes, probably a mistake but Jack was feeling in positive mode.

The day dawned, the day that would prove that his decision to join a dating site was worthwhile. In casual smart wear Jack arrived at the meeting point ten minutes early, it didn't matter because he was undercover and the day was reasonably mild, ten minutes passed, then fifteen, then twenty. Jack had been glancing anxiously at his watch, he was slowly reaching the conclusion that he had been stood up, then twenty minutes after the arranged time a breathless and apologetic Rosina arrived.

As she approached Jack could see that Rosina was indeed passably attractive and although she was late she had at least arrived.

Then came the disappointment, it was not a deal breaker but it was something that made Jack cringe, as she spoke Jack saw a lipstick smear on her teeth. She had probably been in a hurry and had been careless but it was just one of those things that Jack did not like.

They walked to a nearby restaurant and ordered a meal but Jack could not take his eyes off the lipstick smear. Nevertheless the conversation was quite pleasing, there was an openness about Rosina as she explained her background and there was no attempt to avoid any aspect of her life.

Rosina responded to Jacks questions which he weaved into the general conversation, without any hesitation. At the end of the meal when it was time to part they both acknowledged that they had a pleasant time. Jack was not sure that he wished to pursue the meeting with another one so, to get round his unsure mind he explained that he was currently on a project which was taking up most of his time but he would call her at a later date if that was agreeable, that was how it was left, Rosina had merely nodded in agreement as they went their separate ways.

Jack had been somewhat buoyed up by his recent meeting, the date had gone well and the lady in question, although not necessarily the perfect choice for Jack, was at least someone with whom he could spend a pleasant enough time. It was a great improvement on past experiences.

Once home Jack wasted no time in returning to the laptop, he had renewed hope which resulted in renewed vigour. He decided to scroll through the detailed list of ladies on the site concentrating on the posted photographs, this was hardly a recommended way of looking for a compatible companion but Jack knew that there had to be some physical attraction to begin with, at least it was the only way that it would work for him.

During the scroll he paused at one particular line of photographs, the lady had an online name of Helen.

There were four photos posted but one in particular caught his eye. It was a photo of her in a velvet beret, jauntily worn to one side. She wore a slightly cheeky smile and the tilt of her head held a special appeal to Jack, he couldn't quite put his finger on it but the photo spoke to him in a way that no others had.

CHAPTER SEVEN

The photo of Helen had made an impression on Jack, but a photograph is just a small part of the chemistry that is needed in all relationships, in any case, who was Aurora seeking, the detail in her profile should answer that.

Jack looked carefully through that part of the profile that sets out the preferences listed by the ladies seeking men as companions. He was immediately disappointed, according to Aurora's requirements he was both too old and too short, although he did seem to fit in pretty well with the rest but…

Jack decided to sleep on it before considering whether to leave a message, was there any point?

He had continued looking through the various profiles on site but it was that photo, there was something in that picture that said, 'contact me', he couldn't put his finger on it, there was that unexplainable something that overtook both common sense and probability.

Sleep didn't really help, that photo stuck in his mind, perhaps Helen was more flexible than her profile suggested, there was only one way to find out, send her a message and wait for the response, if there was a response.

Jack hadn't always received a reply to the messages he sent out; it was natural for the recipients to view the photo and profile of the sender before instigating any reply; obviously there had been many to whom he did not appeal. Helen may very well be one of those.

The following morning Jack opened his laptop and went straight to the dating site, he found Helen on the site and typed in his standard opening line, it was merely a message expressing an interest and suggesting an opening communication to decide if there was any possibility of a continuing conversation.

There was nothing else that he could do except wait for that potential word of encouragement, that reply that did not immediately shut the door but acknowledged the interest that he had shown.

He knew that as soon as Helen checked her messages she would visit his site entry where she would be able to note the various inconsistences with her own. He could only hope that his site photos were good enough to overcome any of the objections that she may have in other areas. He also hoped that she could see through the pictures and imagine the person within, at least that may give him a chance to prolong any opening gambits, until he could convince her that a meeting may be mutually beneficial.

Jack spent the next hour or so checking through other photos, some which he had already seen but had discounted; he was looking for the person within, just as he was hoping Helen would do, he was attempting to practice what he preached, but he didn't find anyone of real interest.

There were one or two who appeared possible where the photos were reasonably appealing, but the compatibility rating, the interests, hobbies and the companion they were seeking, was far too low, he was just not the type they were seeking.

The following morning was bright, the sun was shining and although the temperature was not high it was a day to be outside rather than in. He considered giving his son a call, perhaps for a visit but then cast the thought from his mind, it was a workday and although HE was retired others were busy working.

The morning sunshine reminded Jack of the personal project that he had been considering, it was an idea principally for the local school. As a nature enthusiast he wanted the children to share his enthusiasm and learn about the flora that existed around them.

His idea was to photograph local trees with close ups of their leaves and fruits, then include the individual photos of each tree, together with their fruits and leaves, on separate sheets of paper, so that every one of those miracles of nature could be recognised on sight and could be appreciated. He intended to name and describe the trees on each sheet so that any child looking at the pictures would be able to name the trees when they saw them.

It was a fact, that most people would find it difficult to name the trees and the plants that surrounded them, trees that they saw each day, and took for granted, but plants about which they either knew nothing or took no interest in.

As a nature photographer Jack felt that if he provided a collection of photographs then it may be both educational and interesting for the local schoolchildren on school trips, to be able to locate the trees and learn about them. It would, most likely, be an education for the accompanying teacher as well.

At least that was his idea, there were of course many books on the same subject, but none would be localised for a particular area, they would be for general interest only and not suitable for individual schools.

Jack needed to fill his time, he needed to occupy himself, to do something useful, some way to spend the long hours that he was alone. With this in mind he thought he might begin his educational exercise on this day. He knew that he would need to research each photograph because he was no better informed than most, but the research would help to occupy the lonely hours.

Jack spent the best part of five hours wandering around the streets and parks, snapping the many trees that grew there, he took close ups of each tree's leaf.

The tree fruits would not be out until autumn, his favourite time of year, but he would look forward to completing his project at that time.

He wandered through the neighbourhood with enthusiasm and it was only when he returned home that he realised that he had not thought about Sylvia whilst he was out. She was of course not forgotten but perhaps he was beginning to accept that she was gone. Of course the loneliness would remain but he was able to think about his late wife without tears welling up.

He thought about the garden, her pride and joy; she spent many hours tending the plants, and even near the end, when she could no longer get about, she still received pleasure sitting in the conservatory and gazing out at the pond and flowering plants that she had helped to nurture. Jack recalled the poem that he had written, before the willow tree in the corner of the garden had been cut down, it was Sylvia's favourite poem, verses written from the heart by Jack, he had named the poem. 'The view from my window';

> The view from my window is special to me,
> The Zinnias in bloom and the old willow tree
> The Copper Beach hedge so tall and so wide,
> where Robbins and Blue Tits have chosen to hide.
> ....

The view from my window looks over the lawn
That sparkles with dewdrops just after the dawn.
The beautiful stripes both dark green and light
Encourage the Blackbirds till onset of night.
……………………

The view from my window is a vision of flowers
Whose colours and textures can spellbind for hours
The bees and the butterflies just flitter around
Until golden nectar from blossoms is found.
……………………

The view from my window has lilies abound
That peep through the water with pads green and round.
Whilst goldfish and boatmen both silently glide
And frogs with their tadpoles neath lily pads hide.
………………………

The view from my window is summerhouse grand
Each side of the doorway the flower troughs stand
A place to escape from the hot summer sun
Or a room to relax when the day's work is done.
………………………

The view from my window is all of these things
The beauty and majesty give my heart wings
and even in winter when lawn grass is white,
the view from my window is my heart's delight.

Jack believed that his words were an accurate description of the garden that his late wife had so carefully and lovingly created; but now he could reflect on them without feeling remorse.

In the early evening he returned to the computer, curious but with no great expectation, he was therefore pleasantly surprised when he found that Helen had responded with an agreement to chat. The next step was to send her his phone number and leave her to ring back whenever she had the time or indeed the inclination.

Jack was also surprised that he felt hungry, he hadn't felt like eating for what seemed to be months, in fact he knew that he had lost weight, a symptom of both grief and failure to have proper meals, but today was different. Perhaps it was that photo?

It must have been about eight-thirty when the phone rang and a female voice announced that she was responding to his message. It was Helen, or as he was to find out during the course of their first conversation, her real name was Sarah.

That first conversation was lengthy, it was a voyage of discovery, a test of compatibility and mutual interest. They found out quite a lot about each other although it must be said that Sarah was not forthcoming on some matters, it was necessary for her to be guarded until she felt comfortable with this new introduction.

Jack fully appreciated her point of view but they did agree to speak again and Sarah provided her mobile number with an override that she was out during the daytime so it would have to be evenings for any call.

During the following ten days Jack and Sarah spoke many times, each time with more openness and friendliness, they were learning about each other in some detail although, to Jack's chagrin they had not yet met. Sarah had explained that she had workmen in her house making various alterations and they worked into the evening. There was no possibility that they could be left on their own. At this juncture Jack had no idea if this was merely an excuse to postpone their first meeting, but they had been so frank and open with each other that he doubted that she would use subterfuge, most likely it was exactly as she was explaining.

There was also no doubt in Jack's mind that there was a certain synergy between them, a meeting of minds, a definite connection; this of course made the waiting to meet even more frustrating. Eventually after twelve days Sarah had a free day and agreed to meet, the workers had completed the house renovations and she had no plans that day.

They arranged to meet at a London mainline station at twelve-thirty, at last Jack would be able to see the 'girl' in the velvet beret.

Jack had high expectations, something he had told himself not to do, but they had spoken so many times he felt justified in expecting a successful outcome. He arrived at the station almost thirty minutes before the time agreed. His timing was largely due to train timetables, but Jack was always early for meetings, it was his nature.

It wasn't cold in the station; therefore the thirty-minute wait was no hardship, but of course the time dragged and thirty minutes seemed much longer than half an hour. Twelve thirty arrived and Jack looked around anxiously seeking the face that he had been checking online for the previous fortnight.

It was another ten minutes before his mobile rang, it was Sarah explaining that she was in the station and was wearing a red coat.

Jack gazed through the crowd and spotted a red coat, then he saw the face that had haunted him during the past two weeks; it was Sarah.

Their first meeting (date) was innocuous enough, it was pleasant and they chatted over a meal and a cup of coffee in a café close to the station. There had already been hours of conversation between them during the previous days so the ice had been broken beforehand, nevertheless there was still a little tension which was natural it being their first face to face.

After Jack's previous meetings, dates, there had been no doubt that there would be no follow ups, except perhaps with the lady who had been careless with her lipstick; but Jack knew that this time it was different, a second meeting was never in doubt.

The second encounter followed in a similar pattern to the first, a cup of coffee and a 'getting to know you' chat. It was most pleasant and there was a connection that was quite apparent. However that could have been spoiled by Jack who in a moment of idiocy stole a kiss on a surprised Sarah who indicated, not by words but by bodily language, that it was far too early for that form of familiarity.

It was not until they met for the fourth time that their embryonic relationship moved to a slightly higher level. On this occasion they travelled to central London and visited one of the Capital's famous museums. Following this excursion they enjoyed a meal and then went walking in the park. Jack, at this point was to discover Sarah's love of walking, a pursuit that she had followed during the many years since her husband had passed away. Jack had not discovered his own walking shoes, partly because of his months of caring for a sick wife but also because he had always thought of walking as a means of getting from A to B, and not as a leisure pursuit.

However, Jack had no argument with Sarah's wish to travel by Shanks's pony, if that was her wish he was more than glad to follow suit. There was now a growing realisation that their meeting, although occasioned purely by fate, had a deeper and more significant meaning that a casual or simple explanation would justify.

On this fourth meeting they walked through the park with arms around each other. They found a bench and in the cold of a late winters evening cuddled to keep warm. It was a familiarity that seemed natural.

The next meeting was to be a trip to the theatre, Jack had organised to meet Sarah close to her home and then travel to the West End of London on public transport, the only way to successfully get around the Capital. Without any feeling of concern he asked Sarah for her home address, (something that had not yet cropped up), explaining that he would park outside the house and then escort her to the nearest underground station.

Jack was surprised even mortified when Sarah expressed extreme reluctance in disclosing where she lived. He argued that he merely wished to collect her and he did not expect nor wished to be invited inside. Sarah tried to explain that it had been many years since any man had called on her, it had not been something that she had encouraged.

But of course Jack had wished or hoped that their relationship had progressed beyond that point, then to discover that it had not, was a devastating blow, he just could not understand the problem, if indeed there was a problem.

Jack argued that it would be dark when he arrived, he did not know the area or where to park if it was to be anywhere other than the house, after arguing the practicality of meeting at her address there was a few moments of deafening silence before Sarah, somewhat reluctantly, gave way and agreed to his request.

When Jack pulled up outside the north London suburban terraced property, he noted an avenue that was well kept and where most of the properties had been maintained with some degree of care. The front gardens were small and most had been altered to accommodate a car. Although designated as an 'avenue' there were almost no trees lining the sides of the road, no doubt the local authority had reason to remove them, but it seemed a shame.

It turned out to be a most successful evening, the show was excellent, the company superb and a turning point in their relationship.

Now that the mould had been broken and Sarah's address was no longer a secret, there was no reason for Jack not to be invited inside, the relationship had moved forward in leaps and bounds.

He discovered that the property was, in its natural state, a three-bedroom one-bathroom house, but Sarah had converted the loft into a fourth bedroom with an en suite. She had done so to provide space and privacy for herself. The other bedrooms, for part of the year, were tenanted, mostly by students, on short term lets.

There followed six weeks of dates, theatres, restaurant meals, excursions and hand in hand walks, it would be fair to say that they now considered themselves to be a couple. It was of course still early days in their relationship, however they both had the feeling that they had known each other for ever. They were totally relaxed with each other and being together on almost a daily basis was the most natural thing in the world.

They had walked hand in hand over the Golden Jubilee Bridge asking passers-by to take photographs; and before that a visit to the National Portrait Gallery was an interesting adventure, particularly because Jack had studied art when he was young.

They saw each other frequently and when they weren't together they were sending emails. At one-point Jack forwarded an email saying;

> *I recently rechecked your online profile, under the heading Do you want children, you have ticked the box which says, ask me later, don't you think they may be a bit of a tie for us?*

And then Sarah's response to one email was;

> *Harry and Meghan fell in love after two dates. What took YOU so long? They were also very tactile in public; you must try HARDER.*

There was no doubt that their affair had progressed swiftly and with meaning, it was a satisfying, exciting and unexpected time. It was true to say that their spring blossom had burst forth in the autumn of their lives.

Jack was now a frequent visitor to the house, he stayed over on many nights, sharing the double bed, as couples do. The downstairs front room became their haven when the evenings were cold and when they had no plans to go out. The front room settee became a place to cuddle and canoodle and they did so as though they were teenagers in the first throws of intimate discovery.

Jack had also been fully introduced to Sarah's love of walking, he joined her through the many parks that were close to her North London home. Walking, hand in hand had a magic of its own, and if Jack was unfamiliar with the joys of walking, he certainly realised that being with Sarah made all the difference.

It was an enchanting time, an unforgettable time, a time that neither would ever forget.

It was shortly before a planned but forgotten trip, a trip slightly overshadowed by events, that Sarah recalled the visit she had arranged months before.

And then she dropped her bombshell. Sarah had been swept along in her new romance and had overlooked that she was due to visit her family in Ottawa,

Canada. She had purchased the plane tickets six months previously, before she had met Jack, and the trip, a regular event each year, had been arranged as a five week stay in the family's Canadian home.

'Five weeks, five whole weeks', Jack couldn't believe it, he had become used to an almost teenage style romantic situation and five weeks seemed like an eternity. But of course there was nothing he could do, he tried to persuade Sarah to shorten the trip, to return to the UK earlier, but the tickets had been purchased and it was a trip to her family, a family she had not seen for many months, but a family he had never met.

The next couple of weeks flew by and before they both realised it the day for her to leave was upon them. With a very heavy heart, on the evening before her departure he said his goodbyes. Sarah promised to Skype so they could enjoy face to face chats, but in Jack's mind this hardly compensated for their separation.

On the other hand Sarah was obviously not feeling the strain in quite the same way. She was visiting her daughter and grandchildren whom she had not seen for some months and, quite rightly, it was an exciting time for her. Although this was not a sentiment felt by Jack he understood that for Sarah it was a visit that she looked forward to.

The day of her flight seemed to last forever, there was no way to get in touch and therefore it was just the case of having to wait for her to arrive, get settled, then contact him when the opportunity presented itself. In his mind he imagined that she would phone as soon as the plane touched the tarmac in Ottawa, but this was a pipe dream, an unreasonable dream, she would, of course, go to the family home, enjoy the welcome she received, settle in, all before she would find the time to make contact. Jack was new in her life and he had to be patient and wait for the phone to ring.

Very late that evening, (Ottawa was five hours behind Greenwich time) Sarah made her call to tell him that she had arrived safely, it was a brief call, merely a contact call and nothing else.

Sarah was busy with her family, the grandchildren, Roland and Charlotte were excited to see her and that excitement had to take priority, for the moment Jack had to take second place.

That evening Jack sat in front of the television, something was on, what it was he couldn't say, his mind was elsewhere, many miles away. It had been but a few hours since he had last seen Sarah but it seemed like an eternity. He was so used to chatting with Sarah, even when they were not physically together, that his life had suddenly and abruptly become empty.

He was at a loose end, imprisoned in the house merely because there was nowhere to go. How was he going to spend the next five weeks, it was a lifetime?

On the second day he sent an email to express his feelings, it read;

> *It could be that much of our communication will be by email, make sure that you check yours frequently. I need my arms around you to make sure that you are real, that reality seems at the moment to be a lifetime away. Why is the time standing still? It never does when we are together. Skyping is ok but the timing can be difficult, do not forget that tomorrow evening I will be leaving the house at one pm your time and I will return at five pm your time, if those times make it awkward for you to contact me, let me know.*

During the day, time moved slowly, Jack only came alive when he received a Skype from Sarah, and on the days that she was busy with family outings and had no time to talk, the waiting was overbearing.

When he was eighteen he had studied Shakespeare, many of the words that the great man used were foreign to Jack but there was one poem that at this moment he truly felt. He couldn't remember it word for word so he went to the bookcase and selected the complete works of Shakespeare, he knew exactly where to find the words that he had in his mind. He thumbed the pages until he found the text and read aloud:

> Who is Sylvia? What is she,
> That all our swains commend her?
> Holy, fair, and wise is she;
> The heaven such grace did lend her,
> That she might admired be

Of course Shakespeare had used the same name as Jack's late wife, but Jack and Sylvia had drifted into their marriage following a long courtship, it had been natural that at some point they would 'legalise' their relationship in a registry office. There was no great celebration not even a following meal. Sylvia was his first love but it lacked the sensuality, the passion the excitement that everyone saw on the silver screen, it was just an expected event.

Therefore, although the poem had some significance because of the title, its meaning, its intensity, did not directly apply to those early years, but they seemed to apply now, to Sarah. In his mind Jack felt that the poem typified his newfound love.

Jack decided at that moment he would call Sarah to see if she would be open to the suggestion that he may make the journey to meet the family while she was there.

Five weeks was a long time so Jack thought a few days after the third week would break the time apart into more acceptable time periods, at least for him; Sarah would be with family and she would be busy, Jack realised that time would not drag for her.

True to her word, late the following day Sarah Skyped, and they indulged in a lengthy chat. Jack put the proposition to her and was pleased with her exited agreement.

Following Sarah's enthusiastic response to the visit suggestion Jack emailed her;

> *Hi Sarah, I'm thinking of you as you share your evening meal with the family. I feel blessed that I have found love and that it is returned, it was something that I never expected. I will promise you Sarah that I will try my best to make sure that all the days ahead will be the happiest you have ever known. I will visit the travel agent tomorrow and I will let you know what happens.*

Jack's vision of being five weeks apart was now over, he was ecstatic, he could now spend the next few days looking forward, he felt an inner peace.

Some hours later Jack received Sarah's reply;

> *Good morning Jack, I am home for the day. I will be wondering all day how you got on at the travel agents. I certainly did not expect to fall in love either. Although in my dreams I went on site and hoped it may lead to this. Like you*

> *I would have been content with a companion, albeit not just for lunch.*

Jack made his visit to the travel agent, he was successful in obtaining a plane ticket for the six day stay that he intended and as soon he arrived home he messaged Sarah, he did not even check the time difference he just wanted to let her know the result of the visit;

> *Hi Sarah, I will be travelling to Ottawa and my ticket is not refundable, so I hope it's ok. I will send you full details shortly.*

The arrangement had now been made and it was time to consider the coming visit and his introduction to what he hoped would eventually be, his new extended family.

As he had never met the family Jack thought that it may be nice if he made a gesture, an olive branch that would soften the initial impact of a stranger in their midst.

Since her childhood Sarah had always loved bears, cuddly bears, teddy bears. It may be that they were some consolation for the fact that she had never owned a pet. So Jack decided that he would write a children's story, one that could be read to her youngest grandchild Roland.

The story should have some meaning, some connection to Sarah so he decided to write a story about a bear.

That evening, after he had spoken to Sarah, he sat at his computer and wrote;

Mister Bear was a brown bear, he lived in a large forest in Canada. Mister Bear was not like the other brown bears who lived in the forest because he was very kind and very gentle, but best of all he loved children.

Mister bear also loved the forest, he knew almost every tree. There was one tree that was his favourite, it had a knobbly trunk and so each time Mister Bear had an itch on his back he would go to his favourite tree and rub his back against the tree until the itch had gone.

Mister Bear was a happy bear, especially in the summer. He loved to eat berries and he would wander happily through the trees looking for his favourite berries. He would eat as many as he could then he would find a gap in the trees where the sun shone through and he would lay down for an afternoon sleep; he was always sleepy after eating a lot of juicy berries.

One day he was walking slowly through the trees when he heard someone crying, it sounded like a child and it sounded as though the child was in pain. Mister Bear followed the sound until he came upon a small boy lying on the ground holding his knee. The boy had tripped on a fallen branch and tumbled over twisting his knee as he fell.

Mister Bear looked down at the small boy who was of course very frightened to this big bear looking down at him; but when the boy looked into Mister Bear's big brown eyes he knew that the bear would not hurt him. Mister Bear noticed that there was a name on the small boy's shirt, the name was ROLAND. He also noticed that the boy was wearing a belt around his waist and on the belt was a large buckle.

This gave Mister Bear an idea, he knew that he would have to carry Roland to somewhere safe so that he could be found. He could not take him to the village because the villagers would be afraid if a large brown bear should wander into the village. However, close to the edge of the forest was a log cabin and Mister Bear thought that if he carried Roland close to the door of the cabin and gave a noisy growl then someone would come out and find Roland lying on the ground.

Roland's buckle was a help for Mister Bear, he gently leant forward and took the buckle between his teeth. He lifted Roland up and headed for the cabin. It did not take very long and soon Mister Bear was standing a short distance from the cabin door. He slowly lowered Roland to the ground, gave a loud roar then turned and walked away.

Mr and Mrs Thornton who lived in the cabin heard the roar of the brown bear. Mr Thornton was a little afraid but he went to the door and opened it just a little. He saw Mister Bear going away in the distance and he also saw Roland lying on the ground holding his knee, 'quick', he said, "there is a child here who has hurt himself".

Mr Thornton carried Roland into the cabin and laid him down on the settee, Mrs Thornton examined Roland's knee and decided that nothing was broken it was just badly bruised and swollen.

"I know this young man" she said, "I think we should get him home as soon as possible; his parents may be getting worried".

A short time later Roland was back home with Mummy and Daddy who had been very worried. They thanked Mr and Mrs Thornton who told them the whole story of the brown bear and Roland lying outside the cabin door. Roland explained how the bear had carried him to the cabin and left him there to be found.

Roland's mummy and daddy were amazed, their son had been saved by a big brown bear, it was a wonderful thing to have happened. Roland's daddy decided that this special bear should have a name, his own name, just like the children in the village.

"What do you think we should call him?" he asked,

"I know," said the boy, "let's call him ROLAND".

Jack had the notion that if the story were read to the grandchildren they would have been introduced to him, in a way, before he eventually arrived. He thought that perhaps it was a short circuit method of eliminating any first meeting awkwardness. It was a novel idea but children being children, who knows how they are going to react to a stranger in their midst?

Jack and Sarah chatted to each other every day, sometimes for over an hour. Sarah would take the phone to a private place in order to be discreet and in order to have privacy, especially if the conversation was to be warm and personal.

However there was a little consternation in Jack's mind because Sarah's family gently complained about the amount of time they were talking, they felt that Sarah should be more engaged with them. This was understandable, because of the time difference some conversations took place at inconvenient times and may have interfered with family plans, after all Sarah's daughter and grandchildren saw Sarah only intermittently and therefore family time was important.

But at the same time the corner of a red flag did appear on the horizon. Jack was the new boy in the equation, they had never met him and they were used to having Sarah's company exclusively. Jack just had that niggling feeling that he was not entirely welcome, he was an interloper, an added complication into the family setup.

Sarah had been on her own for many years, she had not been involved in an intimate relationship for all of those years. During that time the family had exclusive call on her, she was always there when they needed her, as it should be. Now that normality seemed to be changing, there was a stranger who was interfering in the existing structure of the family life, interfering in the way their lives had been for those many years.

It may have been different if Sarah had been younger, but a beau, an intimate relationship at her time of life, was both a surprise and was an unwanted one at that. It was not that they did not want her to be happy, far from it, although not said, it was more likely to be the intensity and demands of her new relationship that concerned them.

However, for the moment Jack put aside his concerns, he was in a new relationship and Sarah's family had a right to feel protective. It was reasonable for them to wonder why at this time in her life, Sarah had chosen a different path to tread, a path foreign to them and possibly unwise for her.

The days passed slowly, Jack spoke to Sarah on most, there were times when the family undertook an excursion together and on their return it was too late, because of the time difference, to make the call. Apart from those occasions Jack and Sarah spoke constantly, always in romantic terms and both enjoyed the close and intimate conversations. They were both looking forward to the coming reunion.

When Jack was not in communication with Sarah he had time to kill, time to reflect on everything that he and Sarah had done together, time to recall all of their romantic excursions, of their romantic embraces, in fact all of their life, as short as it was, during the past weeks. It had been a joy, a revelation.

It was during these moments of remembering, that he was impassioned to write an email to her; to let her know what was in his heart, it was there waiting to come out, he could not hold it back, no matter what.

It was late in the evening, late for him but not for Sarah, that he decided that he could hold back no more, he opened his computer, clicked into his emails and wrote the following;

> *Hi Sarah, it is midnight here but only early evening in Canada... I was thinking of the days after I arrive and the days that follow and as I thought I wanted to say that whether we are walking, travelling, watching television, cuddling or making love, life will be complete from now on. We will live it to the full, each day will be an adventure.*
>
> *We will teach each other things that we have only read about, our passion will reach heights*

that you only imagined before, there will never be a dull moment.

We will diet and we will exercise but most of all we will laugh, our roller coaster of love will not die, it will grow to a point that it is all consuming, but it will be glorious.

Even as I write, I can feel your hands roaming over me, bringing me to life. You do it because you love me and you need to feel and see my reactions to your touch.

Never be afraid to show me how much you care; it is the nectar of life for me. My hands will bring you to the pinnacle of ecstasy, it will surprise you.

So think of this during the busy days ahead; you will be weary from each day's exertion, but as each day passes the nearer our reunion becomes. Sleep tight and God bless."

The message was ended with three kisses and sent.

The very personal nature of the message concerned Jack a little. As far as the internet was concerned he was somewhat of a dinosaur, he always worried about security once you have sent a message to the clouds just how secure was it. Maybe it could be intercepted by others, how embarrassing would that be? However, it was done now, it had been sent. There was nothing more to do except to wait for a reply; Sarah may be busy during this evening; she may not even pick it up until her bedtime or the next morning. He could wait, but the effort of writing, the intensity of the content had left him tired, it was past one o'clock in the morning and it was time to sleep.

Jack slept well and he was up, showered and dressed before eight thirty. It was the middle of the night where Sarah was but Jack wanted to know if she had read it the night before and had responded. To his delight she had, her words were short but encouraging, she had not taken offence at the bluntness of the text, she had appreciated that he had been merely telling her how much he cared.

> *Ohh., Jack, what a wonderful message to receive before going to bed. It actually moved me to tears.*
>
> *Your genuine kindness and thoughtfulness were just a couple of the reasons I fell in love with you.*
>
> *I cannot wait for you to arrive here so that I can be in your arms. Xxx*

It was the answer that Jack had hoped for, his happiness was complete.

The departure day arrived and Jack boarded the plane for his first trip to Canada, he was both excited and a little nervous.

CHAPTER EIGHT

Jack boarded the plane at ten o'clock in the morning and it amused him to think that he would arrive in Ottawa at eleven o'clock in the same morning local time.

He did not realise at the time he boarded the plane that the next six days would be his most challenging, not from the point of view of difficult and dangerous activities, but it would be challenging for his character. He was also not to know that the challenge would be a step too far and he was going to come up short.

Throughout his adult life Jack had been in charge, his late wife Sylvia had been an only child, her parents had passed away early in their marriage and in the case of her father, before they had met. Jack had shared his personal time with no-one other than his wife and immediate family.

His children had left the nest as soon as they were able and there was now only a tenuous link, family wise. Each member of the family lived their lives apart from the others both geographically and emotionally. In a way this was as opposite to Sarah's family experience as it could be.

That personal family experience, where as head of the family he had called the shots and pulled the strings, was going to prove to be the hurdle that Jack had in front of him and the hurdle that he was not going to be able to overcome.

He was expecting Sarah's complete and undivided attention, he was about to experience a rude awakening.

Sarah had visited Ottawa many times, her daughter Anne had lived there for ten years. In the beginning the visits were restricted to holiday times, but since the birth of her granddaughter four years ago, at which time Anne had ceased to work, the visits had become longer and more frequent, now, well to be precise, eighteen months ago, there was an addition, a grandson.

The frequency of the visits had given Sarah a wide knowledge of the city and during their online chats she had become quite excited about showing him around, Jack was equally excited about seeing the city, a capital he had never visited.

As luck would have it, in the pocket of the seat in front of him there was a pamphlet giving details of his destination. Some of the listed facts were known to him but others were new.

He discovered that Ottawa was situated on the south bank of Ottawa River, a river whose name meant 'traders'. Apparently it had been the centre of trading in furs, skins and tobacco. He also learned that the population now exceeded one million, not large compared to cities around the world, but substantial enough to be the home of the country's government.

Sarah had told him that there were plenty of places that they could visit and plenty of places that provided fine dining.

They would have a wonderful time together during the six days of his stay.

The flight's duration was six hours but that did not concern Jack, he and his late wife Sylvia had often visited the southern states of America with their three children and the flight times, on most occasions, were in excess of eight hours.

During those flights, the children occupied much of his time, but on this flight the one thing that helped him to forget that he was many thousands of feet above mother earth, apart from dozing, sleep being the best antidote for lengthy air travel, was the inflight movies and these combined with frequent meals helped the hours to pass quickly.

Jack mused that the time length of air travel, as opposed to car or rail, was not so much the time spent in the air as it was the time it took to travel to the airport, book in the luggage and oneself, and the time it took to pass through customs and collect the luggage at the destination. Virtually an entire day was spent, toing, froing and waiting, and it could be quite frustrating, particularly the delay at the luggage carousel with the luggage trolley and a jostling crowd, only to find that your case was the last to emerge.

So it was with some relief when he arrived in Ottawa airport that he was able to collect his suitcase without any delay. He located the taxi rank, and finally sank, with a sigh, into the rear seat of the cab. He gave the driver his destination address and was told that it would take about fifty minutes to arrive.

The driver was chatty, he recognised Jack's accent and asked if this was his first visit to Canada. Jack wondered how many times the driver had used those words to visitors from all over the world, it must be hundreds. Jack did not hear much of the driver's following conversation, he was on the last leg of his journey and the stress of travelling had now waned, he was relaxed and content that he would soon be at Sarah's daughter's home, meanwhile the view from the taxi window absorbed his concentration.

It was true that he and Sarah had been skyping during those past weeks but skyping always ended in goodbye which in turn brought home the realisation of the distance between them. The trip would eliminate the distance and bring them back together.

Jack had been daydreaming during the journey and it seemed to be only a few minutes when the taxi pulled up at the address the driver had been given.

It was an imposing residence, a white exterior gave it a rather grand appearance and although the front garden was not big, just two or three metres in depth, the large porch which led to impressive double doors that were the entrance, helped create the illusion of affluence.

Sarah had seen the arrival of the taxi and opened the doors with a warm inviting greeting, although just a little muted, Jack thought.

Jack left his suitcase in the hallway and he noted the shoes that were neatly lined up at one side, he bent down and removed his. He never took off his shoes at home, it was probably laziness it just didn't occur to him, but he knew that it was common practice.

The interior was open plan and Jack saw the marble staircase and the extensive living dining area. Through the French windows at the back of the family room he could see the small lawn which fronted a swimming pool. Although the rear garden space was not huge it appeared to accommodate pretty much all of the family's needs.

Sarah was alone, the family were out for a short time, deliberately so in order that the two could be reunited in peace. It was a kind and thoughtful action that Jack did not realise at the time. Jack could see the excitement in Sarah's smile and reaction as he entered, they were together again, just where they were meant to be, he too was elated.

It was an hour later when the family returned, Sarah's daughter and her two grandchildren; his new family to be.

He was introduced to Anne, Sarah's daughter, and the two small children Alexandria aged four and baby Simon almost two. Jack had arrived at a time set aside for lunch and he was therefore quickly directed to an armchair in the main living area, whilst mother and daughter continued to look after the two children, a maid hovered around the kitchen clearing away dirty dishes.

Anne was a strict mother in regard to mealtimes and bedtimes; she had instilled the regimentation into the children so that they understood and were comfortable with the boundaries that had been set.

Jack sat silently waiting, he had arrived expecting an accolade, a welcome fit for a king, he had travelled over three thousand miles just for a few days with Sarah, but instead he was left wondering why it took two women and a maid to feed two small children. It was difficult for him to accept that family came first, yes he did understand that scenario for Anne and the children but he had believed that Sarah would set aside her grandmother's duties during his stay. He could never have fully understood the bond, the tie, the attachment between mother and daughter. It was something he had never encountered in his own experience.

He hadn't realised just how full-on Sarah was with her family, she was unable to tear herself away. He was being naïve, he was the interloper, he was the stranger and in addition the family were aware that the relationship was still short lived. Naturally they would expect their mother to be fully attentive, it was as it should be; Jack would have to wait, he would need to integrate slowly, he would need to ingratiate himself until he was accepted, but instead his mind was removed from reality.

Jack had it in mind that as Sarah had been with the family for three weeks before his arrival, and as she would be there for a week after he left, that he would have her more or less to himself during his six-day visit. In his mind this belief appeared to him to be the natural consequence of his trip, that was why he was here, that had been his motivation, but he was about to discover that, with Sarah, family took priority, as it should, and he would have to understand and accept that although their relationship was important he was not the only star in the sky; it was a new situation for Jack, but one that he would need to come to terms with, if he could.

Jack had never met or spoken to the family, they were complete strangers to him, as he was to them, but now he felt unwelcome, being shunted away from the feeding process as he was, he experienced a slight tinge of awkwardness, this may well have been an unfair attitude, it probably was, but we all feel and act in accordance with our experiences, Jack was no exception. Patience is a virtue but with Sarah, Jack had lost sight of her other priorities, family were more important than he, they were the foundation of her existence and he needed to recognise that, but his weakness was that he was having difficulty coming to terms with the fact that notwithstanding his long journey he was still just a guest in the house and he was still a newcomer into Sarah's life.

Jack, in reality, as far as the family were concerned, was an interloper; he was a distraction, the family were busy, it was feeding time, it was family time, for the moment he was a nuisance, he was in the way, (those were the thoughts that dominated Jack's mind), he was taking away a mother's affection from a daughter; an affection that had been without interruption for twenty years. Of course this was nonsense, the family were having no such thoughts, it was a figment of Jack's imagination but he couldn't shake it from his mind.

Jack had the impression that he had been parachuted behind enemy lines. He had arrived in a strange place, amongst strangers, he needed to assimilate when the time was right, but that was not right away.

Jack sat in silence, waiting patiently, the traveller forgotten, a lonely, detached figure midst people he did not know.

Small children take an age to eat, they play with their food in a most frustrating way. No-one seemed to notice Jack as he sat there in a strange house with people he had never met. He felt alone, an intruder into the family scene and as he sat waiting he had the urge to go outside. It was a need to escape, to breath freely, to try to understand this situation that was new to him and how to reconcile this Sarah with the one he had been with for the past two months or so.

Without disturbing the children's lunch he decided to get some air and take a brief walk for a few minutes whilst family duties took place. He did not believe that his absence would be noticed, in fact he was convinced that it wouldn't be, he would only be gone for a short while and in any case he was used to doing his own thing.

Once outside he noted that the area was typical suburbia and although the houses were large and architecturally quite pleasing they were very much the same. It crossed his mind that the appointed architect did not have too much imagination. However although the homes were all similar they were all detached, well cared for and gave the impression of being expensive and sought after, should any come available for purchase.

Jack wandered around a couple of streets, he noted a small children's playground and some well-maintained public gardens, it was a pleasant area although not overly exciting, but then suburbia is rarely exciting.

He'd been out about twenty minutes when he decided he'd better go back. Hopefully, the children had been fed and watered and there would be time for a more leisurely, 'getting to know you' introduction.

As he entered the front gate he was met by an agitated and annoyed Sarah; "Where have you been? You didn't say you were going out; we were worried, I've been out looking for you, you don't know the area you could easily have got lost."

Jack was flustered, what was all the fuss about, he'd only popped out while the grandchildren were being fed, and as for getting lost, he was hardly a child. As far as he was aware he was all grown up. In addition he was an elderly, well-travelled, educated man, and he was not used to being challenged in this way, in fact he felt that it was quite insulting. In retrospect he would come to understand that they were genuinely concerned and that he should have announced his intent before stepping outside, not just disappear into the ether without a word. He was wrong to think that they wouldn't notice, of course they would, their attention was on the children but they knew he was there and waiting for the meal to finish.

Jack mumbled a response explaining that he had only gone for a short walk, he apologised for not saying that he was going but in all honesty he didn't believe that his brief disappearance was as important or worrying as everyone seemed to think; he was yet to understand that being involved with family meant fully involved, fully integrated. Wandering off without notice was not an action that was tolerated, it was an action of indifference, of lack of care and respect. But Jack did not and could not see it that way, he was his own man and he did what he wanted to. Naturally, he did not see his actions as disrespect, they were what he always did, he had never before had to consider others, it was all new to him.

However it was very apparent that his jaunt had upset the entire family and consequently his feeling of being a man amongst strangers was enhanced, he felt uncomfortable and disappointed, it wasn't a great start to the trip.

The rest of the day passed without incident, nevertheless he still felt awkward. Sarah continued to be busy with the children, she was a full on, caring grandmother and it wasn't until the youngsters were put to bed did he feel that he had her attention.

Even then the family, that is Sarah's daughter Anne and son-in-law James, were busy making a vain attempt to ensure that he was comfortable. They were most polite; a family dinner was being prepared and they hoped and trusted that it would meet with his approval.

In truth Jack was not in the least bit hungry, food was the last thing on his mind, the day's events had left him feeling tense and he knew that whatever the meal was going to be it would be difficult to digest; but how does one explain that, you can't, he would just have to get on with it.

Jack would have much preferred some time alone with Sarah but that was not going to happen, or so he thought, he would have to accept the situation as it was.

Fortunately, as the meal was being prepared Sarah must have sensed his unease and suggested that they take a brief walk whilst the cooking took place. Jack was greatly relieved, he did need time outside, time to chat to Sarah, time to get used to the idea that he was in unchartered territory; it was second nature to Sarah, she had been visiting for many years and it would be, it was, extremely difficult for her to understand why he felt so awkward.

In normal circumstances Jack was amenable, friendly and sociable, but he had just travelled three thousand miles to be with Sarah and the initial greeting and first hours of his arrival were not as he had anticipated or expected.

Small doubts about the wisdom of the trip began to creep in, particularly when Sarah announced that the family had suggested that they all go out on the morrow but perhaps on the day after that he and Sarah could visit the mall and spend some time together. Sarah honestly believed that he should be grateful that the family were giving them time to be together, she appeared to have overlooked the fact that being together was the entire reason for making the trip.

Of course it was nice that Sarah felt open to introduce him to her family, to welcome him into the fold, to introduce him as her companion, but for Jack that would all come in time, this trip, as far as he intended was finding time for them to be together after being apart. He was more than happy to meet all and sundry, but most of all it was Sarah that he had come to see.

Jack had sometimes stayed over at Sarah's house when it had become late and travelling home in the car was a dangerous option. They had shared the same bed, cuddling and romanticising, it was fun, meaningful and the family probably thought, had they known, rather naughty, but as life is short neither of them really cared what others may have thought, they were not interested. It is common for the younger generation to believe that those older than themselves are unable to enjoy the passion of an embrace, a kiss or intimate moments. They will learn in time when their younger generations treat them as though they were long past strong emotion.

In consequence it was with some surprise and gratitude that he discovered that the family had allocated just the one bedroom for them. It was apparent that they were not sure if it was the right thing to do, they were unaware that the pair were passed the point of sleeping in separate rooms.

Sarah was very private and when it came to it, a rather shy person in regard to very personal matters and therefore she would have never discussed sleeping arrangements with her daughter in advance. They had anticipated correctly, and thankfully personal life in Ottawa was going to be normal.

Jack had no doubt that the family felt a little awkward, their mother and grandmother sharing the same bedroom with a strange man, when they had been aware that she had been sleeping alone for many years. He imagined that it had been a difficult decision for them to make and he was convinced that Anne was not comfortable with the situation.

The family tended to retire quite early, mainly because the children woke at an uncivilised time in the morning and would not resettle. It was therefore with a certain sense of relief that he and Sarah retired at the same time.

That first evening Jack and Sarah made their way to the allocated room and discovered two single beds. It was not too surprising; the family were not to know that the pair normally shared the same bed. However Sarah had decided that the relationship, on that very night, should reach the next, and some would say, the ultimate level. The level at which couples announce their intention to make the relationship permanent. The result was a night of passion when their level of intimacy reached its apex. At the very height of the moment Sarah murmured, “I wish this could last for ever”.

That first day had started like a damp squid but ended in a golden explosive shower.

The following day was a family day, it was true that Jack would not be spending the day alone with Sarah, however her daughter was making the attempt to bring Jack a little more into the fold, after all he was her mother’s choice, for better or worse.

The grandchildren had not known how to react to this stranger in their midst, that was to be expected, but today was to be a little different because the outing was a visit to one of the family’s favourite places, Mooney’s Bay Park.

As it was Jack’s first visit to Ottawa Anne decided that, on the way to the park, it would be a good idea to make a stop at Hog’s Back Falls, a sixty-foot manmade waterfall at the junction of the Rideau River and the Rideau canal. It was a popular tourist stop off, a must see for all visitors to the city.

The Falls were a magnificent sight, and the sound of the falling and cascading water was relaxing as well as visually spellbinding. But Sarah and the children had seen it all before and they were anxious to get to the park. Children need to be active and to be actively entertained, gazing at falling water, for any length of time, was not sufficiently enthusing.

The Falls were east of the park and the beach, it was only a short journey to the children's preferred destination.

When they arrived Jack was not surprised that it was a favourite place. Sandy River Beach was, as it was named, a sandy beach alongside the river. The consistency of the sand made it perfect for building sandcastles and as soon as they arrived the children grabbed their grandmother to help them play, so with bucket and spade they began creating bucket shaped structures set in a circle.

Jack looked on, he held back a little because the children were still unsure of him and he did not wish to worry them, so when Sarah beckoned him over he waved one arm and said; "in a minute, I'm enjoying watching you".

As a stranger, playing with the two small children when Mum and Dad were there made him feel a little uncomfortable. He didn't know them well enough yet, hopefully there would be other times.

The group remained on the beach for a little over an hour, but the children were anxious to go to the Park's children's playground. Jack was soon to discover what a wonderful playground it was.

There were swings, roundabouts, climbing frames, slides, a tree house, sandpits and many other structures for adventurous children, a play area packed with activities, more than Jack had ever seen before. It was the largest children's activities centre that he had visited and looking back he recalled that there had been nothing like it when his own children were growing up.

The day passed quickly; Jack had been annoyed that he had not been alone with Sarah but on reflection he realised that they were all trying to make him feel at home. It had been Jack's intention to make his stay one for just himself and Sarah, that was of course unrealistic but it was the way he felt, the way he had envisaged and anything short of that would be less than his desires.

In the evening, after the young ones had been fed and tucked up in bed, Sarah's son-in-law prepared a meal with a fish base, Jack guessed that Sarah had told him that fish was one of his favourite dishes; there was general conversation around the dinner table, at this stage of Jack's inclusion into the family circle, a very tight family circle, he had not yet been fully integrated and so the chat did not include any serious topics. No politics, religion, sport or colour, just reminiscences of the day past and the thoughts for the morrow.

That night Jack snuggled up to Sarah on the single bed that she had chosen and not until she had fallen asleep did he move to the other single bed. It had been a good day and tomorrow the day had been set aside for them, no children or family until later in the evening.

The following morning, at the crack of dawn, Jack heard the sound of children's voices. They were both awake and ready to go, Sarah also woke to the sound and, in a flash she went to the bathroom, dressed and was gone.

She always assisted with her grandchildren's breakfast both in preparation and in feeding, Jack still did not fully understand why the children's mother, with the maid's help, could not manage without Sarah, after all she did so when Sarah was not there, but that was Sarah, she had always been there at breakfast, the children expected it, as did her daughter.

It was not his role to reason why, he had no option but to try and understand and to accept. It would be fair to say that when he was told that Sarah was, being given the day off, (not the family's words but Jack's interpretation) it made him feel just a little agitated. On later reflection perhaps this was unreasonable, he was after all a stranger imposing himself on the family's affairs, a situation that they had not before encountered.

Nevertheless the day was theirs and after they had eaten, Sarah's daughter drove them to the centre of town where they were able to board the pick-up drop-off bus that would enable Jack in particular to see the sights of the city.

Sarah loved to travel by bus, or any form of public transport and, although she had visited her daughter many times she had never taken this tour of the city.

They went to the upper deck of the bus, it was an open top, as are most of the city tour buses. Today was a little colder, spring in Canada was as unpredictable as spring in England, but it wasn't raining and always the best place to view any sights on a bus is upstairs.

This bus, known as The Grey Bus (although it was red in colour), travelled past many of the city's well-known landmarks. Sarah thought it best to stay on the bus for the whole round trip, there was insufficient time to hop on and hop off to see the attractions, Jack's visit was not long enough, there would be other times.

The city tour took two hours and gave Jack a reasonable flavour of Ottawa city; they went by City Hall, the War Museum, Canada's Parliament buildings on Parliament Hill, Rideau Hall (the official residence of the Governor General of Canada) and past Byward Market, an old and large market, a must place to shop, but not today.

Following the bus tour they decided to take in the canal trip, Sarah wanted Jack to see as much as possible and there was limited time; too little as far as Jack was concerned.

The visit was only six days, a short stay for the distance travelled and the sights that he wanted to see.

When Jack was alone with Sarah time flew by, the moments were fleeting and too short, he needed this quality time, this alone time, their time, but what Jack had not quite understood was the closeness of the family ties, Sarah had been living alone for many years and quite naturally those circumstances automatically culminated in a closeness between mother and daughter.

The Rideau Canal Cruise was both relaxing and educational, as with the bus tour there was a complete audio explanation and description of all the Ottawa historic buildings and attractions as they were passed. The trip lasted ninety minutes but sailed by different places of interest, such as, the Museum of Nature, the National Arts Centre, Ottawa University and others. It was a most pleasant way to see the city.

After they disembarked they made a beeline for the Notre Dame Cathedral Basilica.

They both enjoyed visiting any city cathedral, which were more than places of worship, they were places of history, of conflict, of beauty and whenever they had the opportunity Sarah would light a candle and under her breath mutter a short prayer. In normal circumstances she was not religious, but in a cathedral or old church, the quietness and the sombreness brought out the early beliefs she had been taught.

After the sightseeing they made their way to the French area of the city, not that they were particularly enamoured with France or the French, but because the best restaurants, they were advised, were located there. It had been an exhilarating and enjoyable day, a day to be repeated whenever possible.

Sarah's family approach was natural for her, Jack had not spent his life alone, his ties with his family were close insomuch that he cared for his children, but they had their own lives and he had his, the family get-togethers were pretty infrequent, mainly high holidays and birthdays. It could be described as a much looser relationship, the family were there, or would be there when needed, but they did not live in each other's pockets.

In a way neither Jack nor Sarah really understood the other's family perspective, both believed that their family lives, their family ties, were absolutely normal, and so they were, given each other's particular circumstances.

But they were different and being different they were difficult to comprehend. Sarah did not appreciate Jack's apparent need for more time and attention away from her family, her approach was that he,

Jack, should be more appreciative of the fact that he had been invited to spend time in their home and he should be more open in displaying that appreciation, of course she was right, but Jack believed that he had travelled thousands of miles to spend a brief few days with Sarah, but the family neither understood his desire nor were willing to indulge in it. It was adolescent, a childish approach, but Jack was seventeen again and his thoughts and actions were immature.

Jack and Sarah, over the weeks had built a love, a bond, a closeness that sometimes takes years to develop. They, to coin a phrase, an old adage, were 'soulmates'. They felt that they belonged together and that they were lucky, at this stage in their lives, to have found each other. But the friction of the past few days, arising mostly from misunderstanding, was bound to take its toll.

However, on the day after the visit to the city, there was still some time to go and there were more places to see, there was no time to waste reflecting on differences.

Sarah always made sure that breakfast time was allocated to the children and she more often than not made sure that she was home in time to read them a story at bedtime. These preferences did tend to shorten the day as far as alone time was concerned; but Jack knew that on no account should he attempt to change Sarah's natural habits, it would be a mistake, but the knowledge that he had to remain silent whilst inwardly protesting made him feel morose..

In addition, Jack and Sarah, on the days allocated for them to be together were reliant on being taken to the city in the family car, it was too far to walk, there were always taxis available but the house was not on a public transport route. The need to be ferried made independence difficult and although Sarah's daughter was always happy to give them a lift to whatever location they wished to visit, they were reluctant to be a nuisance.

The following day had been set aside for a 'mother daughter' day. That meant a trip to the beauty parlour for a massage, facial and nail treatments. A day of pampering that they both deserved but a day that interfered with Jack's visit.

It was only a morning but it was a long morning. Jack now had a fair idea of the area around the house so, as the weather was holding up he decided to take a walk and waste a little time until Sarah returned. There was a picturesque canal nearby with a path alongside, it was an ideal walk on a pleasant day and the distance travelled was entirely up the walker, it was most certainly an ideal way to kill time.

The rest of the day belonged to the children, Jack did get involved, amusing them as much as he could; they were getting used to him and were not quite so shy. He did feel that they may accept him, given a little time, but the adults would take longer. He still had the feeling that he was 'in the way' as far as Sarah's daughter was concerned.

Sarah had been able to give her daughter undivided attention for years, and as far as Anne was concerned her mother was always there and available when needed, but now things were changing and she made it fairly plain, in a nice sort of way, that she didn't like it. In their family there had always been a special bond between mother and daughter and there was no distance between them to accommodate anyone else.

Jack could sense the opposition to his intervention and it unsettled him, he asked himself the question, "doesn't Anne want her mother to be happy?" But that was the wrong question at this time, he needed to wait, the future would take care of itself if only he were patient, a virtue he didn't have.

Looking back Jack could see that there was no reason why Anne should believe that he would make her mother happy. She didn't know him, did not care to know him, and for all she knew he could have been a pig of a man who had stolen her mother's affections. At the time of this first visit, this first introduction, these were reasonable, protective thoughts, but for Jack they seemed both unreasonable and divisive.

There was still another day, another Jack and Sarah day to enjoy. There were other venues in the city that Sarah was keen to show Jack, and they would be better seen and enjoyed on foot.

Ottawa was blessed with many parks and springtime brought forward a plethora of colour, they could not visit all of them but Sarah was enthusiastic about another return visit in the not-too-distant future so that they could explore the places that they had not seen this time, together.

On this day Sarah wanted to visit the Royal Canadian Mint to see how Canadian coins were manufactured. The Mint was just a stone's throw from Notre Dame which she felt was worth a further look. Finally there was Byward Market, a blend of old and new Ottawa, there were bound to be keepsakes they could acquire that would be a reminder of the trip.

That evening was the eve of Jack's return and it was to be a family meal and glasses of wine to say farewell. It was bittersweet for Jack; this first visit to Sarah's family had been a little fraught for him and he suspected that Anne felt the same way. He was sure that she would not be disappointed that he was leaving.

However Jack was very sorry to say goodbye to Sarah. It would be over a week before he could see her again, and at this stage of their relationship a week seemed like a long time.

The final day of the trip arrived; Jack was due to fly at two thirty but during that morning there had been no private time with Sarah. It was true that they had spent each night together but they were in separate beds and tiredness, and a slight feeling of tension, had mostly kept them apart.

On that final day Jack was feeling particularly peeved, perhaps sullen would be a more accurate description. His visit had ended, he had not spent enough time alone with Sarah, he felt frustrated and unhappy, he was a mature adult but was acting and feeling like a spoilt teenager. He was unable to change his mood and perhaps that was an indication of insecurity and childishness, a trend that describes the feelings and actions of most of the male population.

He was no mood to be jolly or friendly. Of course he should have been both but he was unable to mask his true feelings. In reality the entire visit should have been a joyous occasion; Jack was meeting his love's family and they were meeting their mothers/ Grandmother's choice of beau, a man she expected to spend her life with. Perhaps that was a recipe for tension perhaps not, but either way the visit did not turn out as expected. Now it was over, and the tensions still simmered beneath the surface.

It was a normal workday for Sarah's son-in-law and as he departed in the morning he bade farewell to Jack, in an out of character response Jack mumbled a reply but did not stand or shake hands. It was a miserable and pathetic response but once Sarah's son-in-law had left the house there was no possibility of turning back the clock. Jack's inept attitude did not go unnoticed but nothing was said,

It had been raining that morning and there was a flood alert, the news indicated that some of the roads close to the airport were under water. Not wanting Jack to miss his plane a taxi was called and it arrived at ten o'clock over four hours before the flight was due out and the airport was less than an hour away.

Jack had the immediate feeling that he had been given orders to remove himself, it was probably not the case but the timing of the taxi persuaded him that it was so. His case was pushed into the boot and he departed to a somewhat tepid goodbye from a quiet and subdued Sarah,

The journey to the airport took less than sixty minutes, there were no flooded roads and Jack arrived with more than three hours to kill. He spent some time in the airport lounge reflecting on the week's events. He knew that on the whole things had not gone too well, and he was worried.

Sarah was due to remain in Ottawa for another week before flying home, it would be a week of deep concern for Jack, he had no idea how Sarah would respond when she returned but he had a sinking feeling that it would not be the way he wanted.

He was also not looking forward to a week's worry and loneliness. But there was nothing he could do about it:

Whatsoever a man soweth, that shall he also reap.

This was the biblical phrase that came to his mind, a phrase that he had himself quoted once or twice, now it had come home to roost.

The flight back was smooth and without incident, it did seem to take longer than the six hours of its duration but at least, on arrival, after the baggage reclaim, the ordered taxi was there waiting.

It was dark when Jack put the key into the front door lock and the house was cold and uninviting. There was no-one there to welcome him and it was a little late to make any calls, all he could do was make a cup of coffee and feel sorry for himself.

Fortunately, the following day was camera club day, he would be able to meet some of his friends. He wasn't really in the mood to see them but he decided he would make the effort. There was also indoor bowls that was one of Jack's hobbies, that would pass some time before Sarah returned, it was something to do.

Jack did not call Sarah the following day, he decided to leave well alone. It was forty-eight hours later when he made contact to find out how she was. There was no immediate response, he waited on tenterhooks but it was some hours later before he received a reply.

Sarah told him that she was unwell, she had contracted a virus that was going around and had arranged to call the doctor, meanwhile she was confined to the house and did not feel well enough to indulge in too many online chats.

This was a slap in face for Jack and his heart sank, perhaps she really was unwell or perhaps she did not want to communicate with him, or perhaps it was both. He really did not know what to think or what to do. He did not want to accept that their relationship was over, it had been too intense, too meaningful, too real, it could not just suddenly end, could it?

Over the next three- or four-days Jack made several attempts to make contact, finally he received a reply from Sarah telling him that it had been necessary to cancel the flight home because she had not recovered from the virus. It was an open-ended reply in that Sarah gave no indication when she would be able to return home, it was up to the doctor.

Now Jack was really concerned, he had no way of knowing how serious her illness was. It had been over a week, quite a time for a virus to be so active, particularly as Sarah had been taking medication. The signs were ominous, it seemed to Jack that she was avoiding him and bearing in mind the way that he had left to go to the airport, her reluctance to communicate was understandable although saddingly unwelcome.

Jack could only hope that it would blow over and that their relationship could return to normal and by normal he meant the loving feelings that existed before he travelled to Canada.

The days passed, they passed beyond the time that Sarah was due to return. Jack knew that all was not well, not with Sarah's health but between them. He did not know if she was thinking over their relationship, whether she was feeling so unwell that she preferred solitude or whether there was more to it.

It was several days later when he received the email, the bombshell, it said in no uncertain terms that she could never live or be associated with a man who was so rude and ungrateful to her family.

The message had no other concluding remarks, that was it, the romance was over.

CHAPTER NINE

Jack woke from a fitful sleep; he reached for the pillow, his comfort pillow, the pillow that he had placed beside him the night before. It gave him warmth, it was almost as though there was someone beside him, someone to share the bed. But last night he could find no comfort, there had been no warmth, just solitude and a deep feeling of loss and loneliness.

A few days ago his life had been full, the future was certain, it had stretched before him filled with joy and expectancy, however, this morning, in the cold light of this new day fear gripped his heart; once again he was alone. It wasn't the fact of being alone that left him devastated, it was the loss of the one person who had appeared in a miraculous way to give hope for happiness in his autumn years. The very meaning of the days ahead had been snatched away just when they seemed to be within his grasp.

Jack gazed out of the bedroom window on to the rear garden, the colours were grey, perhaps it was the dark grey clouds that blocked out the sun but more likely it was the colour that his mindset beheld.

I need to see someone, anyone, I'll give Bill a call.

The words raced through his mind, and then he remembered, Bill had left for Albania the day before Jack had boarded the plane for Ottawa, he would be away for three weeks.

The house on his left side was in the process of being refurbished and the family were staying with relatives until the completion of the work. Jack had no immediate neighbours, no one next door to alleviate his woes, he was alone on the oasis of misery.

Jack turned over and pulled the covers up to beneath his chin, he didn't want to get up, what was the point, Sleep would be his escape, his salvation his way of eliminating the deep sadness he felt; where was Sarah, why didn't she understand?

But how could she understand, he had acted like spoilt child, he had broadcast his insecurities, he had been rude and insolent, in fact he deserved to lose the one person who had been his salvation; the only cure was oblivion.

It was almost two hours later when he woke with a start, he glanced at his bedside clock, ten fifty-five, the day was almost half gone, he needed to stir himself; it was the house phone that had woken him, the extension was on the bedroom wall just above his head, Jack reached out and took the phone from its cradle, it was Peter, a courtesy call to ask his father how his trip to Canada went. Jack grimaced but he decided to lie and make light of his predicament,

"Hi Dad, how was your trip?"

Jack responded in the lightest tone he could muster. "It was fine, Ottawa is a lovely city, I saw most of it."

Peter replied; "How was Sarah and her family, did you say she was staying on?"

Peter had given Jack a get-out, there was now no need to go into details he could lie with deference.

"Everything was great, Sarah is staying to help her daughter with the grandchildren, her son-in-law is going away for a short while on business, she will stay as long as she is needed."

Peter accepted the bait and left the subject; "*What are your plans over the next few days, I thought I might drive over to see you?*"

Jack hadn't expected that and he wasn't ready to see his son, he needed more time to reflect and compose himself.

"I've got the camera club tomorrow and bowls the day after and I'd promised myself that I would crack on with a pet photography project that I've started. Maybe you could give me a call next week and we will arrange something."

That seemed to satisfy Peter, he had done his duty, checked on his father and confirmed that everything was ok.

"Okay dad, good to hear you feeling chipper, oh by the way I went over to mum's grave while you were away and left some fresh flowers. I'll ring in a few days."

And with that he hung up.

The call had woken Jack, he decided to get up and think of something to do, he could call his daughter but what would he say, he didn't really feel like talking to family just now. If Bill had been home he could have unburdened himself, as it was he would just wallow in self-pity.

When he had dressed Jack went to the kitchen cupboard, he should eat something, he wasn't hungry but he should eat something anyway His stomach was rebelling, that wasn't unusual if he was stressed, his stomach was always the first of his organs to signal that all was not well, but Jack knew that starving himself was not the answer, it was the easy way but not the best way.

Unfortunately, he had forgotten that he had been away for a week and the cupboard was looking decidedly bare, he needed to shop.

Shopping for Jack was a necessity not a past-time and the less time he spent in the supermarket the better.

Some snacks, some microwaveable meals, something sweet and something to drink would satisfy him for a few days, that was all he needed.

Within the hour he was back home munching on a packet of crisps and sipping a cup of tea. He had no desire to do anything so he switched on the television with the idea that he could lose himself in the programme content, but his mind kept wandering back to Sarah, what was she doing? What was she thinking? What....?

Jack's mind could not escape the past weeks, he was caught in a recent past from which he could not escape and could not recapture; a wonderful time gone forever, never to return.

The rest of the day dragged on, the television was blaring but it could not hold Jack's attention, sometimes he could concentrate on the on-screen antics but not for long, Sarah was there, she was always there, she would not leave his mind. Even his beloved Sylvia was pushed to the back of his conscious thoughts, he could think of nothing but the feelings that he had for Sarah, feelings that he had to dispel, somehow, someway.

At ten o'clock that evening sleep overtook him and oblivion became his salvation.

Jack slept for almost nine hours, a sleep he needed, a sleep which provided some escape. When he awoke he realised that although he had lost his soulmate he had to move on, there was no choice. Perhaps the pain of his loss would remain with him, he would have to bear it. His family and friends would never know the deep feelings that he would have to suppress to survive.

Jack was in no mood just yet to face family or friends but he did need to have some company. If it were to be a female companion then just a companion it would be.

He could not imagine meeting anyone like Sarah, perhaps a pleasant person, a person with whom he could chat, share a meal with or maybe an excursion, would suffice. That would be better than the loneliness that threatened the long days ahead..

Jack turned once again to his trusty non-human companion, his laptop; or was it his poisoned chalice, a chalice from which he felt compelled to drink, he shook his head and punched in the letters for the dating website.

As he began his search through the list of profiles that were a near match, he remembered 'Rosina', the lipstick lady, at least she was relaxed and easy to talk to, if she were not with someone perhaps they could link up. At their previous meeting she had mentioned that she had been dating someone on a friendly but casual basis, she explained that he would disappear for weeks on end and then suddenly give her a call.

Jack had wondered why she had bothered but logically if he were only a friend and she was not meeting anyone with serious or long-term possibilities, then why not have males as casual friends?

Notwithstanding Jack supposed that he would have to give some explanation for the long gap since his last communication, but what the hell, there was nothing to lose.

Jack scrolled back through his emails until he found the last one that he had received from Rosina, then under 'reply' he typed;

> *Hi Rosina, sorry I haven't been in touch but I've been abroad and I've been working on my pet project, so I haven't had much free time of late. But I'm taking a rest from work and I'm trying to catch up with all those I have neglected, I thought of you first, you were top of my list.*
>
> *If you are still free and unattached, perhaps we could meet and chat over lunch in order to catch up.*
>
> *Please be in touch, I'm still on the same mobile number.*
>
> *Jack*

Jack felt a twinge of guilt at the outright untruths in his message, it wasn't his style to lie, but on reflection he concluded that there was nothing wrong with contacting a previous date, he had no ill intent. Rosina could only ignore the message or respond in negative fashion; it was up to her; he would just have to wait and see.

While he was typing his string of untruths to Rosina a message popped up, they had probably noticed that he was online; the message was from Rose Marie asking him to contact her. She had noted his profile and the site had advised her that he was an ideal match.

Jack completed his hangdog appeal to Rosina and went to the profile of the new contact. He noted the photograph of a woman with very dark hair. It was cut short not boyish; the picture depicted an attractive woman who Jack estimated to be no more than forty-five or fifty. Her looks were not particularly Jack's choice but he was in no position to be overly choosy.

During his site search for a companion Jack had realised that certain types of face, of look, in the shape, the fullness of the lips, the position and brightness of the eyes, of the proportion of the features, made a significant visual and mental impact on the appeal to him. He also realised, from his discussions with Bill and his preferences, that everyone was magnetically drawn to different features, it was inherent in the nature of things that we liked different things. He had thought to himself that it must be the scheme of things, otherwise we would all like the same woman, in the case of men, or the same man in the case of women.

Rose Marie lacked that special appeal but she was sufficiently attractive for Jack to read her profile. He read through her preferences and the various boxes that she had ticked.

Under 'age preference' she had entered; From one to one hundred.

Under 'location'… Anywhere in the world.

Under 'Height'… 120 centimetres to 210 centimetres.

Under 'language'… Any.

And so it went on, her preferences were in fact anyone, they covered every man that had subscribed. Jack immediately thought that any lady casting her net that wide must be desperate or was an opportunist; it was a danger signal but Jack believed that he could look after himself, he had enough decades under his belt to make him wise.

Bill had already primed him that it was likely that he would encounter fortune hunters, sugar daddy prospects, jokers, meal tickets, and more, they all relied on the natural arrogance that men had; so he should be ready for anything.

Jack did feel that he was 'ready for anything' therefore there was no reason why he should not respond, she may be genuine, and like himself she may be lonely. He therefore responded in his usual manner with politeness and interest;

Thank you for your message Rose Marie, I would be happy to chat with you, my mobile number is .... Please call me at any time.

Jack took the view that a chat could do no harm and he was certainly in the market for talking to someone, anyone, he needed a distraction from his thoughts of Sarah, thoughts that permeated his mind, thoughts that he could not dispel.

There was nothing further he could do at present except scroll through the website and leave a number of messages where there were matching profiles and of course appealing photographs, he ignored any profile that may match but had no photo attached.

Jack had eaten nothing that morning, he had no appetite, but common sense told him that he should eat something even if were something sweet, probably unhealthy but the only thing that he could comfortably digest. So it was a breakfast cereal, loaded with sugar, followed by a sweet weak cup of coffee, a meal that would sustain him for a few hours.

After the meal Jack loaded the dishwasher and sat gazing out of the kitchen window on to the back garden.

It wasn't a bad day, the early spring sun ventured out from a cloudy sky at frequent intervals. Rain was not forecast but he wondered if you could rely on that. He sat there for half an hour; he was not keen to go out but he was depressed staying indoors in an empty house. Neither option appealed but as there were no other he had to choose one or the other. In the end he opted for a short walk outside, the nearest open country area was a little too far away so a stroll through the streets it was.

Jack donned a coat; it wasn't cold but the spring air was cool even though it was approaching midday.

He lived on an avenue, a street lined with small trees, ones that would abound with blossom in the near future and although the walk was not particularly therapeutic it was not unpleasant.

As he passed the driveways and the front gardens shielded by privet hedges, his thoughts turned to Sarah. He chided himself for his inability to think of something else, but he could not cast from his mind the idea that she was on the site seeking someone new, someone to take his place. Could she have forgotten him so soon? He blinked his eyes and wiped away the moisture that had dampened his cheeks, he desperately needed a distraction, the intervention of another human being, he just needed to see someone, anyone, and he needed that meeting to take place today, now.

Jack had reluctantly accepted that Sarah was in the past, she had moved on even though he could not. The recriminations, the desires that perhaps he could go back and rekindle the dreams of the past had to be pushed to the very back of his mind; he was unable to extinguish them entirely but they should not be pre-eminent.

It was a pity that Bill was away, he could have helped, he would have listened to Jack's woes, his cries for help; Bill would not have been too sympathetic it was not his way, but he would have been a listening ear and his lack of sympathy may have provided a shot in the arm.

But Bill was unavailable, Jack's only hope was the two online messages that had not yet borne fruit. One of them, Rosina may be able to provide immediate company, a spot of lunch, a face to talk to, that would suffice temporarily. The other was a whistle in the wind, a chance for tomorrow.

Of course, there was always family, the photographic club, or his bowls club associates, but he could not go through the process of explanation, it was too painful. Strangers were an easier and better option. They were the best and less painful antidote for the emptiness that he felt. He would not be required to mention Sarah, they would have no need to know, he could be comfortably emotionless, that was the best medicine it would be easier in the company of someone who didn't matter.

Jack's walk did not last long, he had little appetite to trudge the streets, so in less than an hour he was back at his computer, hopeful that there would be a message, or more than one message, that would be his salvation for the day.

He had not taken his mobile out while he was walking and it suddenly trilled, a reminder that he had a missed call. It was Rosina. He rang back immediately; she must have read his thoughts; it only rang twice before the familiar voice responded.

"Hello Jack, I thought that you had forgotten me."

Jack recalled that Rosina was a great talker, not so much by the importance of the content but from the point of continuous non-stop flow. It was almost an art form but it was what he needed;

"I wondered why you hadn't been in touch, but to be honest, just after we last met my son and his girlfriend, well his fiancé, came to live with me. They were looking for a flat to buy, they had been renting a place but when the lease was up they decided that it would be better to buy something, meanwhile they needed a place to stay and of course they couldn't tell me how long they would be here, it could be months.

"Needless to say they did nothing around the house, no cleaning, no cooking, nothing at all, they didn't even make their own bed, I've been running around after them from morning to dusk it has been exhausting. What with all that work, my daughter had a row with her boyfriend, not for the first time, I really don't understand why they are still together,

I never really liked him she could do better. Any way she turned up on the doorstep in tears wanting her old room back, I don't mind but I know it will be more work; then Topsy my dog became ill, I took her to the Vet and she needs an operation, I've got insurance and..."

Jack listened in silence a somewhat vacant expression on his face, there was no need for him to speak, he just had to be patient and wait for Rosina to stop for breath. Eventually she did pause giving Jack the opportunity to speak;

"Sounds like you have had a hectic time Rosina, I hope things have settled down a little. As I told you in my email I've been busy myself but I hadn't meant to neglect you, I picked up the phone on many occasions but something always cropped up to stop me making the call. I wondered if there was a chance that you could find the time for a catch up, perhaps over a bite to eat; what do you think?"

Rosina responded as though there had been no time lapse since their last encounter, that was her way, she was not one to inspire a deep meaningful relationship, it was all fluffy stuff, light-hearted banter, general conversation very little personal discussion, the sort of relationship that could best be described as a loose friendship.

It was not the companionship that Jack was seeking but it was satisfactory for now. Rosina was quite amenable for an early meeting, maybe she needed to escape from family and the chores they were creating, or maybe she was hungry, Jack made himself a promise that he wouldn't be so cynical in future.

A lunch meeting was arranged for the next day at the same restaurant they had met on the previous occasion. Jack knew that the 'date' would be a mirror image of the one before, lots of talking a swift farewell and a promise to keep in touch. It was no wonder that Rosina was still unattached and Jack wondered if she preferred it that way. Nevertheless it was company, a precious commodity for him, perhaps it was the same for her.

Within minutes of making arrangements with Rosina his phone rang, it was Rose Marie, she may have called during his marathon call with Rosina and received an engaged signal.

"Hello is that Jack? This is Rose Marie you gave me your phone number."

Jack responded in the affirmative and the subsequent conversation followed the usual pattern, as he was talking he cast his mind back to her profile and photo, he remembered the lady with the short dark hair and young-looking face, now they were talking it was apparent that English was not her first language, she had looked Spanish and she sounded Spanish although the subject of nationality never arose.

Rose Marie was quite enthusiastic about meeting for coffee, she explained that she worked unsocial hours but would be free the day after next during the mid-afternoon. The time was fine for Jack, he had nothing better to do and he was curious.

The meeting was organised for coffee in a department store café in a London suburb some distance away, not ideal but not a game changer, as he concurred he mentally made a note that he should get away before the rush hour, he hated driving in traffic that moved no faster than walking pace.

Jack was now spoilt for choice, two dates in two days, a perfect distraction, or was it. He knew in his heart that neither date would match up to his requirements and they would never match up to Sarah, he was beginning to believe that no-one would; but time is a great healer, that was someone's philosophy, but not Jack's, nonetheless he prayed that it was true.

The next morning he kept himself busy cleaning his camera lenses, he would have been better employed cleaning the house, instead he had employed a cleaner who had agreed to call one day a week; cleaning house was never his forte but his cameras were his lifeline, his way forward, his means of getting over the departure of his true love.

An hour before he was due to meet Rosina he chose casual dress for the occasion, he wanted to look smart but modern; he then set off for the thirty minute drive to the restaurant, he had not booked a table but he was aware that the day of the week and the time, precluded that necessity.

He was probably going to be early but he always allowed time for traffic holdups or road problems.

There were no delays so of course he arrived early, he parked the car close to the entrance of the restaurant car park and waited. As anticipated Rosina arrived ten minutes after the agreed time, it was a woman's prerogative. But it did seem that leaving home too late, or not predicting the length of time that the journey may take, was part of her character.

After she had alighted from her car Jack was there wating, they engaged in mutual smiles and Jack was, as last time, drawn to her painted lips; yes, there it was again that faint smudge of red on her teeth. This time he wasn't fazed, he had expected it, he was able to ignore the smudge, he had company, the one thing that he desperately needed, he could relax and listen while Rosina chatted away.

The time passed quickly, the food was reasonable and the Budweiser he downed tasted cool and refreshing. It was a pity that Rosina could never be a part of his permanent life, it would never work for Jack and he surmised that it would not work for her. Meanwhile, they could keep each other company, Rosina loved to talk and Jack was content to listen. But in the coming weeks Jack was to discover that she was happy with a once-a-week lunch as a rest from the family, but of course that was a long way from satisfying Jack's needs, it didn't even scratch the surface.

By the time Jack reached home the light was beginning to fade, the evenings drew in early. He would be alone that evening but he was not too concerned, the television would occupy his time and he would think about giving Laura a call, just to keep in touch. In the end he fell asleep in front of the screen and when he eventually woke up the TV had automatically switched off.

The next morning the weather was typically British, cloudy with a hint of rain in the air, always a good excuse for putting off any work that was due in the garden. His meeting with Rose Marie was not until that afternoon therefore a session on the computer would help to pass the time.

In any case it was necessary that he kept up with any contacts received, there could be one that was from that elusive someone that he was seeking; but even those vague thoughts were depressing, he had thought that Sarah was that special someone and even now, with all the water that had passed under the bridge he still could not stop harbouring the thought that she may get in touch. But her last words had been so final that he knew they were words from which there was no return.

Although it was early morning there was a message from the site, it came from a lady who called herself Lena, most likely not her real name. There was a photograph attached and the image was of a woman of thirty something. She had posted a profile which explained that she heralded from Russia but had family in the UK and was a frequent visitor. Lena was seeking companionship with an Englishman who could keep her company during her visits and there was a further discreet indication that if she found the right person she was not averse to a stronger relationship.

Jack was no fool, Lena had obviously read his profile and seen his photographs. She knew his age so the question was, why would a woman of thirty something wish to meet a man of seventy something? it didn't add up.

It was a question with an obvious answer but of course Lena was relying on most men's arrogance regarding their own looks and personal attractiveness, men can be so stupid at times. However, Jack was intrigued and he decided to return to the message later that day by drafting a suitable reply; it would pass the time and could prove to be amusing. He was aware of the time difference; she was five or six hours ahead and so she would be unlikely to read his words until the next day.

There were no further responses to the messages he had sent out earlier, that was disappointing, but it was early morning and he knew that many ladies did not check in until later in the day and some only checked the site once or twice a week.

Jack made himself a brunch. Brunch? It was a toasted cheese sandwich and a cup of tea, but it was enough. He dressed as he had become used to on these dates, smart casual. And also, as usual, he gave himself two hours to travel a journey that his satnav told him would take ninety minutes.

The journey, the shortest route, took him around the South Circular Road, a road that he had not used for many years. Now it seemed busier than he ever remembered, the traffic was heavy, there were multiple roadworks and the result was a journey with traffic jams every few yards. The construction workers really were out in force; it was a nightmare, the minutes ticked by and Jack grew anxious. He hated being late.

Fortunately, the additional time he had allocated for the journey was just enough and he pulled into the store car park with a minute to spare.

The store café was not full and it was quite small, Jack had no problem in identifying the dark-haired woman seated alone at a corner table. He approached, she rose and introduced herself in a voice that carried the accent that he recognised from the phone call.

He had been open minded as to the woman he was to meet, on a previous occasion his 'date' turned out to be considerably older than the photo she had posted, Rose Marie's picture was also of a woman who appeared much younger than the years she professed to be; on this occasion Jack was pleasantly surprised to find that the woman in front of him was exactly like the photo, it was recent.

Jack smiled, politely asked if he could buy the coffees, sought her preference and with cups in hand returned to the table.

The ensuing conversation was surprisingly relaxed, Rose Marie was easy to talk to and her accent made the discussion even more pleasing. But Jack realised immediately that there was no attraction from a mental or physical point of view. As they chatted he discovered that she was the victim of a bitter divorce that had taken place some years ago and that there was still an ongoing argument related to the division of the proceeds of the marital home which had been registered in her ex-husbands name. Meanwhile, while she waited the outcome and the receipt of the substantial sum to which she was entitled, she was, by financial necessity, employed in two part-time employments, hence the reason for the unsocial hours.

Because of her unfortunate circumstances she lived in a flat provided by the council but she struggled to find the rent. However, it was only a temporary situation which would be alleviated when she received the proceeds from the marital home.

Her story, as sad as it sounded, appeared to be well rehearsed and Jack formed the unshakeable impression that Rose Marie was seeking a financial provider, a man of any age that would keep her in the manner to which she believed was her true station.

Jack also found it difficult to accept that she was as old as she had described in her profile. There was not a line on her face nor a strand of grey in her hair; of course Botox and hair dye could be the answer but he believed otherwise.

Jack's face was expressionless as he listened to her sad story, now and then he offered a sympathetic nod and at one point asked if she had received any indication when the ordeal with her ex-husband would be over. She had responded with a pained expression that she did not know.

They finished their coffees and Jack's offer of a refill was declined; he knew that when he left the café and offered his thanks for a delightful meeting that there would not be a second one. He realised that it would be cowardly to delay the truth by not saying… I am sorry but I do not believe that we are compatible, but I do hope that you meet someone who will be ideal… or something similar.

The problem with not being open and honest is that the other person is left with the mistaken impression that another meeting is a possibility. Jack was aware of his inability to be honest but he could not bring himself to say words that may be hurtful, that was his weakness, one that he always had and could not conquer.

The journey home was even worse than when he came, the London rush hour had begun, workers were leaving their places of employment in their droves, the road works were still in full swing and the stop start driving experience was frustrating in the extreme. Jack knew that every Londoner going home after work had to have the patience of a saint or suffer heart palpitations, it was so bad.

The journey home took three hours, he could have driven three quarters of the way to Yorkshire in that time, what a waste of petrol, but there was no relief in sight for those unfortunates who were unable to avoid travelling in the prevailing conditions.

When he finally, with a profound sense of relief, pulled into his driveway, he looked back on an afternoon that had been stressful and unrewarding, it was an afternoon to forget.

A cup of tea was his first port of call before he opened his laptop and respond to the earlier message. When he did enter the site he noted that there was another communication; it was Rose Marie thanking him for a pleasant time and that she was looking forward to their next meeting.

CHAPTER TEN

Jack shook his head, not in denial or frustration, it was dismay. Now he would have to contact Rose Marie with the news that he did not wish a further meeting. He could of course lie and say that he had met someone who he was continuing to see and he thought it only fair to give the relationship a chance. Or he could merely ignore the email.

Jack had wondered why Rose Marie had cast her net so wide, she was not unpleasant in appearance, she certainly did not look her age if she was being truthful, was she really just seeking someone to pay the bills? Or was there another reason? Whatever the answer he knew that their personalities, their experiences, their outlook on life were so different that even companionship was out of the question.

It was a dilemma he decided to face later.

He had been back a week and it crossed his mind that Sarah was due back about now. She would be home working out her daily schedule, it would probably be similar to the way she lived her life before they met.

He was curious to know if she would join the dating site again, if she did it would most likely be a different site, she wouldn't take the chance of him noticing her on the same one, the one that had originally brought them together.

He tried to imagine her meeting someone else, enjoying his company, even forging a new relationship, his thoughts were painful, physically and mentally, his eyes moistened as the realisation that they would never meet again, drove home.

With a grimace, an expression of anger with himself, he wondered why he was still thinking of Sarah's movements, they should not concern him. He had to push them to the back of his mind no matter how difficult, he had to move on. There was nothing that he could do that would make any difference.

His mind had finally concluded that he must accept his current situation and try to move on. That was easier said than done, he had found his true love and lost her.

His mind reluctantly wandered back to the time, before they met, when they were spending hours on the phone talking about everything, she had told him that they were soulmates and he believed they were, but somehow being soulmates had ended in not being enough. She wanted, needed, something more, something that Jack had been unable to supply.

Notwithstanding he was still grateful that Bill had persuaded him to join the dating site. His experience with Sarah should have taught him something, the weakness in his character perhaps. Whatever it was, no matter the pain, he could not be sorry that he had met, loved and lost his 'soulmate'.

He had not yet benefitted from his membership, benefited in the sense that he had met the person who was destined to fill his life in the future, he had come so very close, but it was not meant to be. He had to believe that there was another Sarah somewhere in the ether, his lips curled in sardonic humour as he wondered if she had a twin sister of whom she had omitted to tell him.

In reality his membership had been somewhat disastrous and disappointing, it had left him broken-hearted and distraught but it was early days, he had to believe that he was being tested, that he had been found wanting but that with God's forgiveness all would be revealed and would come right in the end.

That evening Jack did nothing but snack and watch TV, he could have replied to the message from Lena, but he could not raise enough enthusiasm to go back to the site. It was easier to slouch on the settee and look at the screen even if for most of the time he was lost in his thoughts.

Later in the evening he received a call on his mobile, it was Bill. He had cut his trip short, apparently there had been some political problems in Albania and although it was perfectly safe to remain he had decided not to tempt providence.

It was too late that evening for a visit so Bill suggested they catch up the following day. This was good news for Jack, another day with company, it was something to look forward to.

His life had now been reduced to the attempt to fill it with company, any company, he believed that the occupation of the mind, driven by the person you were with, should eventually stop you thinking of the one you wish you were with.

That was Jack's philosophy, his goal, the answer to his dilemma. It was mind over matter, he had to concentrate on anything but Sarah, anything at all.

Jack slept a little better that night, he still required his comfort pillow alongside him, it persuaded him that he was not sleeping alone, a ridiculous notion but Jack had not slept alone for almost half a century, it was difficult to come to terms with the vacant spot beside him, but in any case, during the winter months in a large bed, the pillow did provide genuine warmth.

The following morning he woke early, there was no point in turning over and going back to sleep, he was wide awake. He didn't want to disturb Bill at this unearthly hour even though he wasn't actually aware of Bill's normal early morning movements, but he was aware that many people who live alone are not in too much of a hurry to leave their beds as soon as their eyes are open, for them laziness or lack of effort is the best way to spend time, the one commodity that is often surplus to requirements.

Perhaps it is the foetal position, the child in the womb, but there is something warm and safe in bed.

Jack wasn't always ready to eat when he first awoke, his appetite took an hour or so to appear, but this morning he decided to try a bowlful of cornflakes. They had been lying in the cupboard since Sylvia had died, but they were in a box and the greaseproof paper had not been disturbed; the sell by date had passed but they were still crisp and crunchy.

His principle reason for breakfast this morning was time wasting, he wanted to ring Bill to update him but he felt he couldn't do that until after nine, a civilised time. So he decided to munch and dawdle, look out of the window and watch the birds, particularly the two magpies who stomped their feet every morning on the back lawn, willing the worms to come to the surface.

It was nine-fifteen when he dialled Bill's number, there was an immediate response and it was obvious from Bill's chirpy voice that he had been up and about for some time. Jack invited him over for coffee and a chat, he needed to get the recent events off his chest.

Bill was sympathetic but not surprised when Jack relayed the fact that his relationship with Sarah had ended abruptly.

He peered over his coffee cup and in an understanding manner relayed his own experiences;

“Jack the same thing happened to me twice, just when I thought that the future was roses and wine, it ended. Sometimes it would seem the idea of commitment, of eternal life with one person, is just too much to accept, too much to contemplate, especially for those who have been on their own for a long time and have forged a suitable lifestyle. Being alone provides privacy and a complete control of one’s movements, some people require that freedom. I count myself lucky with Barbara, I have the best of both worlds at present. To be honest I’m not sure what I would do if she wanted to get married and live together as a normal married couple”.

Jack nodded and after a moment’s thought replied; “I do understand, I suppose it is a daunting thought, life with one particular person, but I thought that Sarah was different, I believed that we had found something special; I guess I was wrong”.

Bill paused and responded;

“Not necessarily Jack, you may have had something special, but you told me that Sarah had lived on her own for a long time, people get conditioned to that sometimes and the thought of losing that space and privacy may be just too much. Perhaps for her close companionship will suffice, even though that is not what you want”.

Jack realised that it was true, he had become conditioned to marriage, Sarah had been her own woman, free from ties, free from having to consider anyone else when making plans, it was easy to understand the benefits of that. Jack was lost in thought for a moment then replied;

"I do understand what you say Bill, but you are forgetting the fact that Sarah joined a dating site to end her loneliness, she made a conscious decision to find someone with whom she could share her life".

But Bill had obviously considered that before, he had been in the shoes that were now worn by Jack;

"That's true Jack, but when it comes to the crunch, better the devil you know, it's safer".

Jack could see the point as painful as it was, Bill was correct, Sarah had been in her comfort zone before they had met, Jack had believed that love conquers all but maybe that was naïve; it was time to move on, if he could.

After coffee Bill excused himself with the promise that they would go to the pub for a social beer in a couple of days; he was now about to get ready to see Barbara at lunchtime.

'Okay for some', went through Jack's mind, then he dispelled the negative thoughts and decided that the laptop was his best option this morning. He had to keep thinking, keep moving, keep himself occupied, it was the only way.

Jack went straight to Lena's message, if she were emailing him from Russia then they were hours ahead, it would be afternoon where she was, it would be a good time to reply.

Jack typed his answer;

> *Thank you for your contact Lena, I would love to chat, can you tell me a little more about yourself and when your next visit to the UK will be?*

Jack noted that there was another unopened message, perhaps this one held more promise than the chat with Lena, talking to a lady in Russia was more a matter of consuming time than likely to produce anything constructive. In any case he had yet to understand why an attractive and young woman from thousands of miles away would wish to communicate with him, he was hardly the catch of the century.

But Jack was wrong, or so he believed, because this time the message came from a lady in America who was apparently making contact with British men who she felt had more gentility and style to match her personality, than those from her own country.

Jack immediately thought, 'not the ones that I know'.

It was another interesting or perhaps uninteresting diversion for Jack, another waste of time, of that he was sure, nevertheless he decided that he would go along with it, just for the fun of communicating with someone so far away.

But, as always, his mind involuntarily turned to Sarah, I wonder what she's doing now, is she thinking of me? Probably not.

Just at this moment Jack had no stomach for the ladies from other countries or come to that for women in general; he could not shake Sarah from his mind and that feeling was so strong he decided to have one more attempt at reconciliation.

Sarah had said she had been unwell, perhaps the illness was the driving force behind her breaking with him. It was a long shot; the final goodbye had been so definite but…

Jack, in his time, had penned several poems, mostly written in traditional rhyming verse. They were not in the modern idiom but Sarah seemed to like them, most likely they appealed to a certain age group.

He thought for a moment, his senses and feelings were running high and he was in the mood to attempt to put something on paper that expressed how he felt. It was often his way of releasing his emotions, putting them on paper was a great help.

An hour later he had drafted verses that shouted out his mood, they were far from perfect but he hoped that Sarah would understand. Jack sat at his laptop and typed;

So swift the passing of each day
When thou art with me and love abounds
So swift the daylight hours fade away. Healing
all my heartfelt wounds.

And as the shadows of the night emerge
Calling forth my lonely fears
The comfort of my heart does surge
As you brush away my falling tears...

How can I tell thee of love so strong?
That it stirs my everlasting soul
This beating heart can ne'er be wrong
Only with you can I be whole.
....

So sweet love just hold my hand
And walk with me to distant shores
And as the desert moves the shifting sand
Forever I will be just yours.

Jack sat at the table gazing at the words, Shakespeare it was not, but he hoped that the verses would have some impact with Sarah, he thought 'what the hell' as he pressed the send button.

Jack knew that he would be on tenterhooks waiting for a reply, but he also knew that Sarah may not reply or if she did it may be hours or days before the response came through. Jack was no fool, he knew that Sarah would realise that he was holding out an olive branch, hoping, trusting, wishing that she would grasp it and forgive all, if only she would.

But he could hardly sit by the laptop waiting, hoping that she would respond, He may be sitting there for hours, days, forever, he had to put it to one side for the time being and trust to good fortune, to luck, or to God; there were other messages from the site that he could deal with, reply to, if only he could motivate himself to even read them.

As he sat there contemplating his predicament his mobile made its usual sound, someone was calling. He glanced at the screen, it was Rosina, no doubt advising him that she was free to meet. He looked at the name displayed, he couldn't answer just now, he needed space and time she would have to wait. His mind in a whirl he thought; God, why now.

As he sat there thinking he received a second call, it was his daughter, was she his rescue, or was she a damsel in distress? He would soon find out. He pressed the small green telephone icon.

Jack spoke first in a forced cheerful manner; "Hi, long time no hear, how is everyone, are the grandchildren ok?"

Jack knew that the call from Laura was only to ask if he was alright, she was not one for feeling comfortable when grief or death were about, so she had left it long enough for the first pangs of loss to have passed.

"Hello Dad, the grandchildren are fine, they're at Uni, so they are terribly busy, they don't come home every weekend, God knows what they get up to. But I'm calling to see how you are; are you coming to terms with... you know... with Mum's passing?"

Jack had the feeling that his daughter was hoping that he had settled into an acceptable routine and that she didn't have to worry. He couldn't tell her that he had met someone who had now ended their potential relationship, she would never understand. As far as she was concerned no-one could, or should, replace her mother. She was unaware of his visit to a dating site; God forbid what she would think or say if she found out.

Most daughters, in the circumstances, considering Jack's age, would expect their fathers to live a monastic existence, with mainly male friends for company. No he couldn't mention anything at this juncture, he quite possibly would never mention anything. If he did eventually meet someone he would say that they had been introduced, a little white lie would do no harm.

"Don't worry Laura, everything is ok I'm keeping myself busy, I've got the camera club and bowls, there's plenty to do.

"Peter called and he said he would call in to see me whenever I needed him. Hopefully, perhaps in a couple of weeks I'll drive down to see you, give me an idea when the grandchildren will be home and we'll work something out. Don't worry about me, I will be fine.

"Of course I miss Mum, I expect you do too, but I'm sure she's looking down making sure that we are all okay.

"I will give you a call when Peter lets me know when he's coming, give my love to the grandchildren".

There was nothing further to say, his conversations with Laura were always short, he loved her dearly but their relationship had always been a little strained. She had never really shown her feelings to her parents and he had wondered if autism affected her as it did with her brother, he wouldn't be surprised if it did. Thinking about David reminded him that it was about time that he went to the cemetery and tended his grave, his mind had lately been elsewhere.

At this particular moment, with his life on partial hold while he waited for Sarah's response, he wasn't in the mood for family gatherings; he needed to be left in peace until his mind and future were more settled.

They both said their usual goodbyes, the proposed visit was left open and Jack's daughter was reasonably satisfied that there was no need for her to worry.

The day was passing slowly, there were now several messages from the site that required attention, but not right then. Jack's thoughts turned to photography, he should try and revitalise his enthusiasm, as difficult as that was, it would certainly pass the time, and the passage of time was of concern.

However there was one thing that he could do, now that it had been brought to mind, a long overdue visit to the cemetery to tend both graves. He knew that Peter wouldn't go, Peter hated cemeteries with a passion, it brought home his loss, something he was trying to forget. Jack knew that when he passed both graves would remain unattended and overgrown. However there was nothing to prevent him going, perhaps the visit would provide solace, peace, it was unlikely, it would probably make him feel guilty.

His mind made up Jack put on a warm coat and drove to the cemetery, the place he had spotted the lonely little dog, presumably looking for his master. There were only two other cars parked in the spaces provided, not surprising in that it was cold and it was a weekday.

Visiting a grave is hardly ever an uplifting experience, Jack had never believed that the person he once knew was down there, beneath the soil, in the dark. He had always accepted that the spirit had left the flesh and was unconnected to the bones that would eventually be turned to dust. However he was drawn to the two graves as a matter of duty, of loyalty, of respect, he needed to attend not for himself but for them, if they could see him from wherever they were they would know that he cared.

Fortunately, the cold weather, and of course the cemetery workers had kept both graves in reasonable order, they were not overgrown and the rain had cleaned the stones.

As he stood there gazing at the headstone he wondered what to say or what to think, it seemed silly talking to the ground, he had already said everything that was in his heart during the weeks following her death. He could of course ask for her understanding in his search for a companion, but he knew Sylvia as she knew him and she would expect nothing less. She would be the first to tell him that life goes on and that is a gift that should not be wasted.

Jack left the cemetery feeling better for his visit, duty had been done and he was convinced that Sylvia understood his actions, if the situation was reversed he hoped that he would have the same understanding and forgiveness, it was a thought that he found a little tormenting.

The drive back home was somewhat daunting, the house would be empty and most likely cold; his loneliness and solitude would be acute, there was no Sarah to give him life and hope, there was only the memories. He slowed the car, much to the chagrin of those behind, but he was in no hurry, no hurry at all.

That evening it was the TV and snacks that took priority not that there was anything worth watching, but he could not bring himself to go online to check emails, or call Rosina, not till the morrow. He was not in the mood, even his snacks were difficult to digest, his only passing thought was; 'Will Sarah respond to my words; can she see how much I am hurting?'

Jack's major problem was sleep, he felt tired but the peace that was inherent in sleep seemed to be unattainable. The result was that he sat or slumped on the settee until extremely late or until his eyes drooped, then he would drag himself into the bedroom for the long-awaited oblivion, and in the end it always came.

The next morning Jack decided to visit his emails, he did so with little enthusiasm, he wasn't even sure that he wanted them or whether he would reply if they were there. As he expected and as he feared there was still nothing from Sarah. Then he remembered, she had been a teacher and was still on standby for emergency cover. Perhaps she was working as well as not fully recovered from the illness that she had contracted; that would explain the delay in responding to his last message. That was the explanation that he wanted to believe, the one he had to believe.

Jack had been fairly confident that his poetic overture would find its way past Sarah's resolve, at least he hoped it would. He had poured out his heart, a heart that felt broken, was broken and seemed irreparable.

There was nothing more to do except decide how he was going to spend his day. It would be counterproductive to merely wait inside the house on the off chance that he would receive the salvation that he was expecting; if Sarah were working she would not be online until the evening and he would be on tenterhooks until then.

He decided that his photographic hobby should be given his time and concentration. He had two projects in mind, his social awareness photos, printed in black and white for effect, and his 'the nature around us' project aimed at the younger generation. He had neglected his hobby for too long, now was the time to immerse himself in his pet projects, who knows there may be someone out there who would be able to use the pictures with great effect.

The visual image was a powerful tool of persuasion, it produced passion, horror, fear, and acceptance. If the image was true and not airbrushed it was a reality that demanded attention.

Social poverty and depravity had always been something that Jack had wanted to bring to the foreground, something that he felt passionate about and he hoped that his pictures would make the public aware.

Most people are cocooned within their own lives, their own existences and do not fully appreciate the sadness, the poverty and the feeling of worthlessness of so many who have little to live for.

In the past self-determination had been Jack's strength, he had prided himself that he could obtain any goal that he set his mind to, any goal that he wanted to attain, but in recent times his love for Sarah had weakened that resolve, that weakness was not necessarily a bad thing but it could be, and would be totally destructive if his love were not returned.

He had found new strength in his feelings for Sarah, he had been given another chance.

With mind made up he opened his laptop to undertake some research into local flora, as he went to the main page a message came into view, it was Sarah.

Jack nervously opened the email; it was Sarah's response to his last ditch throw of the dice;

> *Jack... Let it be... Let it be... Don't distress yourself more. I struggled with your demands of togetherness. You are a passionate person wanting more.*

It's your nature, you always will. I appreciate you have tried to change but we both know the type of man you are; you give your all. It would be difficult for you not to. I know you were also confused and unsure which made you more demanding and unreasonable. That made me feel caged, but that wouldn't necessarily be the case with someone else. I am sure that you know that I cannot resume any kind of relationship with you. I wish you well.

Sarah

Jack read through the message several times, letting it sink in, he felt destroyed, his stomach lurched, he felt sick, it was really over, the tears moistened his eyes as he covered them in distress.

CHAPTER ELEVEN

Jack found it impossible to sleep that night, his pain had pushed his adrenalin sky-high, it was almost as though he had taken drugs.

Throughout his life Jack had lived on an even keel, no real traumas, no real ecstatic moments. Of course office politics had sometimes created a modicum of stress, but nothing too serious; when anxiety did occur Jack's way of dealing with it was to turn his mind, to really concentrate on something that had meaning for him. In effect he 'turned off', he deliberately tuned his mind away from whatever was stressing him, to an alternative subject.

But of course this was different, this time his emotions had been stretched to their extremities, both high and low, nevertheless he determined that he would try, if only for a brief time, to push Sarah to the back of his mind.

Jack gazed out of the bedroom window, it was a clear night, the moon was full, many stars were visible, light pollution was at its lowest.

The sight of the full moon, casting its silver light and appearing glorious in the heavens, surrounded by black velvet pierced by tiny flecks of stardust, brought back memories for Jack. Some years previously he had become interested in using his camera to photograph the night sky (astrophotography). He had discovered that he did not require ultra-expensive equipment and the knowledge that it was within his budget enhanced his interest.

He had his digital, single-lens reflex Canon which was sufficient and equal to the task. It had a high ISO number and with his sturdy tripod he had been able to capture some remarkable photos.

As is normal for excitable humans, when a memory comes to the fore and strikes a chord the immediate reaction is to seek the evidence of the memory, usually locked away in a cupboard or drawer. Jack resisted the urge.

He was comfortable where he was, he couldn't sleep but he was comfortable. He remembered how he chuckled when he discovered that the word 'moon-starer' was in fact an anagram of 'astronomer', it was coincidence of course, or was it?

The sight of the night sky and the memories that it induced, increased his desire to recapture his interest in his principle hobby and perhaps, if he could throw enough energy into the enterprise, help in his attempt to put the disappointment of Sarah to the back of his mind.

His mind went back to the time he went to Northumberland, the intention was to visit Lindisfarne, but the magnet was also 'dark skies'. Little or no light pollution enables the photographing of the night sky to be clear and defined, it was in the county that he produced his first beautiful photo of the Milky Way, that wondrous explosion of stars, touching each other across the darkness overhead.

Jack had produced many examples of the Milky Way since that first time, but the 'first time' is always the one you remember with clarity. Those memories convinced him that it was time to call Stan, his camera club colleague. Jack hesitated to call him friend, they didn't see each other often enough to develop that closeness that 'friends' have; but each knew that the other would be there if needed.

Stan was the epitome of what Jack did NOT want from the dating site. He had been married three times, his first wife was killed in a road accident, his second marriage, a hurried affair that was organised whilst he was still on the rebound, was doomed to failure and ended in an acrimonious divorce; his third, five years ago was peculiar, that is to say odd as far as Jack was concerned.

Both had been settled in their own lives and routines when they met, both continued in those routines after the marriage. From Jack's standpoint it appeared that they did nothing 'together', they had their own lives and to coin a phrase ne'er the twain shall meet.

That was not the sort of marriage Jack had lived all of those years, it was foreign to his nature and he wondered why anyone would join hands in holy matrimony if they did not want to share their lives in the recognisable way.

However, Stan was an amenable fellow, easy to get along with and a colleague in whose company Jack felt at ease. They both were keen amateur photographers and Stan was aware of Jack's 'projects' and was eager to assist.

Jack still had the problem of pushing Sarah to the back of his mind, It was easier said than done, she would pop up when least expected or wanted, but forget her he must, it was essential for his wellbeing. He hoped that Stan's light-hearted quips would help.

It was a spring morning, blossom was painting the trees in bright colours, it was a perfect time to get out to photograph the various *Arbor Vitae*, as well as those whose leaves were just beginning to form. Spring was a wonderful time for most, it was the time of rebirth of nature both fauna and flora. But it was not Jack's favourite time, he was enamoured with the colours of autumn; the browns, oranges, greens tinged with yellow, rust and other restful shades. Autumn was the time of year that he preferred to photograph and of course it was the time that brought forth the fruits of the trees that he required for his school's project.

But spring it was, a slightly sad spring for Jack but fortitude brought its own rewards, at least that was the notion Jack told himself.

Stan was his first port of call this morning, he could check his site messages but he decided to leave those for later in the day.

He knew that Stan would want to, no, needed to, go down to his local pub in the early evening. Stan was a keen darts player, he played most nights, he certainly did not spend them with his wife, Jack furrowed his brow, 'most odd' passed through his mind.

Mid-morning, after the early chills had passed and the spring air was warmer, he gave Stan a call on his mobile. No point in calling the house phone, he probably wouldn't be there. Stan answered, Jack had no idea where he was but Stan answered in his usual cheerful manner and when Jack mentioned his programme for the day he responded with enthusiasm, although it was necessary for him to go home to pick up his camera. So the pair agreed to meet an hour later at a venue they both knew.

There was a large park close by and a wooded area alongside, it was the perfect place to begin the operation of photographing the many varieties of trees with close-ups of the foliage. Apart from a few well-known trees neither had any idea what the others were called, they could not distinguish between an

Ash and a Rowan. There would be need for a lot of research and Stan was happy to help in any way he could.

The pair spent a number of hours carefully reproducing accurate and clear photos of the many trees in their location. Jack was amazed at the number of different trees there were, he had never before really looked, but it was clear that both he and the children who would see the photographs, had a lot to learn.

As expected, before it was dusk, Stan said he had to call a halt; he was in a darts match that night and he needed to go home to collect his 'arrows'. They were both tired and Jack was not sorry that it was time to get back; he wasn't hungry but he needed a bite of something and a long drink. Stan's company was more than welcome but perhaps someone on the web was waiting to hear from him.

Home alone once again, nothing had changed since the very first day that he had joined the dating site.

Much water had gone under the bridge and the water had been turbulent at times, but here he was back to square one with memories of a love lost and memories of his late wife. Jack recalled the words that he had written for his late wife's headstone, words that were now emblazoned in gold, but gold that would fade in time.

I thought of you today
I'll think of you tomorrow and the days that follow too,
I think of you in silence, I often speak your name
All I have are memories, and a picture in a frame.
Your memory is a keepsake from which I'll never part,
God has you in his arms, I have you in my heart.

Jack felt immediate guilt, tears welled in his eyes, had he been disloyal? That was a question he would be asking himself again.

He put all thoughts out of his mind, he still had a life to lead and he could not lead it alone, solitude was even worse than death, morbid thoughts he knew but true, nevertheless. He turned his mind to the laptop and to the messages thereon.

'I should call Rosina', went through his mind, but he needed to know if there were any other messengers seeking a meeting. Rosina was fine to call when there was nothing on the horizon, but there was no future with her, only casual company. Of course there was Lena, the Russian lady who he felt sure was not a genuine person seeking a companion, he was quite positive that she had other things on her agenda.

Still, it would be interesting to see what she had to say. Jack had asked her a question about her visits to the UK in terms of frequency, he wondered what she would say in reply.

Sure enough there was a message from Lena and there was a video. With curiosity Jack watched an attractive young woman, probably in her thirties, going through an exercise routine. It was a nice routine, sensuous and feminine, why on earth was she sending it to a seventy something on a dating website, Jack thought he knew the answer, but he responded;

> *Great video Lena, you look fit and beautiful, when are you coming to the UK.*
>
> *Jack knew that he probably would never meet Lena, but the emails passed the time and it was faintly intriguing. No doubt he would receive a reply in a day or so.*

There were other messages in reply to the short introductory lines he had sent out. Jack decided that he would check them all, each time he typed a reply the concentration took his mind away from thoughts of Sarah, and that was a much-needed diversion.

Having decided that Lena was a non-starter, Jack was disappointed to read another long email from a woman who hailed from America, so she claimed. She had read Jack's profile and had concluded that he was just her cup of tea, not actually her words but close enough. Her message was full of praise for his character, his looks and everything about him.

The attraction that she explained that she had, merely from reading his own words, was so far-fetched that it was ridiculous. Jack was annoyed but faintly amused. He forwarded the email to his son and tongue in cheek asked for his opinion.

He decided that he would give Rosina a call the following morning, he needed the company, as light-hearted as it was.

That evening Jack felt depressed, there was nothing planned for the next few days and his loneliness was accentuated by that fact.

He realised that after so many years married to one person had taken its toll on close friendships.

He had been close to two old friends, both from school, one lived a distance away, but his closest friend had died a year earlier. Cancer was a cruel bed mate; his friend had been unable to stand for the last twelve months of his life. Jack had not seen him during that final year, David had no wish to be seen by anyone, he preferred to be remembered as he was before the disease had crippled him. Jack learned later that the wish to be isolated was not unusual.

At this time there was no-one that Jack could honestly call a close friend. There were family and acquaintances, but he needed to turn to someone else, someone closer in his time of acute emptiness. Bill had thrown him a lifeline but recent events had made matters worse, he had grabbed the lifeline only to feel it snatched away; now he was drowning.

It had only been a couple of days since Sarah had sent her final goodbye, but it seemed a great deal longer. The days needed to be packed with activity, it was the only way forward that would help Jack. Keeping busy was his only option. At present it seemed that the dating site was the only thing that kept him going, the possibility of meeting someone, but even that felt as though it was only a very remote chance. He had met his needle in a haystack, but he had dropped it and chances were he would never be able to find it again.

As Jack was feeling sorry for himself the house telephone rang. Most people used his mobile, the house phone tended to be calls that were official.

Jack picked up the phone; "Jack Tomlinson, whose calling?"

"Hello Jack, It's Richard... Richard Moore... Alton bowls..... How are you, I heard about your loss, everyone here sends their condolences."

Alton Bowls club was Jack and Sylvia's club. They had joined several years ago after Sylvia had been diagnosed with diabetes and high cholesterol, Sylvia needed to exercise to control her weight and indoor bowls had been recommended as good exercise, in addition the sport helped both physically and mentally as it was challenging and competitive.

The strange thing was that only the day before Jack had occasion to look into an empty wardrobe, one that used to house his wife's clothes, and there, on the wardrobe floor were the two pairs of Drakes Pride Advantage indoor bowls. As if by magic the club was on the line the very next day. Was it coincidence or was Sylvia trying to tell him something?

"Hello Richard, it's been a while, Sylvia was very ill before Christmas and after the funeral I just could not motivate myself to do anything."

"I do understand Jack but we all support you at the club, you should have come down just for a beer, it may have helped."

"I'm sure you are right but to be honest I was so down that I just couldn't face anyone."

Jack omitted to mention his excursion into the world of dating sites or his time with Sarah, after all it was no-one's business but his own. Richard took on board Jack's explanation and responded in soft tones;

"That's understandable Jack, however I was hoping that you were, or perhaps had, come to terms with your loss. You remember June and Brian Cox? Well Brian tripped and fell down the stairs, just four, he twisted his ankle quite badly and is hobbling about with a stick, he won't be back for a month".

Jack listened but did not know where the call was leading, he was sorry that Brian was injured but he hadn't yet taken his medical degree;

"At the end of the month we're running the spring mixed doubles and when Brian had to pull out June asked if I would give you a call to see if you would partner her in Brian's place."

Jack had known June and Brian for some years, they were a pleasant couple and always made a beeline for Jack and Sylvia when they visited the club, therefore it wasn't a surprise, in the circumstances, that he was June's choice if Brian was incapacitated. But Jack was not ready, he did not feel that going to the club and facing all there was what he wanted. On the other hand he did not want to let June down so he chickened out;

"I'm not sure Richard, I'll have to check my diary, do you mind if I call you later?"

"That's fine Jack, but don't leave it long, the entrance list will close at the end of the week."

Jack already knew that he was going to decline, but that would have to wait until tomorrow.

Jack was pleased to have received the call, not that he would agree to play but it did indicate that he had options. In any case, by tomorrow he may change his mind.

Within a few minutes from the call from the bowls club his mobile rang; it was Bill. He was making a curtesy call to see how Jack was getting on. Jack relayed the sorry tale of Sarah's final email. Bill was sympathetic but not entirely surprised;

"I have an idea Jack, why don't I pop over, that's if you're not busy, we can have a talk".

Jack certainly wasn't busy, far from it, he had just been searching for something to do, something to occupy his mind or somewhere to go, Bill's call came as a welcome intervention.

Ten minutes later Bill rang the front doorbell He wore a smile that said Don't worry everything will work out. Bill was a believer in the old adage 'everything happens for a reason' or as Jack would say 'there's always a silver lining'. However Jack knew that neither was right, all too often experiences ended with disaster and Jack feared that this was one of them.

"Hi Bill, what did you have in mind?"

Jack spoke in a carefree tone, A tone that was designed to say that all was fine and he was perfectly able to move on without Sarah..

"Jack I know that you haven't had much luck so far, but that's quite normal, remember that I told you it took months before I met Barbara and I considered myself lucky that we met each other so soon after joining the site."

Jack nodded, he was fully aware of Bill's earlier words, but Bill seemed to have missed the point, he had already met the person he wanted to be with, it hadn't happened and he knew that it would be extremely unlikely to find that special someone again. In fact he was sure that it would not happen. But he was not going to relay that to Bill.

Jack nodded in understanding; "What would you have me do?"

"Well it's quite common for people who have been unsuccessful in finding the companion they are looking for, to juggle a little with their profile, maybe adding something or removing something. The idea is to write a profile that may attract the person who would appeal to you. You know that words can be misleading, for example you have described your interest in photography, your passion for social justice, your interest in British history, etc., etc. Now do you think that those interests make you interesting or extremely boring?"

Jack mulled over Bill's words, he was right, he sounded like the greatest bore in the country. What about his interest in music, musical theatre, love of animals, enjoyment of comedy, romantic nature, and so on, there was no doubt that serious juggling was essential?

"Yes Bill, I know what you mean, can you help me to get it right?"

"No problem Jack, but I was also thinking of refreshing the photos, perhaps using different, more flattering positions, different clothes, better background and generally trying to present you in the best possible light. Jack you look ten years younger than your actual years, we should make that apparent."

"Bill, if you think that is what we should do, then I'm happy to take your advice. I can see that those ladies on the site have only the photos and the profile to go on, if it isn't done properly then they won't respond."

"Okay Jack let's run through the profile first and then we'll take some new photos on your iPhone for you to transfer to the website."

The next hour was taken up with the alterations to the site profile and a set of four photos, each photo with a change of clothes and a trendier look, that is a trendy look only as far as Jack's wearing apparel would allow.

Jack viewed the result of the work and agreed that there had been considerable improvement, perhaps he would now receive a few more acceptable interested ladies.

Bill had been a great help but he had things to do so he excused himself with the parting remark, "Let me know how you get on and call me if you are feeling depressed".

The problem with calling Bill was the fact that he was rarely at home.

He travelled a great deal and he spent a part of most weeks at his partners house, the chances were that if Jack was feeling down and needed company, Bill would not be there. Still, it was nice to make the offer.

After lunch Jack went back to his laptop, he had a message, it was a bombshell… it was from Sarah;

> *Jack, I feel that we should talk, however I am still unwell and feeling low. I will Skype you when I'm feeling better… Sarah.*

CHAPTER TWELVE

Jack was totally taken aback, the email from Sarah was worded as though her previous email did not exist. His heart had been broken, no it had been shattered, but there it was in black and white, Sarah wished to Skype. It beggared belief that this was happening. Jack read the message once again, he wasn't mistaken, Sarah had returned. He had no idea what had changed her mind, perhaps she had been ill and depressed when she had sent that last message, it hadn't sounded like it. He knew that she had been disappointed with him following the Ottawa visit, but her change of heart was astonishing yet the most welcome news that he could have ever envisaged.

Jack's very first instinct was to feel angry, to feel annoyed, to ignore the email, to tell Sarah that it was over. But of course he couldn't be or do any of those things, If Sarah wanted to be with him that was enough, more than enough. She was his joy his sweetheart, his true love.

*

Jack had always accepted that the past cannot be changed, one can apologise for it but it was set in stone, forever. It was the future that was important, the path of one's choice should be chosen so that the mistakes of the past are not repeated. For many those mistakes are not recognised, or they cannot be learned from, Jack tried to be wary of not falling into that category.

He had from an early age asked the questions that every person asks; "Who am I? Why am I here? What is my purpose? Why am I alive?"

Unlike many fanatical believers he did not believe in the 'grand design', he believed more in the 'random design', which of course meant no design at all.

There have been, during the ages, some humans who thought that they knew the answer; Jack believed that they were misguided, he thought that it was arrogant for anyone to believe that they were set apart from the rest of humanity.

Jack had no idea why some humans were taken at an early age or why others lived to be very old, unless it was the randomness of creation. In consequence his only belief or acceptance was the 'here and now'. And for him, the here and now was Sarah.

Jack knew that he had to respond straight away, he could not afford to lose the moment; Sarah had made contact and that contact had to be sustained;

Hi Sarah, why wait until you are better to Skype when I can help you feel better? You know that we were caught up in the moment and we fell in love, a love that is different from our past loves, so I will wait for you to call me.

Jack had tried to sound light-hearted and not too deep; he did not think that he had succeeded, but the message had been sent, he couldn't bring it back.

He was aware of Sarah's fears, she had lived alone for many years, but alone for her was a little different from the norm.

Although she had her 'space and privacy' there were others living in the house with her. She regularly held dinner parties, visited the gym, saw her family and friends and went out, in fact she was rarely at home. Therefore, in truth she was never lonely in the true sense of the word. What she did lack in her life was a relationship that 'filled' her private moments; a relationship that brought that special closeness between two people, a relationship that would carry her through her autumn years.

Now that they had met and fallen in love, she had become afraid that by the very nature of the new relationship, she would lose all of the freedoms of her old lifestyle. The ability to come and go as she pleased without having to consider anyone else. The special privacy she had by being in her own space, the comfort of being able to please no-one but herself. It was a dilemma that only she could solve.

Jack understood that dilemma, after years of being in sole charge of every moment of life it would take a supreme effort to give that up, nevertheless she had taken the first step by joining the dating site, she knew what that meant, whether she would be able to carry through her decision was another matter, Jack sincerely hoped she would. Jack tried to trade places in his mind, what would he do, privacy and an adopted lifestyle are not easy to give up, he decided that he just didn't know how he would react if their circumstances were reversed However, at present he had no such problem, Jack had been married for most of his life, he was used to sharing both his privacy and space with another, it had become second nature, it did not trouble him one iota, after many years it was second nature, for him the sharing of his life with Sarah would present no problem at all.

Nevertheless he did have a problem, how could he convince Sarah that she need not worry, that he understood her fear and that he would try his very best to make sure that she had as much space and privacy as she needed whilst they were together?

Jack felt the passion of his love rise in his breast, for both their sakes he had to convince her, it was paramount. He knew that it would be wise to sit back and wait for her to reply to his last message in her own time; but he couldn't wait. He had to tell her now, right now, he could not leave the matter as it was, he could not leave it to providence, he had to act, waiting was not an option, so with shaky fingers he typed out a follow up message;

> *Sarah, I'm kicking myself for writing this. And not waiting. Did you really believe that two mature adults could find the love that we have found with each other? When we hold each other time stands still, when we kiss there is magic in the air, when we make love we do not want it to end... Isn't it worth the effort to make it work for us?*
>
> *There is no reason for you to give up the things that you enjoy we have found exactly what we were looking for and more besides. With me you have found passion and real love. I apologise for waffling on but do not let go of the special thing that we have found... Jack.*

Jack read the message through, was it over the top? Probably, but it was true, he hesitated for a moment and then pressed send.

Now he had no option but to wait for Sarah's reply, he had no way of knowing how she would react, he hoped that it would be favourable and that it would rekindle the feelings that they both had. He sat by the computer for half an hour, then reluctantly went to the kitchen to make a cup of tea. He did not want to be away from the laptop in case the reply came through when he was absent.

Jack felt bad that he was being overanxious, he believed that it made him weak, but he did not feel strong, nor was he strong when it came to matters concerning Sarah.

It was some time, it seemed like hours, when at last a message came through from Sarah;

> *Hi Jack, I tried calling you on your mobile but I got through to a local restaurant. I left a message on your house phone, at least I thought it was your house phone. I guess my mobile needs changing after the accidents in Ottawa, it's not working very well… I'm home if you are free to chat… Sarah*

There was no hint that she wanted to meet, not yet. Jack assumed that it was because she was still suffering from the virus that had been around for a couple of weeks. However agreeing to chat was a big step forward; he picked up the house phone and dialled Sarah's number.

The chat was warm and friendly although Sarah was tantalisingly distant. They chatted about general matters, Sarah mentioned that she intended going to Yorkshire in the near future to see her sister. Jack had never met Heidi but had heard a great deal about her. But it was when Sarah mentioned that she had received a notification from her walking group that they were organising a half marathon walk, that he got upset.

Sarah had actually completed the application form and returned it. How could she? She had been ill for many days, was feeling weak and lethargic, everything was problematical, a half marathon was the very last thing that she should be doing.

Jack became annoyed, he told her that she should rethink her decision to enter, it was madness, but of course Sarah was stubborn and Jack got nowhere at all. The chat however finished amicably and they promised each other to meet soon although no date was set.

Later that evening Jack could not resist putting his thoughts in an email;

> *Hi Sarah, I'm so glad that you are feeling better, but I need to hear that you are not going to create new health problems by entering the half marathon... We can enjoy wonderful times together if you are fit and well. You have been unwell recently and you know that it has put a strain on our relationship, that strain was traumatic for me. I realise, like any wild thing, when you are unwell your preference is to retreat to a corner and lick your wounds; but until we are back together and I am in a position to keep an eye on you I will feel impotent.*
>
> *I was chatting to a friend today and I explained the difficulties we were having. I told him that it was my hope that we were in a long-term*

relationship. He advised me that I should give you time and space. I told him that because of my current solitude there was a chance that I may become too demanding.

But I honestly believe that if we are both forgiving, everything will work out as it should. We could have a wonderful, loving, passionate life with only happiness as its function. It will happen that way if we work at it together. I will tell you more when we Skype.

I am now going on to the dating site to tell each contact that I have met my MATCH.

My love is permanent, have no doubts, I trust that you feel the same. Let us be happy together as we were walking through Hyde Park with our arms around each other, or as we were walking hand in hand along Golden Jubilee Bridge. We must repeat those times again...Jack.

Jack knew that the message was long winded but he needed to get his feelings across and he had all night to do it.

Jack spent the next day mooching around the house, finding jobs to do and then deciding not to do them. He was waiting for Sarah's response. He didn't want to go out so the TV had to take precedence in order to pass the time. But he waited in vain, he even delayed his normal bedtime routine, thinking that perhaps Sarah had gone out and had not returned home until late; it was just wishful thinking, there was no message that night.

Jack could not combat the sleep that overtook him in the early hours of the morning, but still his body clock was overridden by the need to be awake whenever the message came through.

It was almost mid-morning, as Jack sat patiently by his laptop, when the message came through;

> *Jack, I was too exhausted to Skype last night... I am going out now for a swim then a visit to the steam and sauna rooms, they provide the relaxation that I need.*
>
> *I think that you are absolutely right, I cannot tackle the half marathon feeling as I do... Sarah.*

There was nothing more, just the brief email, quite warm and friendly but it fell well short of Jack's expectations. He wondered whether he should reply but decided that the inference in the message was that she would make contact again later. He would have to temper his impatience and concentrate on other things until he received the follow-up.

Concentrating on other things is not easy when your mind is totally focussed on one particular issue, however it was essential that he carry out his normal daily routine of food, housework and family contact. In the event it was only a couple of hours later that Sarah sent a new email;

Jack, I have just been reading our horoscopes and relating them to your last message.

I am sorry my love; I see now why you were upset with me. The marathon question came out of the blue and I responded to the organisers without thinking. I see why you think I'm impossible my love.

We are opposites, I respond without thinking and as a result make an off the cuff remark which on most occasions has no significance. Unlike you, who thinks things through more carefully before making the assessment that you believe would be to my benefit.

I am lucky that you have the strengths that I admire... Plus you are my rock... I really do love you Jack... Sarah."

It was the message that Jack was hoping and praying for, the past problems were forgotten and life could resume as it should. They had found each other and it was important to build on that.

It was apparent to Jack that Sarah was feeling better and that it would now be opportune to arrange to see each other, it had been long enough. It was not natural to stay apart.

As soon as he had read the message a second time he picked up his mobile that lay on the table at the side of the laptop. It rang only twice and Sarah answered.

It was music for Jack to hear her voice without a hint of strain, just a relaxed welcome. It did not take any persuasion to convince her that he should drive down to see her and go out for a meal at their favourite Italian restaurant. Jack knew that their relationship was back to normal and he was elated.

Within twenty minutes Jack was in his car, he had advised Sarah that he would be with her in about ninety minutes, but Murphy's law reared its head and he encountered a horrendous traffic jam. It was almost three hours later that he arrived. But it didn't matter he was met with a smile, a hug and a kiss, all was good.

As they always found, the meal was great, the atmosphere was warm and loving, it was as if the past couple of weeks had not happened.

Later that afternoon following a reconcile cuddle on their favourite settee, Sarah informed Jack that she was arranging to drive to Yorkshire to see her younger sister Heidi and her brother-in-law Sebastian. Jack had heard of them but had not met them, it came as a welcome surprise when he realised that he was expected to go as well. Sarah had not bothered to ask because she thought of Jack and herself as a couple therefore it was only natural that they travel together,

The journey from the outskirts of London to her sister's house just south of York was not too arduous. They shared the driving. The route was almost all motorway and as luck would have it the traffic moved smoothly and there were no holdups.

They did stop at a motorway service just north of Leicester for coffee, a brief rest and a change of driver, Sarah had gauged that it was about halfway.

Less than four hours from their start time they pulled into Heidi's driveway. Heidi owned two dogs, springer spaniels, and they were the first to greet us, barking with tails wagging in warm welcome; there was no doubt that they were well loved animals. Heidi opened the front door and with quick hugs for both of Sarah and Jack, ushered them in.

Sebastian, Jack had already been told, had multiple skills, he was a musician, photographer, but more professional than Jack, a radio ham and keen astronomer. Hence as they entered the hallway they noted framed photos on the walls, all in black and white, which was Jack's own preferred medium. As the main living room door was pushed open the two spaniels could not wait to smell the two new visitors who invaded their territory. They were excited, friendly in the extreme, perhaps in the belief that there were treats on offer.

Sebastian stood up and embraced his sister-in-law and held out his hand to Jack. Formalities over everyone settled to catch up on the latest news.

Heidi's nature was warm and encouraging, Jack hoped that she approved of her sister's choice of partner. Sarah had lived without intimate partnership for many years and Jack had the slight feeling that Heidi was pleased that her older sister appeared to be settling down in a close personal relationship; he thought that perhaps sisters always worried about each other, but he knew that Heidi had no cause for concern, Sarah would be loved and cared for, from that day forward.

There followed a convivial evening of family chatter and Jack and Sarah were entertained by a guitar duo from Heidi and Sebastian.

Combined with a couple of glasses of wine the day ended on a happy note, and Jack was even happier when they were shown their bedroom; a double bed indeed, Heidi was a very understanding sister.

The next day had been set aside for a visit to York, a city full of history. Jack had always been an enthusiastic reader of the time of the Anglo Saxons and Vikings, particularly the ninth, tenth, and eleventh centuries.

York was a Viking stronghold during much of that time and many relics found in the area rest in York's museums.

Jack was pleased to discover that Sarah was also interested in York's history, that was probably because she had spent her early childhood in Yorkshire. Their mutual interest brought them closer together. So much so that Jack acquired a piece of Whitby Jet jewellery to mark the occasion of their visit. It was a very romantic time, a time when they felt close to each other, a time when their relationship was moving from strength to strength.

Strolling through the pedestrian only shopping streets of the city; walking around the great York Minster cathedral; meandering through the Viking Museum and in awe at the household implements they used one thousand years ago, as they so much resembled the kitchen and personal items we use today; supping cauliflower soup in 'Betty's', the best cauliflower soup they ever tasted.

It was a magical time; it was a time of making and creating a mutual memory that would be cemented in their mind's forever.

They returned to Heidi, Sebastian and the dogs for a family meal, Jack had taken to the two Springers, they oozed warmth and affection, it was apparent that they were happy and contented animals. Sebastian had been working away from home during the week and Jack surmised that the two dogs had become companions to Heidi whilst he was away.

That evening they chatted for hours, Jack remembered that Sarah had not seen her sister for some while, however his interest was aroused when Heidi produced some 'tarot' cards with the intent of providing a reading for Sarah. Maybe she wanted to make sure that her sister had made the right choice.

Tarot or mysticism is intriguing, no-one really understands the intricacies of the mind, how it works, how much power it has. Those who study the brain in detail advise us that we do not use much of its capacity, it has unknown and unseen qualities, in consequence those who denounce mysticism as bunkum are not considering the unknown.

Heidi gave Sarah her reading, it was positive although those who know tarot realise that the cards, their meaning and their connection to each other can be interpreted in many ways; it is not an exact science. Nonetheless Jack enjoyed both the reading and the way Heidi elucidated the positive message that the cards portrayed.

Jack enjoyed his stay in Yorkshire, he hoped that it would not be long before they returned.

When they returned to the outskirts of the Capital city it was without doubt as a couple.

Jack and Sarah still both lived in their own homes. Jack still travelled to Sarah's abode, and late at night drove sleepily back to his own house; but there was now a more intense feeling of togetherness, a feeling that they were on a journey through life joined hand in hand, and they both felt that the journey could be lifelong.

Within a few days of their return Sarah travelled to Jack's residence to spend the night. There was of course a stipulation that they would have to sleep in the guest's bedroom. Sarah would not, could not, sleep in Jack's marital bed; the bed he had shared with his late wife. A feeling that Jack shared and understood, he realised and determined that the problem needed to be resolved, a new bed became a priority in his agenda.

Although there was a strong sense of feeling that they would eventually set up their own home, the status quo remained. Sarah had strong ties where she lived; she had close friends nearby, her son lived not too far away; the shops and local amenities that she had enjoyed for the past twenty years were on hand. It would be a momentous wrench to give those up for Jack, the man she cared for.

Sarah had built her 'safe haven' over a long period of time, it was without doubt not at all certain that she could give it up to begin a new life, a different life with Jack, no matter how strong her feelings were.

The fear of change, of the unknown, of the uncertain, is powerful in everyone. To give up a life that has become comfortable, like a well-worn pair of slippers; in exchange for a life like a new pair of shoes, tight, unyielding, slightly uncomfortable until worn in, would be a challenge, perhaps worth taking, but perhaps not.

Sarah was hesitating, with good cause, and the question that arose in her own mind was 'is my love for Jack strong enough?'

Jack's position was the other side of the looking glass. His old life had ended, there was no question of hanging on to the past; it was essential that a new era begin, he desperately needed to discard his old life in order to begin a new one.

The memories of the past would of course be indelibly printed on his mind, they were the memories of most of his life, but Jack had always looked forward, never backward. It was his way of embracing an exciting future whilst remembering a past that could never be changed but that had forged his character and the path that lay ahead.

Jack's philosophy had always been that the past had been lived, it had been experienced, but it could never be altered. One could apologise for regretful actions taken but the apology could only be accepted by those hurt, by actions that needed to be taken in the future; we all make mistakes and we all have the capacity to rectify them.

Jack and Sarah had now reached the crossroads, two paths one of which they must take. Sarah had already once refused to take the path that Jack must take, but she had returned to reconsider. It was a most difficult decision for her, but a simple one for Jack.

Their relationship could not stand still, both had joined the dating site to find a special person, someone with whom they could share their future life. Jack was positive that he had found that someone, he was ready to take the plunge, ready to commit, ready to move forward without the fear that he was making a mistake; he knew that he wasn't. But he had to convince Sarah.

There was a temporary solution, a way of determining what the future may hold, and that was a trip abroad. A holiday away from everyone and everything, a chance to be together without fear of interruption, a chance to think, and hopefully a chance that would allay all of Sarah's worries and concerns.

CHAPTER THIRTEEN

Although Jack and Sarah had decided to take a short trip abroad, Jack still had a dilemma. He wanted to visit a destination that was new to Sarah, but she had been everywhere.

When she was a child the family had moved to Canada, later they moved to America and in her late teenage years she had lived in and visited most of the European and Middle Eastern countries.

She had met and married her late husband whilst she was in the Gulf and then temporarily settled in California, where they became involved in catering and opened restaurants, her son was born in the United States, attaining American citizenship.

There weren't too many places left, perhaps China or Japan but Jack was not keen on a long-haul flight for a short trip, jet lag could have spoiled the first few days. Finally following several discussions they settled on Cyprus, only a few hours away but a new experience for Sarah.

There were other Mediterranean islands that could have been considered but Jack had always been fascinated by Greek history and mythology.

It was still spring in England but the Mediterranean Islands were warm, sun-drenched but not too hot, a perfect solution for a romantic holiday. In addition the tourist season had barely started so they had the pick of the hotels.

Jack had visited Cyprus once before, he felt comfortable that he would be able to guide Sarah to the many places of historical fascination, she was interested in history, both ancient and modern, this was a shared interest that had enhanced their mutual love and respect. As Jack would often comment, "history has moulded the present which in turn will mould the future".

The choice of destination within Cyprus was left to Jack. He did not wish to stay in the same hotel as he had with his late wife, that would not have been appropriate. However, a number of his bowls companions were keen Cyprus visitors and they recommended various hotels throughout the island. In the end he plumped for a four-star hotel near Limassol, he had been reliably informed that the hotel was as good as any five-star hotel in the city.

The choice of hotel was important, not for Sarah who always maintained that as long as the accommodation was clean and the food good, the star rating was irrelevant, but for Jack who was determined to make their first overseas trip a success.

The flight time to Cyprus is approximately four hours, a hop step and jump for Sarah who was quite used to longer flights. The relative short time in the air convinced them that a budget airline would be quite satisfactory, if the flight had been longer then a more comfortable and traditional airline would have been their preference. It was not a case of saving money it was more a case of being practical and not wasteful.

Sarah, an experienced traveller always spent the flying time by watching a film on board and that, combined with a meal, a glass of wine and a brief nap, meant that the time soon passed.

The landing at Larnaca airport, luggage collection and location of the taxi provided by the hotel, went without a hitch, an excellent start. They did note that although the skies were clear, the temperature for mid-afternoon was a little cool. As they were dressed for spring weather in England, which had been changeable, damp and fairly cold, the temperature on arrival was in many ways more than acceptable even though it was less than expected.

The four-star hotel (as good as five), appeared, at first glance, to be really spacious and modern, however it was early in the season and it did seem to be a little understaffed, the lack of welcoming representatives resulted in a lengthy wait whilst check-in and room allocation took place.

The timing of the landing and hotel arrival left them with plenty of daylight time to explore the hotel's amenities before the evening meal. They discovered that some of the family activities were not yet due to begin, but the lack of children and general quietness of a hotel only a quarter full before the season's rush, appealed to both Sarah and Jack; they were bound to get first class attention and peaceful mealtimes.

Jack reflected, during a moment of quiet, on their choice of destination, the land of Greek Gods. It was an odd thing; in over forty years of marriage he had never had a deep meaningful discussion with Sylvia about religion.

Of course he knew that she was Church of England and of course he knew that she was not deeply religious, after all, in all their long marriage they had only been to church for births, marriages and deaths, like many others. Yet deep down Jack did not really know what she thought about 'God'. Whether she believed in the existence of a creator or whether she had considered 'life beyond death'.

It was different with Sarah; he had known her for just an instant but he knew how she felt.

Sarah had been raised as a Roman Catholic, she had knowledge of Mormon practices and beliefs, she also had knowledge of Islam. In all, her general religious understanding was broad and reasonably detailed. Perhaps as one gets older thoughts of 'what comes after', are more prevalent and meaningful than when one is younger.

The autumn years seem so far away when you are concentrating on raising children or striving in one's choice of profession. However, Jack believed that Sarah had always considered aspects of religious beliefs, during most of her adult life.

Jack was also surprised at how much in common he had with Sarah. The 'land of the god's' was a good choice of destination for their first holiday abroad. Sarah had travelled to the central Americas on her own and she had a desire to visit the ancient Aztec and early civilization sites that were prevalent in the general area.

She was aware of the mysteries that experts had not been able to unravel regarding the apparent knowledge that the ancients possessed, knowledge that they could not have logically possessed.

Jack was reminded of an article that he had written for the camera club magazine, a monthly periodical that he had frequently written articles for.

On one occasion beneath a particularly clear picture of the milky way he had added the following;

Every person who has looked up at the night sky has asked one question, amongst others, 'is there anyone else out there?' Delving into possible intelligent life somewhere else in the universe is not necessarily linked to our existence here on earth; however, some hold the view that this planet has been visited in the past, in fact there are many intelligent individuals who believe that human beings may exist as a result of extra-terrestrial genetic engineering who gave nature a significant push.

If this were the case then our current understanding of such ideas as 'soul' and 'life after death', may have been implanted by beings more advanced and more knowledgeable than modern man. Perhaps the clues exist in foregone religions whose ancient scripts may portray and contain teachings from alien visitors.

So the question arises, 'did the human species originate on another planet?'

The answer lies somewhere in the night sky.

It was therefore apt that, for the next few days, Jack and Sarah would be exploring the sites and relics that were apparently linked to ancient Greek gods; or were they Gods?

Limassol had been Jack's choice of the place to stay on the island. In fact the hotel was a few kilometres from the port centre and that distance made the hiring of a car a necessity. Jack discovered that his age added a premium to the cost of hire, he therefore hired the vehicle in Sarah's name, after all it was only for a few days. That innocuous decision was to prove an error of judgement.

There was another reason for Jack's choice of venue, and that was Sarah's love of walking. Limassol is a network of narrow pedestrian shopping streets, a veritable paradise for a walker and a shopper. In addition there is a wide and beautiful promenade with fountains, sculptures, palm trees, cafes and restaurants. As visitors stroll along the promenade there is the smell of the ocean on one side and endless independent shopping on the other.

That first evening in the hotel set the scene for what Jack hoped would be a memorable first holiday with Sarah.

There were three restaurants, two a la carte and one a buffet style. The two waiter service restaurants, although modern, clean and comfortable in appearance, had rather limited menus but the restaurant offering buffet food, looked to have an enormous and sumptuous choice, sufficient to satisfy all diets and tastes. In addition there was no limit to the food that anyone could eat.

Not that either Jack or Sarah was concerned with gorging large amounts of food, it was the variety and choice on display that swayed their decision to eat their fill in that restaurant. The stage occupied by a small group, playing music that was not too loud, was the deciding factor in their choice.

Following a satisfying evening meal, accompanied by the live music and a couple of glasses of wine, Jack and Sarah decided to explore the coastal path that followed the pebbled beach in both directions, to the right towards Limassol and the left in the general direction of Ayia Napa.

Every hotel lining the coast had built long sloping and stepped gardens that cascaded down to the water's edge. The path, on that warm, clear skies and breeze free evening, was lit by the lamps and hanging lights that decorated each of the gardens. It was a perfect evening to stroll and gaze at the varying designs of the manicured gardens that gently sparkled at the rear of each hotel.

There were only a few others walking, simply because the hotels were not yet full of tourists, the lack of that bustling overcrowded atmosphere added to the peace, tranquillity and enjoyment of their hand-in-hand meander along the beach.

It was an ideal end to the first day.

The pair decided to spend their first full day in the Port, shopping was on the agenda, Jack needed shorts and Sarah was generally interested in seeing what was on offer. It was the very beginning of the season and there were many shops offering discount prices, the retail outlets were keen to attract the attention of the early season visitors.

Although Sarah owned a small car, her preferred method of travel was by public transport. She rightly argued that sitting on a train or bus, gazing out of the window at the passing scenery whether it be in the city or countryside, was far more relaxing than gripping the wheel of a car, staring at the road ahead and competing with other road users for the limited space available.

Consequently, on that first full day morning, Sarah had discovered from the concierge that there were several buses passing by the hotel whose route was through the city. The benefit of travelling into Limassol this way was that there was no scramble to find available parking spaces close to the shops.

The scenic bus ride left the couple with a casual morning of shopping and promenade walking, with no worry of car parking charges or limited waiting periods. It was by far a more satisfying scenario than using the hired car; that vehicle would come into its own once they decided to travel further afield.

The shopping was successful. Jack acquired his shorts and the other small items that they purchased were easy to carry and did not deter them from their gentle walk along the sea front. It was early afternoon when they decided to head back to the hotel.

There was a substantial amount of building works along the wide main thoroughfare, some bus stops were not in use because the buses were unable to stop and collect passengers, it was therefore a considerable distance along the route before they were able to find a stop that was undisturbed by ongoing roadworks.

However, the day had not been unduly warm and the weather did not affect the enjoyment of discovering the delights of the port.

On the return journey to the hotel, although short, they missed their stop and had to walk back to where they should have alighted. As they walked they noted that most of the restaurants were not yet open for the tourist trade. In normal circumstances they would have enjoyed their evening meal savouring the delights of local dishes, but it was apparent that this would not be possible within the near vicinity of the hotel, they would have to rely on hotel food.

Fortunately, the hotel buffet was excellent and the loss of the local eating places was not a serious problem.

Sarah was keen to chat to the hotel travel information agent, they were residing on an island that was steeped in ancient history, they had but a week to discover and visit as much as they could, there was no time to drive aimlessly around with no particular destination in mind, they needed to plan their holiday with some care in order to take in as much as possible.

There is so much to see in this world of ours that it had become Sarah's general policy, although not set in stone, that once visited there would be no need to return to the same destination.

Following their discussions with the hotel travel agent, they concluded that there were some popular tourist attractions, although of interest, they would not have time to visit. Mount Olympus, six thousand feet high, although an ancient romantically named mount, was after all just a mountain, and compared with many in America that Sarah had visited, was comparatively small. Aphrodite's rock, just a few yards from the beach, the place from which the goddess emerged, was only a small rock and, as far as Sarah was concerned could be viewed photographically, it was not an attraction worth travelling to see. In effect they were whittling down the advertised places of interest to those that they would have time to view.

The first, nearest and most obvious place to visit was Kourion, an archaeological site, set on a hill just outside Limassol. The acropolis, constructed about three thousand years ago consisted of a theatre, and to the northwest the 'house of Achilles' a sort of reception centre for the ancient city.

Sarah parked in the area set aside for cars and she and Jack climbed the slope to view the magnificent ruins. It was everything that the brochures described, and more. The sloping sides of the circular theatre were a reminder of those ancient theatres found in Greece, and were larger than anticipated, particularly for anyone who had not viewed Greek's famous archaeological playhouses, it wasn't difficult to imagine the crowds seated on the steps cheering the actors or clapping gladiators in the gladiatorial games that took place there.

The House of Achilles consisted mainly of the foundations, covering a substantial area but it was easy to imagine a structure suitable to house visiting dignitaries.

They climbed to the top of the hill of Kourion which was not too steep, but from the summit there was an excellent view across Kourion Bay.

It was an excellent day, romantic from the point of view that they were together, enjoying and sharing the sights of the island and looking forward to the days ahead.

To visit Nicosia was a must, apart from the city being the Capital of Cyprus it was ancient, built fifteen hundred years before the birth of Christ. The history alone was a sufficient magnet to attract anyone staying on the island.

They had the car but with no knowledge of the available parking, nor the geography of the city, both agreed that it would make sense to travel on the bus service that went from Limassol, on the A1, to the heart of the Capital. Sarah had always preferred local transport when visiting any main metropolis and Jack, who had not travelled on public transport for years, realised that she was right.

Nicosia, apart from its history, was also a divided city. There are many border cities and towns that are divided and ruled by different nations but Nicosia is the only Capital city that is still administered by two separate nations, Greece and Turkey.

The bus took them to the centre of the city on the Greek side, it was still before noon which left them time to explore. The day was both warm and humid but, to make the visit worthwhile they felt it necessary to see as much as possible. The two things that stood out as unforgettable were the visit to St Sophia Cathedral, which had been converted to a mosque, and of course Ledra Street, the thoroughfare that crossed the border from south to north.

The crossing was of interest mainly because of the necessity to queue to obtain permission to travel to what was a different country. A weird sensation when only a few yards separated the two nations. However the visit was somewhat disappointing.

There was no doubt that history existed on both sides of the border, but the day was very warm and there was little time to explore the Turkish side. All that they did manage to see were the endless number of tourist shops and stalls, all selling similar wares, none of which held any interest in Sarah and Jack, not even as a keepsake or memory of their visit.

The last bus back to Limassol left early in the evening, too early to see everything that there was to see, but they had a taste of the city, both ancient and modern, and that was enough.

That evening it was buffet time and the offerings were as delicious as ever, too much so for those in the hotel who wished to diet. Not even the strongest could resist the enormous variety of dishes that absolutely required consumption and neither Sarah nor Jack could be described as strong on this holiday. They ate more than they should and downed a little too much red wine with the result that their evening walk became a walk of giggles and laughter, uncontrollable laughter that left them with sore sides. It had been another good day, a day to remember.

It must have been good wine because neither suffered from a hangover. Sarah, the consistent and avid walker of the pair suggested that after breakfast a stroll along the seafront was the therapeutic answer to a heavy meal.

The sea never really went out far and the beach was pebbles. Sarah was nature's child, she not only adored the variety of colours of autumn, but she also loved everything that was natural, was of the earth, was of nature's making. Therefore the beach was a particular draw because of the infinite number of different rocks, stones and pebbles, it was necessary to find and collect any one of those that was of interest. Pebbles that were coloured by veins running through them; stones that appeared to be different in texture and colour. Sarah explained afterwards that she loved to collect seafront pebbles, they were a reminder of her visit and could be used in an ornamental way in jars or bowls.

The morning soon passed, the collected pebbles and stones were heavy but the result was satisfying; the variety of colours would make a fine display when they went home.

That afternoon they decided to revisit Limassol and meander through the shops and walkways, there wasn't enough time to travel too far afield, that would have to wait until tomorrow when Ayia Napa was to be their chosen destination.

If there was one thing that their first holiday had demonstrated it was that they belonged together. Although they had only known each other for six months they had forged a relationship that was lifelong. They both felt that their togetherness was meant to be, they were soulmates, they had miraculously found that someone special that many people do not find, without doubt they both felt blessed.

The journey to Ayia Napa was the longest drive that Sarah had made so far on this trip; but they had been reading the details of the attractions of the town and it had many that could not be found on other parts of the Island. At peak holiday periods it had a particular attraction for the younger set, but this early in the season it would be quieter and more leisurely, suitable for Sarah and Jack to enjoy.

When they arrived they noted that the clubs and music venues had not yet opened for the season, that meant the younger visitors were absent and the stores and other places of interest were not crowded.

As a photographer Jack had an interest in the older sites and the places of special interest, he wanted to create memories, visual depictions that would be a reminder of this special holiday.

They made their way to the harbour, a marina full of boats eager for the first wave of visitors but presently lying silent in anticipation. In the square in front of the harbour was the statue of 'The Mermaid', a unique piece of sculpture in that she had two tails. The story, or legend was, that she was the sister of Alexander the Great. A romantic notion but it was just a legend.

Not far from the harbour was the Medieval Monastery, a revelation for a photographer, both inside and out. In the grounds of the Monastery was the largest tree on the island, with branches that spread out over an enormous area. Jack and Sarah sought the help of other tourists who were delighted to take pictures of the couple standing beneath the boughs but dwarfed by them.

The sculpture park was also on their wish list, but the day had been very warm and there was a long drive back ahead of them so the decision made was to revisit the town in a couple of days, with the park as a special destination.

The next day they had earmarked for their visit to Paphos, a city fifty kilometres west of Limassol. Paphos was known not only as a principle tourist resort but also for its association with the Goddess Aphrodite. In and around Old Paphos there were a plethora of archaeological sites of ancient history that predated the birth of Christ. It was a photographer's paradise, a must visit destination for anyone travelling to the Island.

The fifty-kilometre drive posed no difficulty, the highway was wide and there were not too many vehicles travelling in their direction.

Their first port of call was the Paphos Archaeological Park, a UNESCO world heritage site which held the ruins of Roman villas but also contained the Grove and Altar of Aphrodite, the remnants of a cult that had been established hundreds of years before Christianity.

The 'Tomb of the Kings' was a place that Sarah and Jack wanted to view. It was part of the UNESCO site and was a place that housed eight preserved third century BC tombs, there was a walkway around the site and from there fragments of mosaics and frescoes could plainly be seen. However one of the most interesting elements of the necropolis was the pillar which legend states St Paul had been tied to and whipped.

The day passed quickly, it had been both interesting and educational, a day well spent, but tiring, nevertheless. In the early evening they decided to drive back to the hotel, shower, change and visit the buffet which had become their favourite eating place.

The drive to Paphos had been uneventful, but the drive back took a slightly different route. In order to return to Limassol, the road traversed the Rocky Mountains at a slightly lower level than the road to the city. This meant that at one point the engineers had to tunnel through the high terrain.

Ten years before Sarah and Jack met, Sarah had been involved in a serious car accident, she had been hit by a car whilst crossing a road on a pedestrian crossing. The resulting injuries left her hospitalised for almost three weeks and there were some permanent after-effects. The most disturbing one was the advent of 'vertigo'.

Jack had always believed that vertigo meant that dizziness occurred when the sufferer was at an elevated altitude and took effect when looking down. This layman's view of the disorder was simplistic and there were symptoms of which he was unaware.

In Sarah's case she had serious problems going through tunnels if she was unable to observe the exit as she entered, she needed to see the light at the end of the tunnel. Entering the darkness of an underground or mountain tunnel with no obvious exit in view, appeared to trigger something in the brain that non vertigo sufferers could never understand. It was not just dizziness that she experienced, she also suffered panic attacks and severe anxiety.

As the car approached the mountain, the entrance to the tunnel came clearly into view. This was not a problem in itself simply because as long as the exit was visible on entering, all was well. As the bonnet of the vehicle entered and the way ahead was apparent, Jack heard Sarah whisper to herself; "Oh my God."

He immediately knew that something was wrong, he was aware of her problem but there was nothing he could do, he was impotent.

Sarah's hands gripped the wheel, she was leaning forward desperately seeking the tell-tale light in the distance that would release her from her nightmare. Her knuckles were white, her concentration total, but she managed to keep the car in a straight line until the exit came into view. Sarah was shaking, her ordeal was over but the after effects would remain for a while.

The tunnel exit began to disappear behind them and the road ahead was clear. Limassol lay somewhere south of the road they were on and they knew that there had to be an exit route from the road that would be signposted. Jack was carefully examining the map on his lap, the road to their destination should be clearly marked. As he looked down the realisation suddenly dawned on him, they had passed the point where they should have left the road. Jack explained the situation to Sarah with the words; "Not to worry, we can take the next turning on the right and double back to re-join the road".

Neither Jack nor Sarah was familiar with the roads in the area and Jack made the assumption that they would be able to leave the main highway then re-join it a short distance further back, just before the junction that led to the Port.

As they left the highway it became obvious that the road, a single and one-way carriageway, was heading down the mountainside towards the ocean. As they drove the road became narrower and steeper, the sort of descending narrow thoroughfare that would concern any motorist, but more so for someone who suffered with vertigo. Sarah was panic stricken but she had no option but to still her fears and carry on.

After what seemed a lifetime they came across a fork in the road with the right fork leading back towards the main highway they had left. With just a little expression of relief they took the road that climbed back to their route home.

When they finally reached the main highway they realised with total dread that they were back to their position before they had entered the tunnel, there was nowhere to go but, back through the tunnel, there was no option, no choice, just another nightmare situation.

There was one consolation, Sarah had already been through the tunnel, she knew what to expect and this knowledge reduced the effect that the original ordeal had brought about.

Her mood was now anger; anger at Jack for his pitifully poor navigation skills, he was supposed to protect her but instead had led her to a terrifying experience. It was unforgivable, an error of judgement, a failure to carry out the simple task of ensuring that they took the correct road home; she knew that Jack's incompetence would leave her stressed, anxious and fretful for hours, perhaps days ahead.

They finally arrived back at the hotel, as Murphy's law would have it, the hotel car park was full. It was not an easy place to park at the best of times, now they would have to drive around the car park in frustration, until someone left and released a space.

The day had started out so well but it had ended in terror, tears, frustration and anger.

The next day there was nothing particular on the agenda and nothing particular was what they did. There was a stroll along the seafront path, a collection of more pebbles and an odd day of quiet reflection.

Sarah was not herself; she was introspective, reflective, quiet and generally pensive. It was, as Jack believed, just the result of the difficult previous day, but the passage of time would heal any rift and they would soon be back to their normal interactive existence.

The dawn of the following morning brought them to the last day before their return home. Not wishing to waste time it was decided to revisit Ayia Napa and this time see the sculpture park.

The drive to the resort was slightly moody, nothing much was said or discussed. As before the road was not busy, it was straight and simple to follow, the road signs were clear and the journey to the park was completed without incidence.

Once inside the park both Jack and Sarah had a feeling of disappointment. They had not known what to expect but they were confronted by lines of very modern, mostly white stone statues and sculptures donated by many international artists. It had been in Jack's mind that because the island had so much historical and traditional heritage that the sculpture park would mirror that history. In fact the opposite was the case and the exhibits were not to his taste and not to Sarah's taste either. Nevertheless photographs were taken, purely as a memory of their visit, but no great visual pleasure was experienced.

That night Jack made a clumsy attempt to make love, he wanted to accelerate the normalness of their relationship, to return to where they were before the holiday and to say to Sarah that all was well. Sarah responded to Jack's advances but in his heart Jack knew that the responses were more reactions to their past, they were more dutiful than passionate, they were almost a 'thank you for everything' before a goodbye.

The flight back to the UK was made in comparative silence, it was a budget airline flight but the seats seemed to be closer to those in front than before. Although only four hours the duration of the journey seemed to be much longer. Jack was at a loss, he realised that all was far from normal but he didn't know what to expect, what would happen over the next few days.

The day before the home flight Sarah had lost a filling in a tooth, Jack knew that a visit to the orthodontist would be at the top of her agenda the morning after their arrival. Any thought of a meeting would have to wait until she had dealt with that and had cured the toothache that she was suffering.

They landed on the Thursday evening, Jack knew that Sarah would need some private time, some alone time, time to reflect and time for the dentist, so he suggested that they both took time out over the weekend and talk again three days hence. That was really the very last thing that he wanted or required but he believed it was for the best.

Three days, just the blink of an eye, but not for Jack. The weekend went on for ever, he chatted with his family on the telephone, told them that he had a wonderful holiday and that he would see them soon. He wandered through the house looking for things to do; he had called the gardener who came round on the Saturday to tidy the lawn and raised flowerbeds. But time stood still and Monday never seemed to arrive.

Eventually Monday morning dawned, Jack hovered near the phone waiting for a civilised hour to ring Sarah. He was nervous, hopeful that she would respond in a cheery fashion, but deeply worried that the trauma of the events on the holiday had made a permanent impact.

When he did call Sarah answered the phone straight away, she responded to his enquiries about her tooth (she had been to the dentist), and confirmed that all was well, she also confirmed that she was feeling much better. It was when he suggested driving down to see her that he noted a long hesitation. Then there followed the dreaded conversation that he had hoped would not take place.

Sarah explained, nay repeated, her desires as they existed before they had met. She reminded Jack that her greatest wish was to spend her later years travelling, seeing the world, visiting places that she had never visited, observing cultures and peoples that she had only read about. She reminded Jack that their paths, there roads, led in different directions, then the bombshell,

"Jack, I can never travel with you, I thought I could, I believed our love would be enough, but it isn't. I'm sorry Jack, it won't work, I can't see you, please don't call me again."

Then she terminated the call.

To describe Jack's feelings as 'devastated' would be a total understatement; he felt sick, his hands were shaking he did not know what to do. He wandered from room to room, he had to keep moving, his rapid heartbeat would not slow down. He went into the garden and looked at the shrubs, but he didn't see them, he could not see anything, his mind was in a whirl, it was in total confusion.

It was some hours later that Jack's thoughts began to clarify, perhaps Sarah just needed a little time; she could not really mean that their romance, their relationship was over, it was just not possible. He decided that he would not call, he would send her a message. Telephoning would seem as though he was applying pressure and that would be counterproductive, a light-hearted message was the best thing to do.

That evening he sat at his laptop and carefully tapped out his message:

> *Hi Sarah, I forgot to mention when we spoke that should you need someone to collect pebbles with, or need to laugh until your stomach aches, let me know. The road that you mentioned, has been closed, trust me, there is a brand-new road, a road that neither of us has trodden. Have faith, the old road no longer exists.*
>
> *Why not try a new start, a new first date with someone that you care about?*
>
> *I have a brand-new understanding of you, I would not repeat old errors.*
>
> *We can give each other a future that could be full of fun, smiles and no regrets. Perhaps we could talk so that you would understand. Jack*

The truth was that although Jack had been devastated, he had never accepted that Sarah really meant what she had said. Their love had been too strong to cast aside no matter what the provocation.

As he pressed send he had the strong belief that Sarah merely needed the time and space to reach the conclusion that they were meant to be together.

There was no immediate response, 'a good sign', thought Jack, Sarah must be reconsidering their future together. The rest of the day went by slowly, but Jack was quietly confident that everything would work out well.

The next morning, as he opened his computer, there it was, a reply from Sarah, Jack opened the message.

I'm sorry Jack,

We've been down this road before. Nothing has changed, we just go round in circles.

I promise that I will not contact you again.

Please feel free to use the photos on site.

There will be someone who will delight in the attention you will give them, without trying to change the person that you are, which should be the case.

I also realise that just as I need space, you need someone there around you. There is nothing wrong with that.

It's just as the stars say, we are opposites, attracted to the qualities in the other, none the less it would never endure.

I wish with all my heart that you meet someone soon.

I am better for having known you.

Farewell

Sarah

Jack read through the message a dozen times, there it was, the final goodbye, the end of his life. He had suffered the loss of his eldest son and the death of his wife, this was another loss as great if not greater than the others, it felt too great to bear, his heart felt broken, his world and future destroyed. The tears flowed endlessly, he felt the strength drain from his body, he had to lay down, perhaps sleep would ease the pain.

It was some hours later when Jack awoke from his fitful dreams, there was something he had to do, he had to acknowledge Sarah's farewell. He dragged himself to his laptop and messaged.

> *Sarah,*
>
> *I believe that we both thought that we had something special, a once in a lifetime connection. I am saddened that it was not the case.*
>
> *I will miss the cuddles and the kisses that were very special. I am devastated that my stupidity and insecurity destroyed our love. I should have trusted that your wish for space was not a reflection of our relationship. When you said that you loved me it should have been more than enough.*
>
> *You told me that I was moody, that was because I was in a rush and you were not. You were right Sarah; I was totally wrong. I should have allowed matters to take their natural course, instead I pushed and ended up pushing you away.*

After a very long marriage where I was in the daily company of one person I found it difficult to comprehend your desire for your own space. Too late now, but I understand.

I have been an insecure fool and I have managed to destroy the most beautiful relationship that any two people could have and would have wished for, I am now a wiser fool.

If you manage to get on your pilgrimage, the Camino, you have my best wishes and support.

I hope that you were able to deal with the problems of the house.

I also hope that Heidi's home sale goes through and that your daughter finds the home of her dreams.

Sarah please forgive an old fool for his lack of understanding and his unnecessary insecurity.

You will always be in my thoughts.

Jack

As he sent the message the tears streamed down his cheeks. He did not expect any reply and he received none.

CHAPTER FOURTEEN

During the few days following the collapse of his relationship with Sarah, Jack drifted through the rooms of the house, from one to another with no pattern or reasoning, just a need to keep moving, to allow his mind to take on board an event that he had hoped would never occur. He could not accept that Sarah was now in the past; but he had to, his life would automatically proceed without her, but what sort of life would that be?

The past months had seen Jack reborn, brought back to life from the brink. He had turned his mind back to writing, photography, travelling and enjoying the fact that he was alive and cared for, he had been transformed.

Now that was over, he was back to where he had started, his wife of so many years, gone, but worse than that his soul mate, his newfound love, lost forever. To Jack this appeared to be his blackest moment, he had been cast under the darkest cloud, a cloud that would never move, his heart had been broken, nay shattered and he could see no way back.

He had to keep moving, his eyes had to keep focusing on different views so that his brain could be stimulated to observe ever changing locations, it was not a cure for his malaise, but it helped a little.

Jack wandered out into the garden, he didn't really see the spring colours, the new life emerging, he must keep moving.

Then he heard the sound of a lawnmower, Bill was back, he had been away for several weeks, Jack needed company.

Once back in the house Jack pulled himself together, the tears were still there waiting to flow but he held them back. He was in no mood to do anything, but perhaps Bill would or could help, at least he would be a listening post. He may not be that sympathetic, he was a little cold when it came to matters of the heart and of course he would not be able to understand how Jack felt, how could anyone, but he was a body to talk to. Jack dialled Bill's number;

"Hi Bill, nice to see you back, I hope you had a good trip. If you have a few minutes perhaps you would like to come over for a beer".

Jack waited anxiously for the response, there had been no anxiety in his voice, it had just been a casual invitation.

"Jack, how have you been? I had a great trip, the only problem with going away is coming back to an overgrown garden. Yeah, I'd love a beer, let me finish this mowing, it'll take me an hour or so, I'll come round when I've finished."

At last Jack was back in touch with humanity, it was small comfort but comfort nonetheless.. He had an hour to waste so he busied himself with some superficial tidying, the place should at least appear to be half presentable.

Two hours later Jack and Bill were seated on the settee with two glasses of lager on the coffee table in front of them. Jack was unable to hold back and blurted out;

"Sarah has left again and it seems as if it is for good".

Bill lifted his glass and took a gulp.

"I'm not surprised, I was expecting it. Jack, Sarah is a serial leaver, she is one of those ladies who when a relationship gets serious she can't handle it, she has to go. You'll have to face it, she won't be back, you need to try and forget her, there are plenty of fish in the sea, you just have to keep looking for that special one, Sarah wasn't the one."

Jack nodded, he knew that he would have to move on, there was no choice, but he couldn't face it. Bill could not really understand, why should he?

Bill continued: "The best thing to do is to get back on the site, don't lose the faith and contact as many ladies as you can; you'll have to trawl through those who have registered and leave plenty of messages. The sheer number of contacts that you make will eventually bring you a reward. I realise that you had strong feelings for Sarah, but Jack, it's over, she's gone, you have to move on; there will be someone out there for you and eventually you'll forget that Sarah ever existed".

Jack wished, hoped that Bill was right. Time is a great healer, it can deaden the feelings that you once had, but can it really stop the ache? Jack doubted that, and forget, that would never happen.

But Bill was correct in that he would have to accept the situation no matter how unpalatable and do as Bill had advised, it was the only way. He could also throw himself into his hobbies, the bowls club and photography, but not just yet, he couldn't drum up the enthusiasm, perhaps later he would make the effort.

Bill stayed a little while; the cricket season had started and the conversation turned to sport. In normal circumstances Jack would have voiced his views with a sense of excitement and urgency, but today he was flat, he talked the talk but there was no real interest behind it. Bill stayed for an hour and then left; he had some catching up to do after his trip.

It was the afternoon, Jack had no plans ahead, he'd walked the carpet until it was almost threadbare, it was time to get back to the computer.

Bill was right, Jack decided to flood the site with messages, it didn't matter who responded. He realised that most replies would be of no interest at all, there would be ladies ten years older than him seeking a younger beau, there would be interest from females whose profile would be far from his, there would be those who just wanted a pen pal, and so on. But it was of no consequence, responding to one and all would take up his time, and that was something he had plenty of.

Jack sat at his computer and using his standard short introductory message he typed;

> *I read your profile and it would appear that we have much in common. If you are interested in chatting I will send as many details as you require and we can see where it leads.*

He trawled through the site and left the words with anyone who seemed to be of the slightest interest, hopefully he would be kept busy during the next few days.

As he added the text to multiple members logs, he noted that there was an incoming message, one that he had never opened. Since Jack and Sarah had been together there had been no need to check the dating website, Jack's membership was still ongoing but as he had found his perfect soulmate it had been his unconscious intention to allow it to expire. Now that had changed.

Jack clicked on to the message, as it happened it was only a few days old.

It was from a lady who called herself Janet and she had attached. a photograph. Janet had noted his photos and profile on the site and had been drawn to make contact.

Jack was intrigued, the picture was of an attractive woman much younger than himself, he responded to the message, more from his curiosity than the likelihood of any potential meeting;

> *Hi Janet, thank you for your message, you look stunning in the photograph but I am curious as to why you would contact an older man. Please let me know.*

He sent his response and decided to put it to the back of his mind until there was a reply. Meanwhile 'company' was his deepest need. Being on his own left him constantly thinking and worrying about Sarah.

Then it came to mind… Rosina… he did not know if she were still available but he had her phone number and he could ask. If she were still unattached he would need a story to explain his lengthy absence, he dialled her number, she answered after the third ring.

"Hi Rosina, it's Jack… I'm sorry I haven't been in touch but I've been abroad."

There was a part truth there, but he could not be entirely honest regarding the reason.

"I have family in Canada, distant family, but there was an opportunity to see them following the passing of a family member, someone I had actually never met and my stay ended up being longer than expected."

Rosina took the explanation in her stride and responded as though there had been no gap in their 'friendship'; Jack got the impression that the gaps in communication with people she met onsite were, for her, a common occurrence.

Jack then asked if she were free for lunch so that they could catch up. There was no hesitation from Rosina and they arranged to meet at the same venue as the previous occasion, two days hence.

Jack breathed a sigh of relief; he was meeting someone. He hoped that she had lost her 'lipstick traces', but it didn't matter, he would have company and that was all that he cared about.

Jack could still not bring himself to visit the bowls club or the photographic club, he wasn't ready to meet his friends, or provide explanations as to where he had been and what he had done... they were bound to ask.

Since Sarah had gone Jack's sleep pattern had been so disrupted that sleep was no longer a night-time experience. He could not sleep when it would have been natural to do so, and so it had to be induced. The television proved to be the antidote. Jack would sit in front of the screen until the early hours, until his eyes would not stay open, then he would drag himself to bed and sleep fitfully until sometime the following morning.

Wakefulness did not always occur at the same time, his lifestyle of spending hours in front of his laptop and then in front of the TV meant that he was not getting any exercise, he was lethargic and the lack of physical movement resulted in a situation that his body, rested for most of the day, did not need sleep. His problem was compounded by the fact that his mind, desperately seeking a subject that took its concentration away from thoughts of Sarah, was always proactive which kept him awake.

It was a circle that needed to be broken but one he could not break.

He awoke late the morning after he had received the message from Janet, he was not overly anxious to revisit the dating site to see if he had any messages, but after a cup of tea and a slice of toast, what else was there to do?

There was a message, it seemed to be both long and disjointed but once again there was a photo attached and without doubt Janet was very appealing. The message read;

Hello Jack, how is your day going? I hope you are having a good time, as for me I've been busy with my work and taking my time to write to you. I will love to get to know you. I decided to join the website because I have been advised by my friend that it is a place to meet matured individuals who understand how to treat and care for a lady. Trust me she is so wrong. I have been on the website for some time now and all I have been getting is messages from freaks and horny idiots. I saw your profile and decided to give it a shot, I like your age because I'm already looking for a man who is older than me. I believe that age is only a number and age does not matter at all.

More about me, I am a widow today, not because I asked for it but because death struck and took the most precious gem of my life four years ago, it's all still like a dream to me when Jeffrey passed away. He died of a ghastly motor accident on the M4. It really saddens me anytime I have to talk about this. I am open for a good heart, I live in South London, I am into sales of expensive fabrics and I work for the Red Cross part-time. My involvement for the Red Cross cannot be discussed as it is considered highly confidential, all I can say is I work for them whenever there is a natural disaster. Not like I pray for one, but I do that for free and I don't get paid for doing it.

I'm mentally stable, physically fit, a bunch of laughs, warm, caring, honest, a good listener and a positive person. I am an easy person to talk to and a good listener. My motto in life is, life is to be enjoyed, but in reality I can't enjoy life by myself and I would love to have someone to share and enjoy life with me. I enjoy chilling, I like going to the movies, or watching movies at home, I like camping, fishing, swimming, listening to music and I dance to any kind of music, travelling, going bowling and I'm also a good cook. I can make crepes, pasta Italian and anything from scratch, my favourite foods are chicken, shrimp, crab, and rice.

I'm looking for someone to share the rest of my life with, I'm romantic at heart, I figure that I'll treat people how I want to be treated, I'm the kind of woman who is cautious. I give 100% attention for the right man, being a one-man woman. Why don't you tell me a little about yourself?

I will be earnestly waiting for you to respond.

Jack read the message through twice, it struck him that English was probably not Janet's first language. It also struck him that she had covered every single base with her likes. In fact there would be no-one on the site who would be outside her scope. It sounded odd, but there was nothing to lose so he decided to answer. He was no longer an old fool, the profile photo was of a comparatively young, very attractive woman, a woman who would have no problem in meeting a man, no problem in finding a suitor, no problem in finding someone of her age. It was quite obvious that there was no way that she could be serious in what she said, no way that she could find his photos attractive; it was some sort of game, but a game that would help to fill his time, a game worth playing.

> *Hi Janet, I am a photographer and writer. I was widowed some time ago and I am now seeking that special someone with whom to share my time. I am fit and sport active. I enjoy all of the activities that you have listed. Although I look younger than my years and my outlook on life is much younger than my age, I would still be concerned about the age difference. I am currently writing an article for a magazine and I have been asked for my input into a stage musical. I trust that this message tells you a little more about me."*

Jack forwarded the message and decided to forget the exchange of correspondence. There was something definitely odd about the whole matter. If Janet replied he would respond but only out of curiosity.

Although Jack was intrigued by this recent email, and although he was expecting responses from the many messages he had sent to ladies on site, he needed to get out of the house. He was seeing Rosina the next day but he had nothing else organised, he also knew that Rosina, should they have another meeting, would delay it for a week. It seemed that a once-a-week meeting would satisfy her. An occasional weekly companion was not what Jack required, but for now it had to suffice.

There was something he could do, something that he had neglected, and that was a visit to his daughter Laura. It had been a while; the grandchildren were at Uni but that should not prevent him from touching base with his only daughter.

That afternoon he called Laura to arrange a visit in the near future. When she answered her phone she sounded surprised to hear from him, that was to be expected Jack had telephoned only a handful of time before.

Jack was quite open with Laura, telling her that he needed to get out of the house and it had been a long time since he travelled down to their home, she asked if he was okay to make the journey, it was quite a distance and he hadn't been himself since mum had died. When he replied that he was fine and the journey would be a welcome chance to get away, she offered an invitation for the following weekend; she told him that it was quite possible the grand children would be home at the same time..

It had been almost a week since Sarah had broken their romance and Jack was still suffering the loss.

But with two 'outings' now organised he felt just a little less as though the end of the world had taken place. Tomorrow it would be Rosina, his lipstick friend. Perhaps sleep would visit him without too much effort tonight, he hoped so.

The last few days had left him exhausted; his emotions had been drained; the fight had been taken out of him; but the result was indeed a better night's rest.

When morning prised open his eyelids, Jack decided to approach the day with a little more positivity. He deliberately stayed away from the computer, and he promised himself that he would do so until after lunch.

It would be untruthful to describe his lunch date as something to look forward to, but Rosina would be company, not romantic company, that was not his relationship with her.

The drive to the restaurant was only thirty minutes and as usual Jack was a little early, and as usual Rosina was a little late, it was her way.

As before he waited in the car park until she arrived. This time she had brought her small dog, Jack could not remember his name. Rosina opened a rear window a few centimetres and locked the door. "He will be fine in the car for a couple of hours."

The meal was quite good, there were certainly no complaints about the food. And the company, well

Rosina was Rosina, she talked almost non-stop, mostly bringing Jack up to speed in regard to her family It was not unpleasant, he was more than content to sit, eat and listen. His mind wandered a little from time to time but he made the effort to concentrate on Rosina's 'news'.

When they had finished eating the 'date' was over, Rosina needed to get home, her dog was waiting in the car, it required feeding and walking. Jack knew that he would always take second place to the dog; but he didn't mind, Rosina was a distraction not an answer.

That afternoon Jack was more in the mood to check his messages, perhaps Sarah had changed her mind, but as soon as the thought entered his mind he knew that he was deluding himself.

There were two messages waiting for a reply, and yes, there it was, a further long diatribe from Janet;

> *Dearest Jack, it's always wonderful to hear from you and I long for the day that we can finally gaze into each other's eyes and enjoy the moment. I was in Canterbury yesterday and I'm in Croydon today visiting customers. Tomorrow I will be in Gloucester. With my job there is always a lot of travelling around to do. I am happy that you are interested in learning more about me. I have taken my profile off the site I had to email their support to please deactivate*

my profile because you are the only one I am communicating with from the site. I will really appreciate it if you can do the same so that I know that I am not just building houses on fantasy. I think that you are such a cool person that any lady you say hello to would be interested in you, so I won't take my chances and let someone snatch you from me before I get to meet you in person.

I want to trust and I want you to do the same with me. I was very tired last night here, forgive me for the late reply, I have been busy with work and couldn't stop thinking about you, I think we are getting somewhere.

I just want to tell you the qualities that I seek in a man. A man who will value my heart. I give it all to the one I am in love within a relationship, and I believe that a relationship is built on trust, honesty, faithfulness and love, also passion and caring for one another. This gives the ability to compromise and grow. That is what I call true love, and this includes being there for each other through thick and thin, in good times and in bad times, willing to share your last drop of water to save your partners life in a dying situation.

True love, an emotion so strong that you would give up everything. To feel it once, to knows that you are part of something special. To know that you can feel what love really is, to know, to feel, to love. To love someone is to understand each other, to laugh together, to smile with your heart and to trust one another. I promise to make my one and only the happiest man on earth if only you are willing to accept me as part of you. I will be there whenever you need me and I promise never to do anything to hurt your feelings.

I will love you just the way you are, being blind disabled, deaf or dumb or whatever category that you fall in. I am ever willing to do anything to have my true love forever and sail to the end of the sea with you. I promise to be the woman of your dreams and never let you down. I assure you with my whole heart. I can't tell if that special person is you, but why don't you write to me and let us find out how we get on.

Have a great day and take care sweetie.

She signed the letter Janet, she also attached two photographs, she certainly was attractive.

Jack smiled, Janet had gone too far, it was obviously a scam and he decided to get his son in on the act, meanwhile he would go along with the emails, it passed the time. He thought to himself that if one of his friends had told him that they had received a letter with the content of Janet's message, from someone they had never seen, he would have thought they were joking.

Jack decided to leave any reply until after his trip to his daughter's the following morning, he needed time to decide what to say. As he mused this odd online inter-communication that seemed to be more fiction than fact, his house phone rang, it was Stan;

"Jack, it's Stan, there was a camera club meeting last night, pity you weren't there. Anyway the club decided to feature in next month's magazine pictures of 'the streets of London', I know you must have shed loads of photos lying around, have a check and see if there are any that you think would be good for the mag."

Then he went on; "We haven't been out for a while, fancy a drink later, we could meet at the Stag".

Jack hadn't been expecting a call but it came as a welcome surprise, a beer with Stan was the medicine that he needed; "That would be great Stan, I need a pick-me-up, I'll be there about eight".

Jack downed four lagers that night, much more than he was used to, but they not only acted as a cushion against the emptiness he felt, but they also worked as well as any sleeping tablet.

The following morning he readied himself for the drive to Laura's. It wasn't that far; he had indicated that he would arrive about midday so he figured that if he left about eleven that would be ok.

When he arrived outside the semi, Laura was on the front porch chatting to another women. Jack parked and smiling strode to the two of them; “Hi Dad, how are you? Oh this is Charlotte, she is my neighbour”.

Laura waved her hand indicating the adjoining property, as she did so Charlotte nodded at Jack turned to Laura and said, “I’ve left the wash on, I’ll pop home and put it in the dryer, I’ll talk to you later”.

Laura turned and ushered Jack into the hallway and then into the living room.

“I’ve been worried about you Dad; I know I haven’t been in touch much but Peter has kept me in the loop. We should see more of each other; you must be feeling lonely now Mum has gone, I really miss her.”

Jack nodded and smiled inwardly, Laura had never really got on with her mother, not since she was in her early teens and had been a handful for Sylvia to deal with. Jack seriously doubted that Laura missed her mother.

“Yes Laura, that would be nice, are the grandchildren around?”

“No Dad, they are studying this weekend, they sent their love and said they would catch up with you on your next visit.”

Jack smiled, the twins were like their mother, they had little feeling for 'family', they did their own thing and expected everyone else to fall in line.

"That's a shame Laura, I'll see them next time, give them my love and tell them to work hard."

It had been the tradition when visiting their daughter that the parents would take her, and her children, if they were around, to lunch. Today was not going to be an exception and Laura suggested a local garden centre that apparently had a very nice cafeteria where the fish and chips were highly recommended. Who was Jack to argue and the garden centre it was to be?

After lunch they wandered around the garden centre before Jack, with a harmless white lie, told his daughter that he had to get back as he was due to visit the bowls club later. It was with a slight feeling of relief when he waved goodbye from the car window.

Later that afternoon after giving further thought to the Janet saga, he decided to reply to her last email, then wait for a further reply, before sending copies of the exchanges to Peter for his opinion.

Jack wanted to accelerate Janet's outrageous correspondence and her reactions to the positive responses that Jack was about to make, without giving away his realisation that it wasn't a genuine dating site communication, so he wrote;

Hi Janet, I'm back online. We need to Skype and meet before we take the next step. Would I be correct if I say that Spanish is your first language? If it is perhaps you could teach me. As a professional I am cautious by nature so you will need to be patient. My feelings take time to evolve and if there is to be anything between us in the future it will take time to mature.

He signed off as Jack and wondered how long it would take for Janet to reply. Jack did have another message from the site. The introduction came from a lady called Kanna. His first reaction was to check her profile where he discovered that Kanna heralded from Japan and she was an interpreter and a concert violinist.

Jack was mildly interested; her photograph did not speak volumes and she did seem younger than his preferred age range. Nonetheless her professions were not run of the mill and from that point of view he felt that it was worth making contact. He therefore sent her a little more detail about himself and suggested that perhaps a meeting could be arranged to see if they were compatible.

Jack had now run out of immediate dates. His mind was still firmly on thoughts of Sarah, it was not possible, as Bill had suggested, to forget her and move on, it didn't work that way. He needed to get out of the house, meet someone, and attempt to push Sarah to the back of his mind. There was only one thing for it, he would give Rosina a call.

It took a couple of attempts before he made contact, but when he did she agreed to his suggestion to a latish lunch and perhaps a visit to the cinema to give the 'date' a little more meaning.

However, there was a drawback, she couldn't see him until two days hence. Therefore he had to find something to do during the next forty-eight hours. He could have called some friends from either of the two clubs he attended, but he was still not ready to embark on light-hearted banter. His broken heart had not been mended and there was no indication that it would heal, but he had to keep going, keep occupied and trust that time would help.

Jack racked his brain for things to do for the next two days, the dating site would help a little to take up time. But he needed something more.

As luck would have it Kanna responded that evening with an agreement to meet the very next day. She suggested the foyer of the Royal Academy at noon, she went on to suggest lunch at Fortnum & Mason saying that the café at the back was quite nice.

Jack immediately agreed but secretly thought, 'it'll be a nice price too'.

The evening was back to square one, TV and snacks, Jack couldn't be bothered to cook or find any other form of entertainment.

The following morning Jack examined the tube map to see which station was closest to the Royal Academy, then he gave himself ninety minutes travelling time to get there. He had never been inside the Academy before but it wasn't difficult to find.

Kanna arrived on time, she was exactly as her photograph depicted, it was obviously an up-to-date snap. They crossed the road to the store, were shown to a table and provided with the lunch menu.

As they ate they talked about themselves, discovering their pasts, their likes and their dislikes. It was a very pleasant meal if a trifle expensive. Kanna turned out to be an extremely nice person, honest, forthright yet sensitive, she would have made a perfect companion for someone, but not for Jack. There was no spark, not even a glimmer, however he did not see any objection to their meeting again particularly if he could hear her play. The violin was one of his favourite instruments. They parted after a couple of hours and Kanna promised to get in touch with details of her next concert venue.

He now realised that he could neither forget nor replace Sarah, she had been, was, the one. The very best that he could accomplish would be to replace the pain he felt with a dull ache, an ache that he could live with. The people he had met and the ones that he would meet were merely time killers; perhaps at some point in the future he would be able to conjure up enthusiasm for his hobbies.

By the time Jack arrived home it was late afternoon, there was a note lying on the mat inside the front door. Jack had been unable to bring himself to look after the back garden and rather than allow it to become an overgrown nightmare he had hired a local gardener to come in once a week to, 'tidy up', The note read that the gardener had spent three hours on the garden whilst Jack was out and, if convenient he would call round later to collect his money.

Jack sighed, he had forgotten that the gardener was calling that day, not that it really mattered the gardener had access to the rear garden through the gate at the side of the house.

Jack went to the kitchen and looked out, the lawn was newly mowed and he could see that the paths were free of weeds, and those weeds that grew between the paving cracks were always a devil to pull up. Sylvia's pride and joy was looking not too bad; Jack raised his head, looked at the heavens and silently said, "The garden's looking good and the heron hasn't stolen any fish for ages".

In fact it was probably okay that the gardener 'Bert' was calling later, he was always a mine of local information and a total gossip; he also had all the God-given ailments that had ever been invented and Jack would discover some that he never knew existed, the early evening would be filled with chat, he would learn all the news and he would hardly have to say a word, yes, maybe it was a good thing that Bert was calling round.

Meanwhile it was time to check the site, who knows, perhaps there was a message that would cheer him up.

He was not disappointed, or was he? Janet hadn't wasted any time, Jack's last response had initiated an acceleration of the exchanges, he read;

> *Dear Jack, thanks for the email, I was beginning to wonder if I would ever hear from you again. I'm glad you responded, I want to you to know that I'm interested in getting to know you more and more. I want the same things that you want. I'd like to have some fun and relaxation with you, seeing life in the same direction. I agree one hundred percent in what you are saying about relationships, trust, honesty and everything that comes with it because that is exactly what I want and I can tell that you are independent.*
>
> *Yes of course I can teach you the Spanish language. I was pretty busy yesterday that is why I didn't contact you. I can cook rather good, I love red wine, French table wine and garlic bread. I've been working out more and I eat healthy food. I don't do drugs and I like who I am. Although I think that a terrific man would bring out the best in me.*

I share your high standards, only the best will do. I am blessed and happy to have found you. As I said, all I want is a long-term relationship with loving care and a tender heart man with whom we can always be there for each other.

Thank God I have found that person in you. Please take good care of yourself and also enjoy the rest of your day. Love always.

Jack gave a rueful smile and muttered, that must have been one hell of a profile I wrote on site.

Bert called round and Jack was mildly entertained for over an hour, but that was long enough, Bert was not the kind of man that you could stand for too long.

Before retiring Jack decided that he would reply to Janet, he would keep the conversation going to see where it would lead and after the next reply he would definitely send the various exchanges to Peter. He thought carefully and wrote;

Hi Janet, thank you for your message but please defer judgement until we meet. At least if we talk on the phone you will have some personal contact. My voice may give you some indication of who I am. I hope that we can Skype. If you are on Facebook perhaps we can communicate there

Jack.

Jack knew of course that Janet would not be able either to Skype or Facebook because that would give the game away but the message may bring things to a head.

There was an excursion with Rosina coming up, a visit to the cinema, Jack hadn't been to the cinema for what seemed years, but that night he was in a reflective mood. His life was drifting, with the odd emails, weird discussions with the gardener, nothing was real. His reality, his normality, his happiness had been with Sarah.

Now there was nothing, he was merely treading water, waiting for life to catch up, waiting for some reason to look forward to the next day. He felt empty and with these negative thoughts sleep did not come easily, when it did it was accompanied by strange dreams, dreams that refused to be remembered but strange, nevertheless.

His late lunch with Rosina was fine, she talked most of the way through and this time Jack could not see the tell-tale lipstick smudge. That was definitely a plus.

The film, *The Darkest Hour* was excellent, the actor who played Churchill was compelling, but as before at the end of the evening there was the usual polite goodnight and no future meetings were arranged although the door remained open for future communication.

It was not overly late when Jack turned the key to his front door, he wasn't tired so a visit to his laptop called.

He had two messages one from Kanna and the other from Janet, he read Kanna's message first, it was simple and short;

> *Dear Jack, it was very nice meeting you and having a lovely lunch. I am sorry that it was a rather expensive place to eat. I enjoyed it very much though and am looking forward to seeing you at the concert... By the way my mobile number is...The concert details are...*

The information regarding the time and place of the concert were supplied. It was a normal, friendly message, but that was not expected from Janet.

Jack opened Janet's message; it was lengthy;

> *Dear Jack, Thanks for the email. Loving each other is the most important thing in the world. My love for you is more than anything to me. What else do I want in this world that is more than the honest and true love that I have found in you? Meanwhile, if our relationship still permits me to continue with my business and we both agree on it that I continue with it, I will call you tonight on the phone.*

I enjoy looking at how happy and good looking you are. I will love developing this friendship. I would love for you to communicate with me much more. I'm really looking forward to more and more from you because I have chosen you. At least, I will want to give priorities to our friendship. So give me your time and attention as I give you mine and better things are going to evolve. I sat and wrote this for you because I've been thinking of you.

You are such a wonderful man and I am really and fully ready to establish a lasting relationship with you. The one that will lead us to a wonderful companionship that people around us will also wish to have. I shall always make sure that I have the time to make all this happen. With all my love always.

The email was as usual sent with two photographs of a lady who would never lack for male company. Jack sent the exchanges and the photos to Peter with the note,

What do you make of this?

Jack decided to wait a day or so before responding, Janet's emails were stretching credulity too far.

The next day passed slowly, he phoned his son just after one assuming that it was lunchtime and he would not be working. Jack was wrong, his son was working, he told his father that he did not stop for lunch, Jack was not surprised, but Peter did say that he would use the photographs to see if he could find out who Janet was or who she claimed to be.

Saturday came round, it was Kenna's concert in a church close to Notting Hill Gate tube station. The concert was classical music, Kanna's bread and butter, but music that Jack liked to listen to. Perhaps this Saturday evening would provide him with some peace, some relaxation, some lifting of the tension that had haunted him since Sarah's departure, he hoped so.

The evening was not unsuccessful, the music did lift his spirits a little, Kanna came over to him during the interval and after the concert had finished they enjoyed a quiet meal. It was pleasant, a meeting of two potential friends but Jack formed the opinion that Kanna was looking for more than friendship and that Jack could not give. There was a promise to organise another meeting but Jack felt he was being unfair and he would need to give the matter thought before organising to see her again.

It had been less than three weeks since Sarah's departure and Jack had still not recovered from the breakup. The meetings and the emails were trivial in their meaning, they were merely assisting with the passage of time, nothing more. Jack vainly hoped that time would be a healer, he needed it to be.

The following morning Jack received a call from his son, it was Sunday and even he was taking a break from work. Peter had been amused by the correspondence, although he did agree that the photographs were of an extremely attractive woman.

> *Hi Dad, nice letters you've been getting, I would carry on a bit further and let Her/him get some fun until you drop it on her that you know what's going on.*
>
> *I checked and discovered that this sort of thing is called 'catfishing'. Apparently people set up temporary telephone lines and email addresses so that they can pretend to be interested in elderly lonely people who have joined dating sites. Their interest appears to be just personal enjoyment in seeing the person hooked, like on a fishing line.*
>
> *It's cruel of course because the site members who fall for it are generally the vulnerable, the ones who are left devastated when they discover that they have been played.*

Jack had guessed as much; he didn't know the term 'catfishing' but the general message was understood. He thanked Peter who went on to say that he would try and match the photos with some on the web to see if he could discover who the photos were.

Jack was amused but not amused, it was a time waster but he would play along for a few more days, two could play games, the game initiator would be the loser when he discovered that it was he/she who had been 'played'.

Later that evening another message came through from the site, it was a response from one of the short contact missives he had sent out, it read that Danielle would be pleased to arrange a meeting.

Jack went immediately to her profile. He could see that they were not really compatible, he then checked the photos there were four but only one was a good view of her face. It was one of those faces where the eyes, nose and mouth were squeezed into the centre of the face leaving a large area of flesh around. However Jack thought that perhaps he was being too picky and anyway Danielle may turn out to be a wonderful person, the sort of person whose character overcame her looks.

Jack emailed back saying that a meeting would be welcome and added his mobile so that an arrangement could be made.

He also sent a short message to Janet saying that they should talk or Skype, knowing that she would avoid that at all costs.

He was tired and he didn't want to spend any further time on the computer. His tiredness was mainly his eyes, he wasn't ready for bed, that would come much later.

The television called out to be watched and he spent a long time trawling through the channels. There wasn't very much on that he found appealing, he always avoided reality shows, anything connected to romance and also the news. His preference was a good western or detective story, he could lose himself in the plot for a short time, they were always a good escape.

Eventually his eyes drooped and he nodded off every so often, mostly after an on-screen gunshot he awoke, and after the fourth time he admitted defeat and went to bed.

The next morning just after nine the phone rang; it was Danielle asking if they could meet that lunchtime if he was free. These days Jack was almost always free so arrangements were made to meet at a location they both knew, one thirty was the time agreed.

There was ample time for a cup of tea, slice of toast and a glance in his laptop.

This time Janet had responded almost by return, matters were hotting up. Jack read through her latest communication;

> *Dear Jack, good morning I hope you slept well last night. I will be leaving here very soon. I just put the wedding ring on my finger sometimes because lots of men worry me. (Jack had spotted the ring in one of the photos and had raised the question in his last email). You know that*

I always travel around meeting people for business that is why you see the ring on my finger.

I will give you a call tonight my dear and enjoy true peace in the peaceful island of your arms. I love your 'good morning', just as I love every night and every hour we spend together. It would feel great to start the day looking at your sweet face and listening to your soft voice. Your morning greeting gives me the strength to face any Goliath. You are wishing me a good day gives me motivation to decipher any enigma and to face any giants because it fills me with love and courage. And that's why it feels so great to find you by my side every morning. My love is a journey that starts with forever and ends at never. I will always love you my darling.

Jack felt like laughing but laughter had not been in his heart of late. He did give her marks for the 'ring' explanation; however he did wonder where some of the phrasing and vocabulary had come from. The message and photos were again sent to Peter. There was no doubt in Jacks mind that Janet was edging towards the last throw of the dice so he emailed back asking for a place to meet.

By the time he had read and responded to Janet's missive it was time to leave for lunch with Danielle.

Jack pulled up in the restaurant car park and waited. He had been told the make and colour of the car that would be arriving. He didn't have to wait very long. As soon as Danielle stepped from her car Jack realised that the camera did not always lie, her features were somehow squashed together in the centre of her face.

The meal was passable and the conversation was stilted. He learned that Danielle preferred her men to be down to earth and blunt. Jack knew that she was attracted to, to coin a phrase, a 'Jack the Lad' but it wasn't going to be Jack Tomlinson.

After they parted it was obvious that there would be no further meetings. As he pulled out of the car park Jack in anguish called out, "Where are you Sarah, why have you got me into this nightmare, please come back".

But no-one was listening.

It didn't take long to get home and when he did he saw that there was a message on the house phone, it was Peter.

Jack called back straight away; Peter's voice had sounded excited.

"Hi, Peter, you rang."

> "*Yes Dad, I checked the photos you sent me with pictures on the web and I found a match, the photos were...*"

He named a pretty and quite famous American TV presenter whose website contained many photographs. The ones Jack had received had been lifted from the website. Now he knew who the photos were he could play the game with some confidence.

As Jack settled on the living room settee he felt some guilt about Kanna. He had not been in touch since the concert and the truth was that he could see no reason why there should be a further meeting. Of course the coward's way out would be to lay low and hope that she would forget. For the time being Jack decided to take the coward's way out. Tomorrow would be another day, perhaps his courage may return, perhaps not.

A new day dawned, Jack hoped that the Janet saga was nearing its end, enough was enough.. He made himself a cup of tea, watched the latest news on TV and deliberately delayed switching on the computer. When he did, the message that he was expecting was there, wating for a reply;

> *Dearest Jack, thank you so much for your email. I firmly believe that good communication is at the heart of any successful relationship and therefore honesty, understanding and absolute respect for each other must remain our priorities for a truly happy and rewarding life together. I sincerely hope that we might communicate with each other further.*

I hope you are having a peaceful day. You can trust me with your secrets and I promise to always try my best and bring out the best in you.

For holidays I like to relax, get some sun, swim and have a gym on hand, loved and importantly wanted. I hope that you know that I really want you in my life. When we will wake up in the morning in bed, in each other's arms kissing passionately and start all over again.

I am serious about my intentions and would love to meet you, the sooner the better. Like you I have a lot of love, just as importantly time and attention to give to the right person. I have to say I find you a very intriguing person by the way that you write your emails.

I hope you are relaxing today and have no work. Do not feel too lonely because I am there with you in spirit and thinking about you all the time.

I hope you are well and looking after yourself. I can't wait until I am the one looking after you and giving you all the love that you deserve. If it is any comfort to you I want you to know that I am thinking about you and I am feeling really happy about the lovely thoughts that you are sending to me, my body is simply crazy with wanting you. I wonder if your body wants mine the way mine wants yours... the kisses... the hotness... the wetness... all melting together. Take care of yourself. Many kisses and hugs.

She finished with the address of a London restaurant where they could meet.

In other circumstances Jack may well have been mopping his brow, but not on this occasion, it would seem that this time Janet had rolled two sixes. God knows what the next message would be. But of course Jack knew that there would be no further messages as he typed;

> *Thank you for your email, I would love to meet you as suggested. However as the photos that you have been sending are of !!!!!!. Would you let me know who will be turning up.*

CHAPTER FIFTEEN

It had been just less than four weeks since Jack and Sara had ceased to be an item. Four weeks of torture for Jack, four weeks of heartbreak and disappointment. He had received no word from Sarah, but why would he, she was now part of his past life, a part that he would always remember, but a part that he could never recover.

Apart from Sarah, his experiences on the dating site, thus far, had been, mundane, uninteresting, surprising and disappointing; but as his neighbour Bill had advised, "Don't give up, it is early days, you will meet someone eventually".

But Jack had his doubts, perhaps the person that he was seeking did not use the internet to meet companions, perhaps the person who would be the best for him was too shy to embark on a medium that throws strangers together. It was becoming a strong possibility that meeting Sarah was a one-off miracle, a miracle that would never again occur.

Jack's recent meetings with potential companions had left him depressed, he was alone once again, the opportunity for happiness had been cruelly snatched away and he just could not bring himself to forget, he could only regret what might have been.

He had always been told and always believed that 'Life is what you make it', now he knew that sometimes you have no control and life is thrust on you and does not allow your intervention, you have no control, it becomes a matter of survival, or in the case of many individuals, a matter of permanent escape, as was the case with his own son David.

Jack clenched his teeth, Bill was right he wouldn't give in. It was true that apart from Sarah his experiences on the dating site had proved fruitless; but that was because it was early days. He had been advised that sometimes it took months, even years, to find that special someone who would make life seem worthwhile. And if that someone proved too elusive then loneliness need not be the only alternative. There were many clubs and institutions that offered both activities and social structure to alleviate solitude and provide an opportunity to engage like-minded people with each other.

However for those who are sceptics, the clubs and the institutions appear to offer the same thing, a chance to meet someone.

Many people, like Jack, are not interested in the casual friendships that may be gathered from the membership of the many and varied clubs. They have a need for something deeper, a close companionship, a meeting of minds and souls; so it was for Jack, his club memberships, his various hobbies were just that and none satisfied his desires; they were superficial, necessary perhaps, but not the answer.

So, back to the internet it was, back to the dating site for another try. Bill had said that the one he was looking for was out there waiting, and eventually she would make contact. But in his heart Jack was unable to forget Sarah, he was still harbouring the possibility that she would forgive all and come back. It was of course pie in the sky, but hope cost nothing, except perhaps heartbreak.

That evening Jack called his son, the incidence of the 'catfishing' had oddly brought them closer together. Perhaps it was the sharing of a peculiar situation, perhaps it was because Peter had been able to help his father, whatever the reason talking and laughing openly now became easier; maybe there IS a silver lining lurking there behind every dark cloud.

Talking to his son helped to diminish Jack's tensions and despair, with the result that the dating website would be given another chance to redeem itself.

Jack noted that there were a couple of messages, 'a good sign', he thought.

The first message he read was from a lady who called herself Josephine, a lady who he had talked to some months earlier and to whom he had explained that he was 'with someone', this was a term on the dating site used to terminate ongoing correspondence. However it was not unusual for site members who had been unable to find the companion that they sought, to return to old correspondents in order to discover if the person with whom they had been talking was still with 'someone'.

Josephine was using that tactic; Jack had first replied to her opening email during the period following Sarah's departure after the visit to Ottawa and she had discovered Jack's interest in writing. Jack never met Josephine, in fact he never discovered her real name, but he had reached the conclusion, even before their discussions were terminated, that Josephine was a most unusual lady.

Josephine's new message read;

> *Dear Jack, I realised after not hearing from you that you did not want to pursue any sort of relationship and that is okay. I do apologise for contacting you but there is no-one else I can think of who is experienced in connection with publishing.*
>
> *I have been talking with an elderly man who is a poet, his first message to me was a poem. Suddenly I started to write back in a similar mode, it was almost as if Pandora's Box had opened. Once I started to write back I could not stop, I have probably written enough to fill a book already. I have been told so many times that I am a writer but did not know how to start. I have written a dissertation on art so I can*

write but writing something that is not a formal piece is quite different.

Not only have I written all this prose/poetry, I have now written a two act play but I think I will expand it further. At first I thought, 'is it any good?' But then I began to think where is this coming from?

Then my poet said, "I think your work is outstanding, I am getting in touch with a friend of mine, when I sent him a sample he liked it and he has asked for the four best poems of mine to read.

I can illustrate the book too and they said that it would save money. Now I am thinking what I do next to copywrite my work, art, etc. I am totally at a loss here, please help me with some good advice. Incidentally, I have not spoken to anybody but the poet, but of course I have all the emails so it can be seen which is my work and his. I do hope that you can advise me. I would like to discuss with you the way I write which I don't think is usual, but maybe you can tell me differently.

Jack read the message several times, he thought; "She certainly is a strange one, and I don't believe a word of it".

Jack was uncertain how or if he should respond, their earlier exchange of messages had been interesting, confusing and certainly different. Josephine had informed him that she had shared her home with a monk who had lived with her for a considerable time. Jack presumed that it had been a 'monastic' relationship but the exchanges between them had left him wondering. She had also indicated that her neighbours spied on her and whenever she left the house they made attempts to enter if the house was empty. Jack had assumed that this made it easier for her to delay any suggestion of arranging a meeting.

Perhaps in other circumstances he may have ignored the message or sent back a reply saying that he could not assist; but he was alone, he needed a distraction, what should he do?

He decided to respond by asking her to send samples of her poetry so that he may decide where best to seek a publisher. He had no doubt that she would engage in further correspondence, he just had to wait to see how the saga would unfold.

Within two hours of his short message Jack received a further email from Josephine;

> *Dear Jack, delighted to hear from you, to further explain simply, I have been told so many times from published authors, that I am a writer. A famous author told me that I wrote in the style of James Joyce and my tutor (when starting a second degree in law and psychology a few years ago) did not know how to start.*

Then I met a man on one of the dating sites, he wrote to me in verse and I replied in kind. With that came the freedom to write whatever came into my head and as the verses from the poet became more erotic so did mine. After a while, the poet told me that my work was extraordinary and that he had a friend with connections and he had sent one piece of mine to his friend who then asked that the four best pieces of mine should be sent to him.

I do have every single email with my work shown and it's easy to distinguish between my work and the other chap. He usually writes a poem each day, he is considerably older than me, a well-educated man with a sharp mind, he is still working part time as a clinical pharmacist.

This is why I needed to talk to someone about the body of work, what is acceptable as erotic verse? Furthermore I could illustrate it as an artist and other artists who also could do illustrative work.

Once I started it became difficult to stop, writing every day, I wrote two acts for a play which needs expanding. I have a granddaughter who is at Uni doing drama and Spanish, she is interested in reading this.

Jack read through the text a couple of times, there were repetitions of the previous email but now Jack was convinced that Josephine was a fantasist,

Jack didn't really know how to react so he merely wrote back;

I will wait to hear from you further, if you wish to chat please call.

Meanwhile Bert had left a message on his answerphone and that was welcome, he had known Bert for years, enjoyed his company and at present he needed it.

Bert was a 'twitcher', an amateur twitcher, that is to say he enjoyed, every now and again, bird watching. He had provided on several occasions bird photographs for the club magazine and although he only used a digital camera with a spotting scope, the photographs had considerable merit.

Jack had accompanied Bert only once before, photographing birds was not his genre, but it was relaxing and whilst Bert was patiently waiting for a rare bird to come into view, Jack used a pair of powerful binoculars to survey the area generally, not necessarily seeking out birds but looking at anything that attracted his interest. After a session of bird watching the pair had rounded off the day with a visit to the local pub.

Bert's call was to ask Jack if he would join him, on the morrow, to a bird watching hide about twenty miles away where a Common Nightingale had built a nest not twenty yards from the hide. It was, so Bert said, an opportunity to obtain a great photograph for the next issue of the club magazine. He went on to explain that these nightingales were not common at all, there had been a diminishing number found nesting in southern Britain over the past fifty years. The breeding pair had been spotted only recently in coppiced woods near a lake that they both knew, and the local pub The Dog and Duck had a wonderful reputation for fine food.

Jack did not need any persuading, he had nothing better to do and a trip to the Dog and Duck seemed like a good way to spend some time away from the house. He told Bert that he would be delighted to join him, he wouldn't take his camera but he would bring along his binoculars, and, if it was okay with Bert he would write a short piece for the magazine to accompany the photograph, assuming of course that Bert managed to get one.

That settled, Jack was in a better frame of mind to go back onto the dating site and check the other message that he had received.

This was a simple message from a lady who called herself Felicity, it was no doubt not her real name but no-one used their real name for the initial contact. Felicity explained that she had read Jack's profile and believed that they had some things in common and it would be nice if they could exchange information to find out a little more about each other.

Jack went immediately to Felicity's online photo and profile, if they weren't of interest he would only reply that he was talking online to someone else and was therefore not currently available. This was the kindest way he knew of terminating any further exchanges with the messenger.

On this occasion the photo of Felicity portrayed a lady who was quite attractive. She gave her age as seventy-one, a fraction older than Jack would have preferred but age had been kind to her, assuming that the photo was current. She was educated and had obtained an Oxford University degree, she also had multiple interests including writing. It was an interesting profile and Jack was keen to respond.

As Felicity sounded more promising than many of the other contacts received he decided to put a little more effort into his personal detail response. Jack told her that he wrote articles for a photographic magazine in which some of his photographs had appeared. He told her that he had written poetry and some unpublished short stories. Jack described his fitness level, his interest in bowls and added general matters such as walking, social history and the like. As a university scholar he thought that social history, social awareness and the advertising of the plight of the underprivileged may appeal to her.

He sent his email and was fairly satisfied with the day's events. Matters weren't static, it was Stan tomorrow and he was now in touch with two dating site members. He had things to think about and although Sarah was uppermost in his mind he was desperately trying to squeeze her out.

That night he slept a little better, for the first time in weeks he could not recall that he had dreamt. A coffee to wake him up and a bowl of cereal was all that he needed before he left for his bird watching rendezvous.

He met Bert at a pre-arranged car park and they set off for the hide. Neither had any idea where the nightingale nest was or whether they would find any eggs. Bert had already described to Jack that the small nest was cup shaped, it would be low down in the undergrowth and if there were any eggs they would be olive green in colour. He had told Jack to check on the web for the famous poem about nightingales written by John Clare. The poem may give him a flavour of the small bird that Bert wanted to photo.

The day went well, there was one other person in the hide when they arrived. An elderly grey-haired gentleman who, in a whisper, told Bert where to look. As luck would have it, in a little under three hours a male nightingale returned to the nest where the female was sitting, presumably bringing her food, and Bert was able to get an extraordinary photo of the two birds together. The female bird may well have been sitting on eggs but they were not visible, notwithstanding Bert had got what he came for and fingers crossed the resulting picture would be engaging enough to grace one of the pages in the magazine, perhaps even the front cover.

The late afternoon meal at the Dog and Duck was appetizing and well received but they restricted themselves to just one pint, they were both driving and neither wished to take any chances.

When Jack arrived home the sun was just setting and as he parked in the driveway he noticed that the sky was streaked in red, Jack mumbled, "red sky at night a shepherds delight", he had no idea if the old adage was true but he took it as a good omen for the next day's weather.

As was the case whenever he arrived home after being out somewhere, the house seemed dark and cold. His perception was worse than reality but still it drove home the actuality of his loneliness. He could give one of his family a call, but he was loathe to pester them, the computer had to be his companion that night.

Before he embarked on his evening visitation, a cup of tea was the first thing on the agenda. It was an hour later when he lifted the lid of his laptop. Josephine had wasted no time in getting back to him and Jack read her latest message;

> *Dear Jack, I have some news, the poems went with my friend to a possible publisher, sadly he did not require any of my friend's poems but he took ten of mine, apparently saying that they were very exciting written by a woman giving a woman's perspective. I don't agree with his*

dismissal of my friends work I thought it was brilliant, however he has been quite wonderful about the whole thing. As I have been writing up to three poems a night now for the past three months I do have many left. I wrote two last night.

I'm not sure what happens next, I will be getting the chosen list next Friday, then I shall start thinking about illustrations. I will be guided by you because I am sure you know what to watch out for, whether I can use you for help with publication, it's early days but I'm so excited. But I am prepared for it to fall through which does happen. I certainly did not expect this to happen in my wildest dreams, you hear of writer's works being rejected and never first attempts being considered.

Hopefully, warmer weather will arrive soon and then we can arrange to meet.

P.S. When you reply can you give me your landline; the internet is awful here.

Jack was again bemused by the content of Josephine's message; it sounded a lot of baloney, so what was she really after?

He decided to allow the exchanges to continue for now, they were wild, total fantasy and would definitely remain only as computer messages. His mind went back to the cat fishing episode, but he had spoken to Josephine on the phone and her enthusiasm was not made up. Jack thought that perhaps she was merely lonely and deluded.

He realised that Josephine was an ‘armchair’ site member. A member who desperately wanted, needed companionship, but for a variety of reasons did not wish to physically meet anyone. Mostly it was because they were insecure about the way they looked, they believed that their online ‘companion’ would be disappointed if they met.

Jack’s guess was that obesity was the principle cause of this insecurity. He also realised that his own reasons for enlisting on the dating site were the opposite of Josephine’s dream and that he would have to conclude the message exchange at some point.

Felicity was a more likely prospect, she seemed to be perfectly normal and like himself just seeking companionship. He had provided her with his personal details it was just a matter of waiting for her response and seeing where it led.

The following evening was a night when many of his acquaintances would be at the bowls club, he hadn’t been for a while and although his mind was not entirely on his chosen sport, it was about time he picked up where he left off, weeks ago.

Jack knew many of those who played the sport and although they were only ‘distant’ friends he was sure that if he made the effort they would accommodate a closer friendship.

In the past his reticence to go more frequently had been his closeness to Sylvia and his reluctance to leave her to her own devices in the evenings; but more importantly it was the inability of many of the members to talk about anything other than bowls.

It was true that topics embracing religion or politics may leave one on dangerous ground and to be honest he was not aware of the political persuasion of any of them, nor did he know which God they sought solace from; but there were many other subjects that could be discussed; but apparently not by them.

Nevertheless he knew that they would be welcoming should he choose to go, and an evening away from the computer would be a good thing. He was already feeling the eye strain resulting from sitting in front of that screen for too long.

Having made up his mind to give the laptop a miss on the following evening Jack decided to give it one more shot that night, he wasn't disappointed, there was a response from Felicity. She had read his personal details and was interested in continuing their conversation.

It was quite apparent that she was sitting at her computer and engaging in conversation by messages rather than the telephone, Jack's preferred way of talking to someone. Felicity was obviously not yet ready for a closer contact, she was being wary, perhaps she had previously encountered unwanted attention on the site.

That evening there were a number of messages back and forth, it was an odd way to have a conversation, Jack would have preferred the direct method, a telephone call, but it was quite clear that Felicity, although warming to her new contact, was not yet ready.

Jack did discover Felicity's love of writing, her passion for mathematics, her Oxford University subject, and her involvement with her old Uni friends. She divulged that she had met her late husband whilst they were studying all those years in the past, but unfortunately he had passed away six years ago. She admitted that she had joined a writing group to learn the art of engaging with others through the written word.

Jack found himself interested in Felicity's conversation, he did not consider himself to be an intellectual, but it was refreshing to engage in conversation with someone who was intelligent and interested in what he had to say. From this discussion he became aware that she was 'old fashioned' in her values and her morals. She was a person who took her time opening up to a new introduction, she was cautious.

As it became late Jack decided it was time to say goodnight, he wanted a drink and he wanted to relax on the settee watching TV before going to bed. It was not comfortable perched on the chair in front of the computer for so long; he needed a break and he could continue his conversation with Felicity later.

And so it was left that she would message him the next day, whenever she woke, Jack jokingly chided that it shouldn't be too early.

That night he dreamt of Sarah, he just could not dispel her from his mind and that made him annoyed at himself. Sarah had gone never to return, he had to move on, somehow. Perhaps whenever he met Felicity he could forge a lasting friendship. Perhaps there would be someone else; only time would tell, time the healer, time was his only hope.

That following morning there was a message from Felicity, a short sentence explaining that she was an early riser and could he contact her when he came on site.

Jack was still a little bleary eyed when he typed out his good morning. Their interaction continued as it had on the previous day, just 'getting to know you' messages. They continued to talk in this manner for over an hour before Felicity told Jack that she was expecting her son to visit and that she would be unable to chat until the evening. Jack explained that he had arranged to go to his bowls club and he would not get home until after ten. Felicity was nonplussed and reminded him that she did not sleep until late and sometime after ten would be fine for a late-night conversation.

That settled, Jack now needed to pass the time for the remainder of the day.

It was still early morning, the sun was rising higher in a cloudless sky and the temperature was conducive for a walk, a stroll outside, a breath of fresh air. Jack had never experienced satisfaction walking alone, he required a purpose so today he decided to take his camera and photograph anything that took his fancy, anything of interest.

He had no idea what he was going to capture today, but the reality was that walking was necessary to get him out of the house and the security of the camera strap around his neck gave him the purpose.

As he strolled he remembered that the garden of the house at the end of the street sported a large 'monkey puzzle tree', the shape and oddity of the tree had always caught his eye as he passed, but today he would photograph the tree and perhaps use the picture as part of his schools project.

He had been strolling for about fifteen minutes, the image of the monkey puzzle tree was safely in his camera, but as he turned the corner into a busier thoroughfare, he came across a road accident. There were two cars, both with collision damage, an ambulance and two police vehicles. There were also a number of onlookers. Jack could not see anyone injured, no paramedics in action, but it didn't matter, the scene overall with all its content made the perfect image for his social history collection.

Jack was now satisfied, his walk had been worthwhile, he could return home and check his laptop, who knows there could be a pleasant surprise in store.

As always, arriving back to an empty house made him feel lonely. Apart from bowls that evening he had nothing else lined up, for peace of mind he only felt comfortable if he had pre-arranged meetings or visits covering a couple of days in advance. When there was nothing on the horizon he usually felt an unexplainable sense of panic. So, as he entered the house he determined to go back to 'old faithful' and call Rosina, (his lipstick lady), to see if she was available for lunch the following day.

Jack was lucky this time, Rosina answered the phone at the fifth ring. Rosina was a member of the U3A (the University of the Third Age) and he was aware that during the week she attended several classes, he remembered her telling him about the painting, flower arranging and pottery classes, but as good fortune would have it she was free the next day, no classes, no daughter visit, no son drama.

Jack was both amused and grateful that Rosina showed no surprise at his call, she gabbled on with her news as though the time gap between their rendezvous did not exist. He was thankful for that, and as soon as he was able to interrupt her flow they agreed to meet at the same venue as their previous get together. As far as Jack was concerned that was another day partly sorted.

After his successful phone call to Rosina, Jack checked his emails and as he suspected there was one from Josephine, it read;

> *Hi Jack, sorry for the delay in getting back to you.*

Jack thought, "what delay?"

> *I needed to speak to the other poet who was arranging a meeting. I managed to talk to him and he told me that he was going down to Kent in two weeks to meet the man with the connection to a publisher. He was taking him the manuscripts to read and he asked me to wait before I sent them to you. I said, not a problem... so in two weeks' time you can read the manuscript. Hope all is well, still writing, will send some poetry as soon as I know what they want to use, if any.*

Jack breathed a sigh of relief, two weeks grace, he knew that when, or if she again made contact there would be another excuse why she would be unable to send him samples of her 'work', well, *C'est la vie*, he had two weeks to work out how he was going to terminate the correspondence in the kindest manner.

That evening Jack was reunited with his old acquaintances and colleagues. He managed to join up in a pairs match, one of the four had not been able to make it, but his bowling was not up to scratch, like any sport practice is the key and Jack was woefully short of that. Although his partner played his part they lost six 'ends' in a row before the lateness of the hour overtook them. The evening had been disappointing from a competitive point of view but satisfying from the point of view of meeting old pals. Jack promised that he would endeavour to practice more in order to extract revenge next time there was a match.

He arrived home just before ten-thirty that evening and made a cup of tea before lifting the lid of his laptop.

He immediately checked his messages and discovered an unanswered one from Felicity, it read;

> *Are you home yet? Be in touch, it doesn't matter what time, I'll wait up until I hear from you.*

Jack responded and during the next two hours the messages flowed from one to the other. He discovered that, as he suspected Felicity was not her real name, which was Emily, she believed that her mother had named her after one of the Bronte sisters and she wondered if that was the reason she desired to write. The exchanges uncovered many personal details and by the end of their conversations Emily relented to a meeting, a lunch at a hotel close to her home in Oxford although the stipulation was that he would not be invited into her home on their first time together.

The day was Thursday, he was meeting Rosina on the next day, which of course he did not relay to Emily, so the arrangement was made for Saturday.

Jack was content with that, he had two 'dates' lined up and if he could arrange a meeting with either his son or his daughter for the following Sunday he would not have to worry about being on his own until the following week.

The next morning, before his meeting with Rosina, Jack went back to the computer to discover that he had a message on the dating site from a lady who called herself, Maureen, and she hailed from the USA.

Jack was wary in connection with messages from anyone outside the UK, he wanted to keep an open mind but earlier he had a 'brief encounter' with an attractive lady from Russia, who had even sent him a video of herself training at her local gym. The lady must have been at least thirty years younger than him and even if she had been genuine the age gap was far too great, he believed that in all probability she was either after a passport or she was seeking a sugar daddy. Jack had responded that he had now found someone and was no longer available.

Out of politeness and curiosity Jack replied to Maureen asking, as he usually did, for some personal details.

There was also a brief message from Emily telling him that she was going to a gathering of her old university chums that day and she was looking forward to their meeting the next day.

At lunchtime Rosina arrived, as was her normal procedure, fifteen minutes late. As before she arrived with her small dog so Jack realised that it would be only lunch and the date would end as soon as they left the restaurant. Notwithstanding she did not disappoint during the meal, keeping Jack entertained with a continuous flow of 'news'. After the meal they parted with, 'keep in touch' and both went their own way.

The lunch served its purpose, taking time out of the day and leaving Jack with the knowledge that he had not spent the day alone. He drove home slowly, there was no hurry, all that waited for him when he arrived was an empty house and the dating website.

When he did eventually arrive home, and after he had carried out his ritual of a cup of tea, he then went to his now most precious companion, his computer.

To his surprise he had received an immediate response from Maureen outlining her personal history; she had also attached three photos, the odd thing was that two of the photos were obviously of the same person but one of the three seemed to be of another person, her message read;

> *Hi Jack, I'm into electrical and electronics engineering, I install ELT appliances for both public and private sectors, houses or company premises. I work for myself.*
>
> *I'm a happy woman with so much love to give but take honesty as the first step in doing anything, and also friends first. We could take it from there and see what develops; I'm a good Christian with a sincere, caring, loving heart and a hope of a better tomorrow, because where there is life there is hope. Our hopes should always be high and we should never give up until we finally make our dreams come true. This is the reason that I'm taking this chance to tell you about myself, and also to get to know you better. I believe no-one is an island.*
>
> *I'm a very honest, caring, family orientated, independent, loving, romantic woman with a nice sincere heart of taking care of my own man, home, respect him and giving him all the love he deserves because I want a man that I cannot live without and same in return.*

I'm an extremely optimistic woman and love to meet new people with my smile. I'm easy going, non-smoker and social drinker. I have a great sense of humour, love to laugh, tease, joke cuddle, go swimming, camping and other things. I would love to know more about you.

I hope we can become good friends and perhaps even more. I understand that great relationships take time to develop. I will be waiting to hear from you. I hope that you understand that distance isn't an issue when there is honest communication between both parties. As I said in my profile I wish to retire back to the UK but with a good purpose (love). There are no concerns with the distance thanks to modern means of transportation. I can pay you a visit anytime if the relationship gets better. I'm a good writer as well and I can tell you are a good writer as well, but we have to be committed to each other so that we can build a long-term relationship, which I do hope will mature from being best friends to soul mates, because the heart never grows old and I know it when I find true love. Please be in touch soon.

The message sounded familiar to Jack, it had obviously been prewritten and he had been through this before. However, as always he intended to be polite if not forthright. So he responded by pointing out that the photographs did not appear to be of the same person. He then gently explained that because of his previous experience of 'catfishing' he was always a little cautious about letters from afar and he wondered if she had any more photos, or a face link, so that they could chat face to face, He sent the message and wondered what the response would be.

The evening, as too many evenings were, was destined to be quiet, but out of the blue he received a telephone call, it was Emily, she told him that she wanted to hear the sound of his voice before they met. The voice can give away many details, information of where you live or have spent most of your life, through the accent; the education or background, derived from the way you pronounce your words and occasionally the masculinity by the depth of voice, but this can be misleading; however as the site profile discloses height, it may assist a female listener to determine whether the tone is to her liking.

Jack and Emily spoke for some time, learning and feeling out just a little more of each other's background. A good idea if the object of the meeting is to create a friendship or longer-term relationship. When they rang off both were tired but Jack was looking forward to the next day's meeting.

Saturday arrived and Jack prepared himself for the considerable journey to Oxford, he dressed smart casual but he did not know what a university scholar expected. A modern girl would not expect anything in particular, you are who you are, but Emily was old school she would have other notions.

Jack timed the journey to perfection and arrived only five minutes before Emily. On meeting there was a polite shake of hands and they were taken to a table.

The meal was passable as was the conversation. Emily was not unattractive but there was nothing sparking that would indicate anything long term. However Jack realised that his diagnosis was unfair, it was early in their relationship, in fact it hadn't even started, so he decided that as Emily had a story to tell, as everyone has, he would wait for it to unfold before drawing any conclusions.

At the end of the meal Jack discovered that Emily had travelled to the restaurant by taxi. He felt that it had been an unnecessary expense and offered to drive her home. At first she was reticent but after considering the offer she accepted on the condition that Jack did not ask to go inside when they arrived.

Jack agreed, in reality he had no reason to enter Emily's home, he was, at this point, not sufficiently interested in it to become an issue, he was more than happy to drop her outside and then drive home.

It had been an interesting meeting, Emily had given Jack the impression that she was keener than he, but he was quite happy to meet again, she was genuine and fair company, therefore a second meeting would do no harm; in fact, he would have been happy to call her a friend when the time was right. But the necessary physical attraction was not there so friendship was all that he had to offer.

When Jack arrived home he was disillusioned, once again a promising meeting was destined to lead nowhere. He was sure that he would meet Emily again, and of course there was always reliable Rosina, but for a long-term companionship or the inkling of romance there was nothing on the horizon; there was after all, only Sarah.

Jack was so disconsolate that in an act of pure folly he turned on his computer and sent a wailing call for help to Sarah;

> *Hi Sarah, there is no need to respond to this message… I now understand that a simple thing like bringing coffee in the morning was wrong, I should have left you to your own devices until you were ready to face the world.*
>
> *You needed space, i.e. no-one around until you were ready. You needed days when you required to be on your own, without anybody in particular disturbing you until you were ready to make contact. In short you needed that special privacy for as much time as it took until you were ready for personal contact.*
>
> *What you did not need was someone, no matter how much you cared for him, being in your face.*

Personal space was paramount for any relationship to work. It was sufficient for you just to know that the special person was around when needed.

I realise now that this would have been enough for me. The connection still exists and I will always miss you; but I wish you every happiness un the future, as long as you realise that I do fully understand where you are at.

I know you tried as you say, one hundred percent, but until now my brain was not functioning.

Jack sent the message; he knew there would be no reply but the act of writing and forwarding it gave him some comfort.

There was a message from Emily, thanking Jack for the lunch, it went on to say that as he now knew where she lived it would be sensible to collect her from her home next time they met.

Jack could not respond that evening, it would have to wait until the following morning, he was tired but more than that, following his misguided attempt at an email to Sarah, he was emotionally drained. He just wanted to sink down among the cushions on the settee and rest his mind and body.

The following morning Jack felt a little refreshed, he was very slowly coming to terms with the fact that Sarah was no longer part of his life. Sad as it was, he could not change the fixed path that lay ahead. Now there was, in reality, just Rosina and Emily, two extremely nice ladies who were happy to be friends. For the time being Jack would have to settle for that. He knew that friendship, although welcome, would not satisfy his need for something more for very long, Perhaps the dating site would eventually put him in touch with 'someone special' if it didn't life would still have to go on.

Jack was feeling magnanimous, he did need a friend and it appeared that Emily wanted to be one. During their period of message exchanges they had discussed many topics, it was obvious that she had been probing to discover just who this man was, did he come up to her expectations, her aspirations, her morality and her academic ability? It would seem that he had passed the test.

During their exchanges they had discussed religion, a difficult topic and one generally to be avoided, however Jack had never been one to back away from a discussion on any topic and before their meeting they had been mulling over religious principles, so in response to Emily's thank you message he responded by telling her how much he had enjoyed her company and that they should arrange a further meeting, he then referred her to the previous email that she had sent and in reply he wrote;

Emily, people follow Christian principles merely because those principles apply to all religions.

What is in a name, God is God no matter what name is given to the creator. Any attraction I have for you has been created by the fact that you have a principled and beautiful mind, virtues that are not easy to find.

I hope that you will find something of the sort in me.

In the past exchanges they had discussed her passion for writing and her desire to learn and become a better writer. They did not have a great deal in common, Jack understood that even if Emily chose not to think about it. But writing was a subject common to both and if they were to be friends then it would be necessary to concentrate on any subject that had mutuality. At this moment Jack desired a friend, a second meeting with Emily would be helpful to ease his loneliness and his loss of Sarah, in truth 'company' was the only drug that would get him through the days ahead.

Emily must have been sitting by her computer because within twenty minutes she had responded with a message, noting his enjoyment of their meeting the previous day and suggesting a meeting on the following day, perhaps she sensed his need for company, perhaps she had the same need. Her message was;

What you say has made me think about writing my memoirs, the only writing course that I had undertaken was a course entitled 'Writing stories of our Lives'. I do have other projects but you are correct in your assumption that I am deeply into the past.

I do not feel the least bit guilty about meeting you, I had been given permission... more of that perhaps tomorrow.

The architect friend who triggered our meeting sent me best wishes this morning. More about him tomorrow as there is a strong writing connection.

What you do not know about me is my part in keeping people together socially, from Oxford students to scattered friends to Oxford Business Club members. I have a huge number of contacts to draw upon for after dinner talks but all the men seem to be married.

Jack read the message a couple of times, Emily seemed to be trying to impress him, that would never work but she was a conundrum. Apparently the permission that she referred to was permission from her deceased husband, he would discover that tomorrow, if nothing more their 'date' would be mildly interesting.

Jack noted that he had received an email from Maureen, the American lady, the lady to whom he had gently mentioned his 'catfishing' experience. The email was vitriolic accusing him of lack of trust of ungentlemanly behaviour and more; it ended with the words that 'she' could never again communicate with a man such as he.

Jack grimaced, he realised that he had hit the nail on the head. There would be no further emails from that source.

There was another camera club meeting that night, especially called to discuss the content of the monthly magazine, Jack felt obliged to attend, but it was no ordeal it was in fact a diversion that was welcome. The rest of that day he was determined he would use to catch up on his personal paperwork, the mountain of unfiled receipts, bills, general blurbs from the local council, the Inland Revenue and so on. It was boring and it was depressing to have to put everything away, but it needed to be done.

The club meeting was short, they had decided to use Stan's 'nightingale' photo on the front cover and Jack was asked to write a piece about the trip to the Hide for the inside page. There was the usual good-humoured banter at the meeting which came to an end at seven o'clock, Jack was home by seven thirty.

He had been home less than twenty minutes when he received a phone call from Rosina. It was obvious that she was at a loose end, it emerged that her son had travelled abroad to interview for a new job opportunity and her daughter had gone to stay with friends for a few days. She only had the dog for company. Jack promised to try and book theatre tickets for the next weekend, failing that there was always the cinema.

The next morning Jack was awake early, he had slept pretty well and he had dreamed, the dreams could not have been significant because he couldn't remember them in any detail. That lunchtime he was visiting Emily and he had decided to take her to a local restaurant for lunch and then play the rest by ear.

Jack pulled up outside the pseudo-Georgian style property at twelve thirty, the time agreed. The house did have 'kerb' appeal, but he had never been inside.

Emily must have seen him coming because as he approached the front door it opened and a smiling Emily ushered him inside. The entrance hall was small, and it was cluttered with hanging coats, a small bookcase and umbrella rack. The main living room, as well as the kitchen, which he noted as they passed, were also small. It had to be said the interior of the property did not match the exterior. Emily sat down in an armchair and waved to a couch where she intended Jack to sit.

They chatted for some while, it was just about general matters, she told him about her architect friend, someone who had been a family friend before her husband died. She briefed him on the activities that she was involved in connected to Oxford University and she told him about her family and her new granddaughter. It was a true 'getting to know you' discussion.

They didn't arrive at the restaurant until two o'clock, not that it mattered they had not booked and there was no shortage of tables. After the meal there was no option but to drive Emily home, Jack didn't want to stay too long, it was a long drive back and as nice as Emily was there was a limit to the time he wished to stay with her.

When they got back Emily invited him in for a coffee, in his usual polite manner Jack accepted the invitation with an under-breath vow to keep the time as short as he could. When seated Emily smiled and produced a bottle of whisky that she proclaimed was very old and very expensive, it only came out on very special occasions and this was one of them. She was in fact holding out the hand of companionship and perhaps something more. Coffee appeared a few minutes later and they conversed for an hour or so until Jack, with a white lie, told her that he had a bowls night later so he would have to leave.

Emily seemed a little disappointed but hid it well, they parted with a shake of hands and a promise to make contact later.

It had been an interesting meeting, Jack realised that Emily would now like to move their friendship forward, unfortunately Jack was quite content where it was. There could be no relationship in the future that would satisfy Emily but Jack hoped that he would be able to retain contact but keep the friendship at a distance, it would be a balancing act but he was sure that it was attainable.

That evening Jack needed to unwind after the day's encounter, he phoned the booking office of a local theatre and managed to obtain tickets for a play a week later, they told him that the tickets would be in the post the next morning. Jack decided that it would be a packet of crisps and a lager in front of the TV for the remainder of the day, enough was enough.

Jack considered his excursion onto 'The Web', it had been the full range of emotions, heart-fulfilment, heart breaking, fantasy making, disappointment, ridiculousness, catfishing, soul searching and many other things. The web had brought to him not only true love but also those who only wished armchair laptop chats, those who wanted casual relationships, those who were lonely, and those looking for a free meal. He thought back to his own youth when the only dating sites were the ads in the local paper, when the young people met in clubs or discos. It had been a different world, a world without the web, perhaps a better world, but then he would never had met Sarah!!!

Jack had nothing planned for the next day, he went back to the dating site and saw a couple of messages, there was one from the classical violinist and two others that after he checked profiles he decided only warranted a polite refusal response. His options for the time being had ended. The next date with Emily could not take place for at least a week because her daughter and granddaughter were coming to stay.

He was on his own unless he could find somewhere to go and someone to meet. On occasions such as these his thoughts always turned to Sarah.

That day Jack rang his son, his daughter, Stan and others, all were friendly but busy. He did have meetings arranged for a week hence but a week for Jack, the way he felt, was a lifetime.

The gardener called in the afternoon, Jack watched him mow the lawn and weed the paths from the vantage point of the seat in front of the summerhouse. The evening was, as the last, snacks in front of the TV. Even Emily's chatty emails were absent it must have been awkward with her daughter present.

The following day was as the last, with the exception that there was no gardener to break it up, and that night Jack could not find anything on TV that interested him; he was both lonely and bored.

The past two days had dragged by each lasting an eternity and it was with no sense of expectation when he logged into his computer midway through the next morning. But what he saw was the very last thing that he expected to see, it was a message from SARAH. Jack's heart missed a beat and his hands trembled as he read;

> *Jack, I didn't come to my decision lightly; but regrets? I regret that I lost the friendship that I had found with you, and you may regret that I am responding when I said I wouldn't.*
>
> *I am afraid to hurt you more. That I will always regret. But I also regret that two old, lonely people have lost the close friendship that we shared.*
>
> *If we cannot be lovers it's sad that we can't be friends, at our time of life we have so few. I would also be there if you needed me.*
>
> *If this is not an option for you then of course I will understand... Sarah*

Jack read the email over and over, he read between the lines, it had taken her a week to reply to his last message, a reply that he had not expected in his wildest dreams, but now Jack smiled, a knowing smile, because he knew Sarah, and he knew that it must have been a monumental effort for her to write the email.

She had been gone for five weeks but Jack was now totally sure that she was back, they were about to be a couple once more and he knew that this time it would be for keeps.

In just a few short weeks they would be walking together hand in hand, towards the copse nearby, admiring the wonderful, the magical colours of autumn, but with the knowledge that 'their; magic, their personal autumn, had only just begun.

Ingram Content Group UK Ltd.
Milton Keynes UK
UKHW011951240723
425689UK00004B/170

9 781803 815022